The Spirit of Franklin's Shoe Box

To Dianne
From
your Neighbor
Stormy

The Spirit of Franklin's Shoe Box

Stormy Davis

51 ALPINE AVE.
WATERBURY, CT. 06706
(203) 756-4550
E-MAIL: Sdavis@AOL.COM

Writers Club Press

San Jose New York Lincoln Shanghai

The Spirit of Franklin's Shoe Box

Writers Club Press
an imprint of iUniverse.com, Inc.

For information address:
iUniverse.com, Inc.
5220 S 16th, Ste. 200
Lincoln, NE 68512
www.iuniverse.com

ISBN: 0-595-19024-3

Printed in the United States of America

CHAPTER 1

Franklin Cooper sat on his couch mesmerized. He had no idea how long he had been in that catatonic state. His eyes were fixed on the object he had placed on the filthy table before him. He then leaned forward and folded his hands in the manner of prayer.

"Help me, please! You promised to always help me. Help me!" he pleaded.

Franklin's supplications were not directed to a "Higher Power" in heaven. He was waiting for some mystical genie to appear from a shoe box and take away his troubles. In the past, he had found comfort in the shoe box. Now its magic seemed to have faded. Nothing was helping him. Giving in to despair, he returned the shoe box to its place on the closet shelf.

"Oh, God! Please help me!" he cried again. His face was etched in desperation and he peered around wild-eyed. The thumping of his heart as it vibrated against his body drove him into further madness. Trying to stifle his depression and anxiety for the past week with booze and drugs had pushed his body to the limit. His lips cracked, and his tongue withered with a white coating. It was becoming difficult for him to swallow. He felt a knot constricting his throat. He reached to massage his tightening throat and shivered at the touch of his own skin. It was cold and clammy. "Fluids," his body signaled.

He remembered the six-pack the gang had brought. The small white object across the room faded in and out of focus. It seemed miles away. His feet were glued to the floor. Suddenly he felt strangely disembodied. With a ferocious lunge, he broke loose and staggered to the refrigerator. He flung open the door and cursed the heavens as he beheld the empty shelves.

He spied a beer bottle on the floor and stumbled forward. He managed to swooped it up. He struggled to control his trembling hand and raised the bottle to his mouth. The liquid was warm and unsavory. He felt a sickening wave of bubbles welling up in his belly.

"Oh, God! Not again!" he appealed, while making a dash for the toilet. Late again. The vomit spewed out, leaving a messy trail. He knew he needed help.

"Where are all of my so-called friends when I need them? Why do they always rush off like that, leaving me alone? Well, I don't need them," he muttered. He reached for the crack pipe, but it also was empty.

"Not you, too," he said, smashing the pipe on the floor. "You're just like them. You're not my friend. When the money runs out, you run out. Just like my other friends."

He mustered his last bit of strength and struggled not to be defeated. "Well I have another friend. A true friend," Franklin added sarcastically.

He rummaged through the rubble on the table and found a whiskey bottle. "Gordon's"the label read, but this, too, was empty. Franklin opened his mouth to scream, but the rage he felt froze his voice. The vein in his neck pulsated and began to swell dangerously. He bashed the bottle against the wall with such force that splintered glass became embedded in it.

Was this the bottom that Franklin was destined to reach? For years now he had tried to drive away the haunting madness with drugs and alcohol. The delusions, the hallucinations, depression, and anxiety, all the things associated with madness remained, but the drugs, the alcohol, his money, and his friends were all gone.

He had no father to turn to, and he was forced to stay away from his mother, sister, and other family members. Now his last comfort, the shoe box, had lost its power. He had hit bottom.

"There's no way out," he said bitterly. Sitting on the edge of the couch, he pondered his next move. Then the voices returned. "What have you done in the past?" they taunted.

"I'll kill myself. Yes. That's what I'll do. I'll kill myself."

Franklin reached for the razor on the table. Tears dropped from his eyes as he raised it to his throat. His breath quickened. "No, not this way," he hesitated.

Franklin gave a startling gasp, then made a swipe across his wrist. He sat dazed as blood oozed from the wound. He opened his eyes and saw that the cut was superficial. The razor had become dull from cutting up crack.

Franklin started to shake with fright from his action. He dropped the blade. He couldn't continue, and for a moment he felt a deepening hue of shame. Deep inside he wanted to live. It was the voices that drove him to harm himself. Whenever they would fade, he could reason.

"Tomorrow's got to bring a better day," he voiced. "If only tomorrow could come today."

He pushed everything on the table aside and picked up the phone. He hurriedly punched in numbers. "Hurry! Hurry!" he implored, waiting for the line to ring.

Nestled in the northwest hills of Connecticut is the small town of Torrington. Once a quiet residential area, Torrington is beginning to experience the problems that plague most American cities these days. Drugs, increase in crime, and a rise in homeless and mentally ill people on the streets have crept into the town.

At the local mental health center, Bryce Wright, a fifty-one-year-old African-American is working the weekend shift. Bryce, a newly graduated nurse, is being trained by John Welsh.

John, a white male of Irish descent, has been working as a psych-nurse for over fifteen years. Unlike Bryce, who stands six feet, John is a small man. Bryce often complimented John on his small waistline. Bryce envied him because he was starting to show a little beer-belly, even though he had stopped drinking years ago.

It had been a fairly slow day at the center. Just the regulars who called everyday had called in for a little comforting support. Their time on the line was limited. If it were left to them, some could talk all day. However, this was the regional hotline, and those who needed immediate help were given preference.

Today, most of the regular callers were encouraged to go outside for a walk. It was a lovely March day, a little windy but unseasonably warm and a nice relief from the long cold New England winter.

Bryce and John wanted to be outside. However, manning the phones kept them at their desks in the small room with no windows.

Then the call came in. Bryce listened as John pleaded with the person not to do anything foolish. He motioned to Bryce to get things ready. Bryce now realized that they would have to go out and intervene with a young man threatening suicide. Bryce was beginning to get an adrenalin rush. But after John hung up the phone, he began to linger. He was giving more attention to his lotto scratch-off than to the caller. This incited Bryce to ask, "What's the matter? Aren't we supposed to respond to these calls as quickly as we can?"

"Oh, no rush. It's only Franklin. We've been getting calls like that from him for years. And he still hasn't learned to kill himself."

Bryce thought that John's attitude toward this caller was strange. This was the place where people were supposed to be compassionate to callers. After all, it was for that reason that Bryce had taken this job. "Does this caller deserve this treatment?" Bryce wondered.

Bryce turned the phones over to a backup answering service, and the two men left to do the outreach.

John jumped into the driver's seat and handed Bryce a manilla folder. "Read this," he said.

The folder was thick. The first page revealed the name of Franklin Cooper. His most recent diagnosis was *Manic-Depressive Disorder with Drug-Induced Psychosis*. Bryce could see clearly that Franklin had a long history of mental illness. Yet he was only twenty-two years old.

"He's just a kid," Bryce commented.

"Yes, but when these kids are full of drugs, they become very dangerous."

"Shouldn't we have a police escort or something?"

"Why? Are you nervous?"

"Yes. I think I am. I would hate to think that I survived a year of combat in Nam just to get whacked by some young drug user here at home," Bryce said.

"I can handle Franklin. He's not gonna do anything to us or himself. He just wants some attention. As a matter of fact, he's one kid I wouldn't mind seeing go down hard. That's why I didn't follow procedure and call for an ambulance and cops to be on the scene."

As rude as John seemed, Bryce had no choice but to follow his direction. He had seen how John dealt with other callers. He had been kind and caring, showing genuine compassion and love for his job and the person. Race, ethnic background, culture, or circumstances in life had not mattered to him before.

Bryce studied the row of New England houses as John drove down the busy street. In the distance an ambulance shrieked an alarm, and for a moment Bryce flashed back to Vietnam. Tension rippled through him. Funny how that still happened after all these years. Maybe it was the excitement of this job. After working twenty years in a machine shop, going back to nursing school was a dramatic change, Bryce thought. He blinked and wiped the sweat from his eyes. As reality returned, an ice-cream truck with a line of kids came into focus. John drove past the truck and pulled up in front of a small flat. Amid the line of two-story houses, Franklin Cooper's one-story building looked like a gap in a row of teeth.

They climbed one flight to the porch. The door stood ajar. John pushed it open, and the two men almost gagged from the horrendous smell that hit them like a gust of wind. They covered their mouths and noses and followed droplets of blood to a tiny sitting room. Amid filth and dried vomit sat a lean young black male. As he struggled to his feet, Franklin stood at least six feet tall. The whites of his eyes were the color of a diluted Bloody Mary. Yet the tears that dripped from his face had a pearly sparkle. He fought to balance himself with his right hand as the left one hung freely, dripping blood. It looked as though he had removed his T-shirt to wrap his wrist. He revealed a hairless chest that matched a see-through mustache and peach fuzz chin. He looked younger than the twenty-two years listed in the crisis report.

Franklin grimaced from pain. His hands were balled into tight fists. His knuckles were turning white, but he barely spoke a word. He responded to John's questions by nodding. However, Bryce sensed that his silence was in part due to some sort of hostility toward John.

From the look of his place, he had been on a crack binge. Bryce still recognized the scene, even though it had been many years since he had struggled with drugs. But this was a clear picture with evidence of cocaine use that speckled a lone clean spot on the table. A smashed crack pipe was partially kicked back under the couch. The amount of empty beer cans, liquor bottles, and cigarette butts in the ashtray indicated that Franklin hadn't partied alone. A small kitchen counter played host to containers of devoured Chinese food. Dishes cascaded in the sink, while roaches ignored their presence.

Franklin refused to let John touch him, but he allowed Bryce to take a look at his wound. Franklin's dark skin flushed as Bryce's eyes met his. Franklin flashed a pitiful look of appeal and turned away.

John neared the end of the evaluation. He whispered to Bryce, "How does it look?"

"He 's gonna need a few stitches. He came close to a vein. I don't see how he missed. Must not be his time."

"Call for an ambulance," John whispered. "He probably hasn't taken any psycho- tropic medication in weeks, and he needs to go in for detox. That's probably what he wants anyway."

Franklin had openly admitted to using cocaine and was willing to go for help.

While they waited, John made a wisecrack: "If I lived under these conditions, I would want to kill myself, too."

Bryce didn't think his remark was funny. As a matter of fact, as he stood staring at the young man, he felt sorry for him. "He bares an uncanny resemblance to someone I knew. It's obvious that he needs help. Why would a mentally ill person turn to drugs?" Bryce wondered.

After reaching the hospital, the Crisis Team's protocol was to notify the next of kin or responsible person. In Franklin's case, this was his mother. John assigned that task to Bryce, but Franklin became hostile and resistant when asked for his mother's phone number. "I don't need her here. I can take care of myself. I'm my own man," he shouted venomously. Franklin took on a crazed look. His face turned red and pinched with resentment. His mouth crimped in annoyance.

Bryce let him rant for a while, then approached him again. He explained why he needed to contact her. With some hesitation, Franklin gave Bryce her number.

When she answered the phone, the woman sounded groggy and confused. She seemed to have difficulty understanding the seriousness of her son's predicament. After a lengthy discussion, she agreed to come to the hospital.

By the time she arrived, Franklin's condition had improved somewhat. His mother, however, looked disheveled and smelled of alcohol. She was distraught and tearful. She began to tell Bryce a muddled story about her son's problems.

"He's disobedient and resentful of authority," she said. "He's unwilling to take part in family activities. He becomes violent and wants to argue when he's confronted about his partying at all hours of the night. He's been arrested for shoplifting and for driving while intoxicated."

When Bryce asked her about her son's drug use, she said, "I know he's been using drugs for a long time. But when I ask him about it, he always says that it's his friends that are doing it and that he's only trying to help them. Besides, he never took any drugs in front of me."

"I understand," was the only comment Bryce could make.

"My Franklin is not all bad," she cried. "He got sick after his father died. He was just a little fellow then. One doctor said it was schizophrenia. Another doctor said it was something else. They really don't know. But I know that there's nothing wrong with my boy."

As she continued to weep, Bryce handed her some tissue.

"It's so hard, you know, trying to raise a boy without a father. My family tries to help out. If only I could get him away from that Raymond. That one," she said, "is a bad boy."

Bryce needed to broach the part of the evaluation that covers family history of substance abuse, but he was hesitant to question Mrs. Brown about her use of alcohol. When he did, she became very defensive and said, "I only drink on special occasions and only in small amounts when I do."

Bryce felt it was best to leave that issue alone for the time being.

Two hours later, the hospital staff informed John and Bryce that Franklin would be admitted for three days to the detox unit. Afterward, they would attempt to have him placed in a long-term substance-abuse rehabilitation center.

Bryce found it hard to relax on the ride back to the office. He was visibly shaken by what he had just experienced. Also, Franklin seemed to have stirred up old memories that he had repressed. Not only did Franklin resemble someone he thought he knew, but he made Bryce remember the days when he, too, was down in the gutter.

Bryce looked to John to see how he was handling the debriefing.

"What's the matter?" he asked. He had noticed Bryce's expression. "After a while you get used to this kind. Do you mind if I stop at the next convenience store? I need to get my weekly lotto ticket and some more scratch-offs."

"It's okay," Bryce replied.

"Well, can I get you something?"

"No. I'm okay. I'll just sit and try to get this off my mind."

Relief came to Bryce when he reckoned that this would be the last he would see of Franklin. After all, the hospital did have plans of sending him away to a long-term rehabilitation center. Franklin probably wouldn't even remember meeting him when he became sober. Through all the chaos, he didn't recall John introducing him by name.

A week passed, and Bryce was sitting at his desk doing paper work. Nick, the team's supervisor, came over. "John told me that you did a good job with that Franklin character. He also told me that you were a little disturbed by him. What is it with you and Franklin?"

"Oh, it's nothing to worry about." Bryce replied. "He just reminded me of someone. I can't remember who though. It may be me."

"That's good," Nick said. "I'm glad you like him, because he's your first case."

"He's mine? What do you mean?" queried a stunned Bryce. "I thought he was going away to some treatment center?"

"Yes. That's right. He's up at the Eagles' Nest Retreat. He'll still need a case manager. They don't stay up there forever, you know. Besides, this kid has been in and out of our system for years," explained Nick.

Nick turned to walk away, and then he remembered. "Oh! You can start by reading his history. The charts are over there. And maybe you'll want to pay a visit to his mother. He's a tough case, Bryce. We know you haven't had much experience with this type of work, but we feel that with your background and maturity, you'll be able to help him. Good luck."

Bryce had sounded a little rebellious, but he respected Nick and his decisions. Nick was a big man. He towered over everyone on the team. Nick was of German descent. He had sandy red hair and had a habit of brushing it from side to side while talking. Nick was also left-handed, and this made his movement seem awkward at times. Nick's years of experience as an emergency room nurse was valuable to the team. He made most of the medical decisions for the team.

"It's a good thing that this job is exciting and pays well," Bryce mumbled. "I went to school to become a nurse, not to do this social work stuff."

Bryce found it incredible that at his young age, Franklin was already on his second set of charts. Franklin's problems seemed to start at birth. He was one month late and was a difficult delivery for his mother. On his arrival, he had jaundice and an infection of some sort.

Bryce stopped reading and pondered. He could not understand the significance of this being in the history part of the chart. After scanning the medical part, he found no details about the infection or what had caused it. Curiously though, the line next to the infection part read *SEE VA FILE CHART #362034.*

The history continued, reporting that for the first three months of his life Franklin suffered from vomiting episodes. Also, he had been prescribed Donetal, a medicine used to help keep heart valves open. Eventually, he was able to outgrow the vomiting.

Franklin had suffered many losses in his early life. His father died when Franklin was only four years old. His mother remarried, and Franklin went to live with his paternal grandparents. They both became ill and died within a month of each other. Franklin returned to his mother only to be mistreated by an abusive and alcoholic stepfather.

Franklin first showed signs of mental illness by becoming quiet and withdrawn. He would isolate himself for months at a time. Other times he would constantly be on the go, seldom slowing down to rest. School became completely out of the picture for him. He couldn't stay in any classroom for one hour. Eventually, he started to hang out with people on the streets and rapidly learned their ways.

Around the age of fourteen, he started experimenting with alcohol and marijuana. By the time he was fifteen, he had done LSD, cocaine, and speed. At age sixteen, he was a full-fledged alcoholic.

To support his drug and alcohol habits, Franklin began stealing from his mother and other relatives. He was arrested for disorderly conduct, loitering on school grounds, and shoplifting. He was put on probation and then was sent away to a detention center for violating it.

His mother pleaded for his early release, and he was released to her. Soon he was back on the streets. He became increasingly violent in public and at home. After a short time, his mother had to get a restraining order to keep him away.

His drug and alcohol use triggered a manic-depressive disorder. It was a low time in his life when depression set in. It was at these times that he attempted suicide. There were seven attempts documented to date. He also had a court date currently pending for arson. He set a fire that burned down a house while attempting to commit suicide.

"Whew! What a record," Bryce sighed.

Bryce gathered his things to visit Franklin's mother. He reflected on his own past. He remembered suffering with bouts of depression. He remembered the struggle he had with his own alcohol and drug abuse. "At least I had good childhood, and my teens years weren't bad either. My problems began with Vietnam."

Bryce had a name for his problems. He called it "Fighting the Elements."

"Poor Franklin," Bryce thought. "This guy has been fighting the elements since birth."

CHAPTER 2

Bryce followed the directions he received from Nick. He arrived at 115 Fairlawn Street and fumbled through his folder to see if he had the correct address. Why was he uncertain? From his one-time encounter with Franklin and his mother, Bryce assumed they lived in a run-down part of the city. The neighborhood was well-kept, far from being run-down. Among a variety of shade trees that lined the sidewalk, a mixture of raised ranch and cape style homes were colorfully painted. Lawns were beginning to turn green, and buds were appearing on beautifully arranged flower beds planted out front. Evidence of kids was apparent from the toys and bikes left scattered throughout most yards. Still, it was a quiet, peaceful looking street with "Neighborhood Watch" signs posted on the block.

Bryce climbed up to the porch and turned to glance over his shoulder. He was still uncertain as to whether he had the right place. Adding to his suspicion, a teenage girl with long black silky hair, answered the doorbell. Her hair was tied back and she was wearing an oversized apron. She reached to wipe the dust from her ebony-colored face. Her eyes were large and almond-shaped. They highlighted the sweet girlish expression that glowed from her face. She had a tall slender body. Her voice was soft and velvety. "Hello, how may I help you?" she asked.

"Hello. I'm looking for Mrs. Cooper." Bryce replied.

"There's no Mrs. Cooper here," the young lady said.

"Sorry to bother you," Bryce said as he hurried to leave. His instinct was right, he thought. Before Bryce could leave the porch, the young lady asked, "Is this about Franklin?"

"Yes! Franklin Cooper. I'm looking for his mother, Mrs. Cooper. Do you know where she lives?"

"My mother is not a Cooper," she said. "I'm Monique. Monique Brown. I'm Franklin's sister. You're looking for my mother, Mrs. Brown."

Not only was Bryce embarrassed by his stupidity, but he was also disappointed. Through grade and high school, time served in the Army, and years spent working in a shop, he had learned not to assume. Now he had critically misjudged this family. Bryce knew in order to help Franklin he would have to get off to a good start with his family. He had read the file on Franklin but failed to do research on Mrs. Brown. He didn't even know that Franklin had a younger sister.

"Come in and have a seat," Monique said while dusting the chair she offered. "I'll go and get Mama. She's upstairs."

Bryce tried to avoid another blunder. He looked around the house for clues of other siblings. He also looked for something to comment on when Mrs. Brown came down. Deep inside he wanted to say something nice in order to make himself feel better about the mistake he had made.

There was plenty for him to comment on. The part of the house that he could see was kept in a spectacular manner. Clear to the kitchen, he could see brightly shining hardwood floors with area rugs placed neatly in position. The arrangement of furniture and draperies perfectly matched, giving the rooms a southern flavor. The three rooms that Bryce could see reminded him of the living-room in his home when he was growing up. That room was kept so neat that no one was ever allowed in it. Everything was covered in clear plastics. Bryce often wondered why it was called a living-room.

Obviously someone had spent a lot of time keeping this place neat and clean. Bryce again felt ashamed for his assumption.

Bryce tried to learn about the family. He viewed the pictures on the coffee table before him. He thought it strange that, other than Franklin, no male was in any of them. They were all of Franklin, his mother, and his sister. The one that brought a smile to Bryce's face was of the three of them when they were much younger. In that picture, Franklin appeared to be in his early teens. They looked very happy together.

In another picture, Bryce found what he thought may have been another sister. After comparing it with yet another, he realized that it was the same person who had greeted him at the door: Monique. He struggled to remember her name. This picture revealed a beautiful young lady with long black hair and a beaming smile.

It was not hard to recognize Franklin in the pictures at all. He had grown quite a bit, but he hadn't lost his baby-faced appearance. The person that concerned Bryce the most in the pictures was Franklin's mother. All of them showed her at a young age; a lovely woman with a face that radiated. She looked as though the aging process had little effect on her. She looked healthy.

Bryce became so engrossed in the pictures that he almost dropped the one he was holding when a course voice from behind said, "Hello. My daughter said you're looking for me."

He had no trouble recognizing Franklin's mother. She looked the same as she did the night she came to the hospital. With the exception of the nightcap and gown, everything else about her was the same. Her facial appearance was unchanged. Her face was ashen and the wrinkles from the side that she slept on were visible. She struggled but managed to open large bloodshot eyes. She made no attempt to smile and her lips curled up in disgust from being awaken. Bryce thought that if she had been sober a day since he first met her, she didn't show it.

She made Bryce nervous. He cleared his throat and said, "Hello Mrs. Cooper." He realized his error and quickly tried again. "I'm really sorry about that, Mrs. Brown. Do you remember me?"

Mrs. Brown yawned and stretched. She caused a rolling crackle of what seemed like every bone in her body. With no sign of embarrassment, she replied, "It would be easier if you just call me Martha. Yes, I remember you from the hospital. What's the matter now? Is Franklin in more trouble? The only time I don't worry about him is when he's locked up somewhere."

"Mrs. Brown. I mean Martha. I'm from the State Department of Mental Health. I've been assigned as Franklin's case manager."

"I know where you're from," Martha said angrily. "They keep sending you people down here to tend to Franklin. It doesn't do any good. Franklin's not gonna change. You must be the fifth one who has come. None of them really cared, except for that girl. Franklin did listen to her, but she fell in love with him, and they took her off his case."

"That's not true," Monique said. She entered the room and handed her mother a glass of orange juice. "And Mama, don't be rude."

Monique turned toward Bryce and asked, "Would you like a cup of coffee or something? Mr...ah. Mr...ah."

"You can call me Bryce. Thanks for the offer, but I've already had breakfast. Were you informed that Franklin has been sent to a retreat? One called the Eagles' Nest."

"Another one of them. Franklin's been in plenty of them. They don't do any good either. He seems worse when he comes out," Mrs. Brown snorted.

"Don't say that, Mama," Monique jumped in. "That place is one of the best. I heard Allison speak about it. She is the lady that was Franklin's last case manager. She didn't fall in love with Franklin. She cared about all of us. Her supervisor took her off the case because they felt she was spending too much time with us. She still calls me from time to time."

"I see you've met my beautiful daughter. You see how smart she is?" Martha sneered. She reached for her glass and took a sip.

Even though he was sitting some distance across from her, Bryce caught a whiff of vodka. For some reason this didn't surprise him, even at ten o'clock in the morning.

"This is my baby girl. She'll be graduating from school soon. She's so smart that she finished all of her studies while the rest of her class is still in school." Martha could change from bragging to taunting without skipping a beat.

"She's only got one hang-up. I believe she's afraid of boys. She has never been on a date. Boys don't ever call here. She don't even want to go to the prom. I keep telling her that she should have a boyfriend. I had a boyfriend at her age. No, she'd rather be here, cleaning up all the time."

"Okay, Mama. That's enough. I told you that all the boys around here and in school are too silly. They all want one thing. I don't have time for that," Monique blasted back. She took her mother's empty glass and left the room.

"Martha," Bryce said, trying to get her to focus on the reason he was there. "Tell me a little more about Franklin."

"Oh, Franklin was coming along quite well. Tyrone, Franklin's father, would not go anywhere without his little boy. Then he up and died. Franklin was crushed. He never seemed to have gotten over that. His father drank himself to death. Did you know that?" she asked, not really expecting an answer.

Bryce did not respond. He just sat there, listening.

"That Tyrone," Martha continued. "He was good to me. We fell in love in high school, when I was about Monique's age. He had a lot of plans for us. We were gonna do this and do that. Then he went into the Army. He was okay until they sent him to Vietnam."

Vietnam. This word really got Bryce's attention. He cut in saying, "Oh, yeah! I was in Vietnam, too."

Whether Martha heard him or just wasn't aware of what he had said, she didn't respond. As Monique passed by with a handful of cleaning stuff, she asked her for another drink.

Bryce now sat on the edge of his seat. His mouth was agape as he anticipated hearing more, especially about Nam.

"He got hurt really bad over there, and they sent him home on disability. He wasn't the same though. All he wanted to do was drink. But we never lacked anything, because he got a lot of money. We were among the first black people to buy a house in this neighborhood. Whenever he wanted a new car, the government would give it to him. They were special-made for him because of the nature of his injury. He just wouldn't stop drinking. It was like he was still fighting something. Something internally. You know what I mean. Poor Franklin never got over his death."

"Mama, you really should eat something," Monique pleaded, as she returned to the room with another glass of vodka-laced juice.

"After Franklin's father died, I married Monique's father, Ricky. Ricky Brown," Martha went on.

"Mama, do you have to talk about him? I don't want to hear about him. He never calls or writes or anything," Monique cried out.

"He was a drinker, too, and he wasn't good to Franklin. For some reason, Franklin didn't take to him. He used to beat Franklin something terrible. I didn't know about this until my sisters brought it to my attention. I finally had to divorce him. That was a little after Monique was born. We haven't heard from him since," Martha said. Her face became twisted with a dark expression. A single tear rolled down her cheek.

"Mrs. Brown," Bryce interjected. "I really need to ask you some pertinent questions about Franklin."

"Mama, let Bryce talk some," Monique said, as she approached with a basket of clothes.

"Okay," she said to her daughter, "but just get me one more drink."

"Really, Mama, it's too early. You're just gonna get drunk and sleep all afternoon."

"That's no way to talk to your mother, young lady."

Martha turned to Bryce and asked, "What is it you want to know?"

"I have just a few questions. For one, what happened to Franklin at birth?"

"Well, he was born with some kind of infection. I believe that Tyrone knew what it was. He went to the Army doctors about it. They were meeting regularly about it but after he died, they didn't get back to us. Besides, Franklin grew out of it."

"Is there a history of mental illness in either your or your first husband's family?" Bryce asked.

"You mean are any of us crazy? The answer is yes. We're all a little nuts," laughed Martha.

Bryce was relieved to see her laugh after he had asked a question of that nature. "What I mean is, is there anyone in your family, other than Franklin, suffering from depression?"

"No, I don't believe so. But like I said, Franklin's father was bothered by something when he returned from Vietnam. What I'm trying to say is, you said you were over there, you don't look like you have a drinking or drug problem."

Bryce thought, "If only she knew what I've been through." However, he simply answered, "I've had my problems."

"Martha, I'll be going out to see Franklin one day this week. Is there anything you would like me to say for you?" Bryce asked.

At that moment, Monique returned with another basket. This one was full of folded clothes. She must have been listening in. She said to her mother,"Please, can we go out on the weekend to see Franklin?"

"Well, I suppose so."

"Oh, Mama, what about that shoe box of Franklin's? He's always asking us to bring it to him whenever he's away. He thinks that old shoe box is something special."

"That's right!" Martha acknowledged. "You see how smart she is. She's gonna make a good wife to some young man. That's if she ever gets out of this house and starts dating."

"Mama!" Monique blushed.

"Bryce," Martha asked, "Could you go by Franklin's house and look in his closet on the shelf? There you'll find a shoe box that Franklin seems to guard like a treasure. Bring it to him for us, please. Monique, get the man the key."

Bryce gathered his folders and stood up just as Monique returned with the key. He said goodbye to Martha, and Monique escorted him to the door.

Out on the porch, Monique wanted to show respect. She said, "Thanks for coming Mr...ah."

"If you're gonna insist on calling me mister, Wright is my last name. Oh! By the way," Bryce said, reaching for his wallet, "Take this card and call me if you or your mother can think of anything else I may need to know about your brother."

Even though Bryce was not going to see Franklin that day, he decided to go by and get the shoe box now.

Bryce parked in front of Franklin's place. He became suspicious when he heard commotion coming from inside. He pushed the door open and caught a glimpse of someone leaving in a hurry through the back door. A silver BMW with darkened windows sped away, leaving tire marks in the street. Bryce could not make out the license plate for certain, although he was sure it was lettered and not numbered.

"What in the world could anyone want in this filth?" Bryce thought, as he looked around at the same mess he had seen weeks earlier. Either it wasn't the shoe box, or he had frighten them off before they could reach it. It was right where Mrs. Brown said it would be.

Bryce reached high above his head and gently brought the shoe box down. He treaded through the trash on the floor as though he was carrying a precious museum piece. Bryce laid the box on the kitchen counter. "Darn it!" he said. "Why so much tape?"

As much as he desired to see its contents, Bryce knew that if he wanted Franklin to trust him, he had better not open this box.

Bryce reflected on his day's activity on his ride back to the office. The BMW incident was the first to come to mind. No doubt that was a drug connection. All the signs were there. What role did Franklin play in it?

Bryce had been very impressed by Monique. She was an energetic young lady who seemed to have her future well-planned. He wondered why Mrs. Brown would want to push her into dating. Evidently, she was much more mature than most boys her age.

Bryce had real concerns for Mrs. Brown. She obviously had a drinking problem. As a psychiatric nurse, Bryce was taught to observe and to make quick assessments. He could see that Mrs. Brown was beginning to develop health problems. There was an unhealthy tinge to her skin, not yellow, but very gray. She seemed to have lost some weight since their first encounter. The radiating glow that he had seen in her face in the pictures was fading away.

CHAPTER 3

Bryce pulled into the parking lot and spotted John outside pacing. He had a lit cigarette in his mouth. Bryce knew that John only smoked when he was troubled. Little did Bryce know that John had been eagerly waiting to offer advice and opinions.

"How did it go today?" John asked.

"It was a pretty good visit," Bryce replied. "I learned a little more about Franklin and his family. I didn't know he had a younger sister."

"Well, let me warn you, Bryce," John barked. "This Franklin character is no good. He's caused a lot of trouble for this agency. He almost got a couple of caseworkers fired. I'm telling you, he's scum. He's a drug user, and he doesn't need to be under our services."

Bryce wasn't sure why John seemed to show animosity toward Franklin. He had others on his caseload that were dual-diagnosed (mental illness and substance abuse). Therefore, his anger must have stemmed from a source unknown to Bryce.

"Anyway," Bryce started, "I'll be going out to see him tomorrow."

"I'm telling you, you're wasting your time."

Bryce had become accustomed to walking out with John at the end of the workday. Today John was preoccupied with lotto scratch-offs. Bryce could hear him swearing every time he scratched a loser. John looked up toward Bryce just long enough to signal him to go ahead.

"This guy is becoming very difficult to understand and to work with," Bryce thought. However, Bryce was trying to make it a practice not to bring any of the day's problems home. Home was for relaxing. He also looked forward to the thirty-minute commute to Waterbury. Usually the dancing classics on the radio helped.

Home for Bryce was a three-room apartment. At times it got a little lonely, but most weekends were spent with his daughter, sons, and his grandchildren. Bryce was trying to salvage his relationship with them. After divorcing their mother, his time spent with them became sparse, to say the least. He especially felt remorseful over not being able to help his oldest son, who had a problem with drugs. Bryce saw him making the same mistakes that he had and felt he hadn't handled the situation with him well. Whenever they agreed to talk, Bryce always lost his temper and began to yell. Because of this, they hadn't talked in two years.

Tonight, though, Bryce decided to have a quiet night alone. Being somewhat old-fashioned, he didn't like fast foods or TV dinners. He did his own cooking.

After dinner, Bryce did some writing on his computer. He had been trying to put memoirs of his experiences in Vietnam into words. Even though this was his first stab at writing, he felt that it was coming along quite well.

However, Bryce soon found himself staring idly into the computer screen. No matter how hard he tried to put the events of the day behind him, John's comments about Franklin hung around like a thunderous cloud about to burst. As the person training him, Bryce had listened to and looked to John for direction. He now felt it was time to break away. It would have to be his decision on how to handle Franklin's case.

Early the next morning, Bryce clocked in and signed out a state car. He was about to embark on the hour-long trip when he remembered the shoe box on his desk. He was surprised to see Nick at his desk. Normally, Nick was a late arrival, even though he was supposed to be taking the lead.

"I see you're off to an early start," Nick said.

"Yes, I'm going to see Franklin today. Remember?"

"Of course I remember. Why else would I be here so early? It's before my first morning coffee. Here's some orders from our doctor for the administrator up there. By the way, have you been up in those woods before?"

"No," Bryce replied, "but John said it was easy to find."

"Well then, here are some directions I drew up. Follow them, and it'll be easy to find. It's really a beautiful drive. If I didn't have all these meetings today, I would take the ride with you."

"Thank God for meetings," Bryce thought.

Nick was an okay guy, but he did not want his supervisor riding around with him, especially in a touchy case like this one.

"Remember, Bryce," Nick continued, "don't take this case personally. He may accept you as his case manager, or he may reject you. Either way, remember we still have other clients assigned to you."

Bryce gathered all that he thought he needed: the doctor's orders, the directions, and "Oh!" he said. "The shoe box." Yes, the shoe box still aroused Bryce's curiosity. Yet he dared not tamper with it. Reaching the car, he carefully placed it in the middle of the back seat. The directions read, *Up Route 4 for 2 miles, then turn on to*

29 Route *272 north. Follow this road for about an hour or so. Eagles' Nest is off this road. You will see signs.*

Bryce, not much of a coffee drinker, thought he could use a cup of it to stay alert. John told him it was a long winding road. Bryce pulled into the fast-food drive-thru at the end of Route 4. Sipping his coffee, he tuned the radio to the dancing classics and pulled out on Route 272 north. The blue sign on the side of the road read: *Scenic road for the next 56 miles.*

The first day of April was pleasantly sunny. The New England landscape was budding, but not all was fully green. Yet Bryce was beginning to see what made this a scenic route. The first set of homes he saw, these being nearer to town, were charmingly adorned. They were large with neatly mowed lawns and well spaced between neighbors. Behind them stood a huge mountain. On the other side of the road, a vast area of farms and open fields filled the scene.

Bryce was fascinated by the different animals he spotted along the way. To him there was always something special about seeing animals in their natural habitat as well as those who were domesticated. He passed ranches with horses right up on the railing, peering down at him as he slowed for a longer look. He recognized dairy and pig farms by the smell. Several times Bryce had to stop to let animals cross the road: family of geese and a family of ducks. He saw a lot of wild turkeys. Bryce thought it was silly to find himself laughing alone on this country road. He thought, "Well, I'm not the only turkey out here this morning."

As the houses became farther apart, other animals that darted onto his path included foxes and a bobcat. Even though he had never seen one before, he knew a house cat couldn't be that big. Several times he almost ran off the road trying to avoid squirrels and chipmunks. They seemed to be playing a game of chance with him.

One thing that puzzled Bryce were the stone walls. It seemed that every house had a stone wall, and there were stone walls or stone fences that seemed to encircle property. "What is all this about?" Bryce thought. "What purpose did they initially have? How long have they been there? Most of all, who took the time to build them?" He was a former military person, and they looked like some type of defensive set-up. "Probably from the patriotic war days," Bryce guessed. These questions went through Bryce's head, and he realized he was no longer paying attention to the road. As a matter of fact, had he not turned his attention to the road, he would have missed the partially obscured sign that read: *The Eagles' Nest this road.* Coming to a precipitating halt, he had to back up and then turn onto the dirt road.

Bryce knew there were several things that were capable of sending him off to a flashback of Nam. This dirt road was one of them. It reminded him of the many trails that he had walked down in the jungle. These paths had been traveled so frequently that they didn't need to be paved. They were frightful times, because someone had to have made the trail, and eventually the two forces would cross paths, leading to firefights and dead bodies.

The bend in the road snapped Bryce out of his flashback. He was very impressed by what he saw. Set in this big open meadow at the base of the mountain was a vast complex of beautifully colored buildings. A huge white one with a red roof and shutters was labeled *ADMINIS-TRATION*. There were a dozen or more cottages that looked like small motels. There were separate buildings clearly identified as dining, recreation, and auditorium.

Bryce drove around to get to the administration building. On his way, he observed tennis courts, swimming pools, basketball courts, baseball fields, and a small park-like area with statues of people unknown to him. "This looks like some type of college campus," Bryce thought.

Bryce entered the building and was greeted by the receptionist. After he stated his business there, she took him to meet the administrator.

"Ms. Langdon, this is Bryce Wright from the State Department of Mental Health. He's here to see Franklin Cooper," she said courteously.

Bryce's immediate thought of Ms. Langdon was that she looked too frail to be in charge of such a sizable operation. As she sat up, he could see that it was the oversized chair that had made her seem so small. He sensed that she was not accustomed to sitting there when she struggled to place her arms on the desk. With sunlight peering over her shoulder, her silver-gray hair sparkled and sent out a glare across the room. She adjusted her wire-framed glasses to focus on Bryce. Her voice had a flare of both authority and wisdom.

"Hello, we're glad to have you here. We welcome other agencies that get involved with our treatment plans," she said.

Bryce was a little lost for words. John had told him that they did a lot of fighting with private agencies regarding treatment. Able to recover, he said, "Hello. I'm glad I can help."

He handed her the orders from the doctor. She anxiously accepted them.

"Have a seat," she said as she turned her back and scanned the letter.

"This does help," she said. "Franklin is a strange kid. I wasn't sure he was right for this place. I mean at this time. That is, I thought he might benefit from a more intensive treatment program until he got a little better."

Bryce didn't quite understand. Then she went into details.

"Franklin has been very difficult to reach. He knows in order to stay here that he must abide by all the rules. This means attending all sessions, and so far he's done that. But he secludes himself whenever he can. He does not engage in conversation. After sessions, he's back in his room, in the dark, on his bed, curled in a fetal position. He only comes out when he needs to. None of my counselors have been able to get through to him. Our cottages are all coed. We don't encourage relationships. However, Franklin acts as if he doesn't even know that there are girls in his cottage. Most of the time, our staff is busy keeping people apart. So, young man, that is why we welcome you. We're hoping you can reach him."

"I'm gonna give it my best try," Bryce replied.

"And, while you're visiting here, all of your meals will be free of charge. We're noted for our fine foods. Some of the best chefs in the area have come from here. We have an agreement with the culinary people at the local college, of course."

"Of course," Bryce repeated.

"I've been in this business for over forty years now. I've seen a lot of kids come through our program. I've seen a lot of good kids that got a bad deal. And I've seen a lot of kids that were just bad. This Franklin is not a bad kid. He's been dealt some bad blows, and he's made some very bad decisions. Overall, he's not a bad kid. Mind you, now, his records do not tell me this. No agency has told me this. After all these years, I've learned to trust my feelings. I know through my own feelings, and that is what I'm going by, Bryce. Bryce, that's right, isn't it?"

"Yes, Bryce Wright."

"Well, Bryce, I've rarely been wrong with my feelings. Once was with a spoiled marriage. Well, actually, my feelings were right then, too, but I pushed them aside because of passion. That was long before I met Dr. Langdon. Vince is my late husband. He founded this place. Well, anyway, I know you didn't come all this way just to hear me talk. I want you to feel welcome, and if there's anything you need, please feel free to contact me or any of my counselors. I hope you will be able to help Franklin. About this time he should be on free time. That means that you're most likely to find him in his room. My receptionist will take you to him."

Bryce had seen his share of treatment facilities during his try for recovery, but none as elegant as this one.

"This is a beautiful place," he said to the receptionist.

"Yes, state of the art. We used to have a five year waiting list, but things have fallen off a bit lately. You could say that people were falling off the wagon to get in here," she said with a giggle. "That's one of our jokes," she said as though apologizing.

'That's okay," Bryce said. "I thought it was funny. It's just that my mind is on Franklin. This place looks expensive. I don't know how he got in here so suddenly."

"Well, it wasn't suddenly. Do you know Allison? She's a social worker for your agency, I believe. She applied here for Franklin some time ago, and he almost got in then. I heard she was taken off his case. After that, he never came in."

"How was she able to get him accepted so quickly?" Bryce inquired.

"Well," responded the receptionist, "Ms. Langdon or should I say the late Dr. Langdon, was in her family somehow. So, you know, family connections!"

"Oh!" Bryce said. "Thanks for sharing that with me."

"Here's your building. If you need to find your way back, pick up any phone, press the intercom button, and just say hello. I'll hear you."

"Thanks again," Bryce said, as she headed back to her office.

Bryce entered the circular lounge area of the cottage. A big-screen TV with its volume blasting faced him. He paused momentarily to see if the person watching would return. Bryce scanned the names on the six rooms in the circle. Three were on one side with girl names, and the boys were opposite. Before he could make a move toward Franklin's room, a young lady with her arms stretched high above her head stepped out of one of the rooms. She yawned and rubbed her sleepy eyes. She then moved quickly to the TV and turned it off. She turned and was startled by Bryce.

"May I help you?" she asked.

"I'm looking for Franklin Cooper," Bryce said, though he could plainly see Franklin's name above his door.

"Franklin's over there," she said, still rubbing her eyes and staggering back to her room.

Bryce knocked on the door, but got no response. He then pushed against the door, and it opened into darkness. For a moment he saw absolutely nothing. As his eyes began to adjust, he saw a body laying across the bed. "Franklin! Franklin!" Bryce called.

"Franklin! Franklin!" he said even louder. He called again and watched as the body rolled over.

"I'm Franklin. What do you want? Can't you see that I was sleeping? I don't want to be bothered. This is my free time. You don't have the right to come bothering me! Go away!" Franklin bellowed ferociously.

"Franklin, I'm with the state. I was with John at the hospital. Remember?" Bryce said almost pleadingly.

"I don't care!" snapped Franklin. "Just go away and stop bothering me!"

"Franklin, I'm your new case manager. I'm here to help you."

"I don't need your help. What makes you think you can help me? You and John can go to hell. Now get out of my room."

"Franklin, Franklin," Bryce repeated while trying to calm Franklin by lowering his voice.

"What part of 'get out' don't you understand? I don't need and don't want your help. Now get out. For the last time, get out!," Franklin shouted.

Bryce was about to inch closer when a shoe whisked by his head. He retreated, closing the door behind him. He turned to see five people staring at him. They all had sleepy eyes. Returning to their rooms, they seemed to nod their heads simultaneously.

Bryce sat in the lounge area pondering his next move. He was perplexed and didn't have a backup plan. He felt like he had been defeated in battle. Everyone was depending on him to make contact with Franklin. Until now, he felt he'd be able to at least talk to Franklin. Minutes passed, and Bryce realized that his trip was a failure. He began to feel very disappointed. He went straight to his car and drove off. He did not want Ms. Langdon to know that he didn't get through to Franklin. "So many people will be disappointed," he thought. What will he tell his boss? How can he face Ms. Brown? What will he say to Monique? John will be the only one getting any satisfaction out of this visit. Maybe John was also right about Franklin being scum. Maybe they're all in this together. Maybe it's an April fool's joke, and they're laughing at him.

"Don't take this case personally. Don't take it personally," Nick's words rang in Bryce's head. But he was taking it personally. How could he think he could help Franklin when he couldn't help his own son? He was taking it so personal that he began to feel depressed. Depression was something that Bryce had suffered for years after Nam. He had fought his way through it and hadn't felt depression of this magnitude for ten years. The thought of stopping to have a drink entered his mind.

He remembered how his depression had been tied in with his alcoholism. It had been over ten years since he last tasted alcohol or used drugs. "I can't go back down that road," he spoke.

The ride back was dismal. A dark cloud covered Bryce's thoughts. He returned to Torrington without remembering a single landmark on the road. In the parking lot back at the office, he turned to get out and spotted the shoe box on the back seat. "Dammed it," he declared. "What a disastrous day."

He didn't even do the one thing that Mrs. Brown and Monique had asked him to do: deliver the shoe box.

CHAPTER 4

It was a busy day at the Mental Health Center. This was not unusual for Wednesdays. All the department heads, case managers, and various private service providers met to discuss issues. Clients also streamed in and out for appointments with the doctor. Sometimes these Wednesdays even got chaotic.

Bryce tried to conceal himself from John under the cover of all this activity. Again, he recalled Nick's words: "Franklin may accept you, or he may reject you." But for John, this rejection would be proof of his point.

Bryce was already depressed and disappointed over not being successful in his attempt to reach Franklin. He didn't need John rubbing it in. Twice during the day, he spotted John, but he was engulfed in rubbing off instant-win lotto tickets.

For the next couple of days, Bryce moped around the office. He had been trying to muster the courage to go see Franklin's mother and sister. Finally, he was confronted by Nick. "How long are you gonna grieve over this guy? We told you that he was a tough case. You're not the first person he has rejected and, believe me, you won't be the last. I want you to wrap up this case. Take a couple of hours of overtime on your way home, and inform the family of your results. Next week we'll start you on a new case."

"Well," Bryce thought, "I guess this is how it goes in this business: win some, lose some."

Bryce parked his car three houses down from Mrs. Brown's. There was no place to park from the corner to her driveway. He wondered if something had happened to Mrs. Brown. He also thought about coming back at a later time. However, his conscience would not let him rest through the weekend without telling her the bad news.

Bryce climbed the five stairs to the porch. He could hear the chatter of many voices. They sounded too cheerful for it to be a sad occasion. He rang the doorbell and blinked in surprise as he was greeted by a beautiful lady. She had large greenish-brown eyes that highlighted her caramel-colored complexion. Unprepared for this pleasant sight, Bryce stood speechless and for a moment they stared at each other adoringly. She introduced herself as Brenda, one of Mrs. Brown's nieces.

"My name is Bryce Wright. I'm here to see Mrs. Brown, but if she's entertaining, I could come back on Monday."

"Don't be silly. We're all family here. She's in the kitchen. Follow me," Brenda instructed.

Bryce followed Brenda as she weaved her way through a bunch of women seated in the two rooms leading to the kitchen. She stopped halfway in to introduce Bryce. There were at least twenty women in those two rooms. The main event seemed to be centered around four card tables set up in the two rooms. Those seated at the tables were engaged in some partner-type game, while the others appeared to be waiting their turn.

Mrs. Brown was seated at the kitchen table. She was holding her favorite orange juice cocktail in one hand and waving a large knife with a broken wooden handle in the other. There were five other women seated around that room. Again, Brenda introduced Bryce, and for a minute there was no response. They seemed to be sizing up Bryce and Brenda. Mrs. Brown was the first to speak. "Well, Brenda, I see you've finally met your Mr. Wright."

By the time the giggling subsided, Bryce and Brenda were looking at each other, speechless. Both were totally embarrassed by the comment.

Mrs. Brown continued with the introductions: "Hello, Brian," she said, with no one correcting her. "These two are my sisters, Mabel and Jessie Mae."

Bryce had already assumed they were Martha's sisters. They clearly had the faces that matched those in the picture he had seen of Martha's younger days. Even though their faces were beefy and much rounder. They were a little broad in the beam. The long dresses that they wore hinted to Bryce that they were probably very religious. Their modest look showed a shy side, but they spoke with eminent authority.

"Stop waving that knife around, " one of them blasted.

"You look like you're ready to throw that thing," said the other.

Mrs. Brown set the knife down and took a sip of her drink. She continued with her introductions. "These three ladies are my sisters-in-law. Two of them are married to my brothers. They're visiting from Hoboken, New Jersey. The other one there is my favorite and my friend from high school. She's Tyrone's sister. All the others in the house are my nieces and cousins, even the Spanish and white ones."

Everyone laughed.

Mrs. Brown seemed to be a good hostess and well-liked in her neighborhood.

"Mrs. Brown, may I talk to you alone?"

"Sure you can, Brian," Martha said while struggling to her feet.

"Aunt Martha, his name is Bryce," Brenda tried to correct.

Whether Mrs. Brown heard her or not, she replied, "Brenda, will you please finish chopping up these onions for me?"

Mrs. Brown reached to pass the knife to Brenda, and the handle fell off. "Why don't you get rid of that old knife before someone gets hurt with it," one of Martha's sisters said.

"You've had that thing for what seems like ages. You're always holding onto things forever," said the other one.

Bryce followed Mrs. Brown as she made her way to the front of the house. She stopped at each table to find out who was winning. Bryce learned then that they were playing a game called Spades.

"Mrs. Brown, I was unable to successfully get through to Franklin. He rejected me. He rejected our services. He refused to accept any help from me. There's nothing else I can do. He has to want our help," Bryce said sounding apologetic.

Mrs. Brown stood and walked over to Bryce. She took him by the hand and led him back into the middle of the party group. She then announced, "Listen everyone. This nice man came all the way out here to tell me that he was rejected by Franklin."

First there was silence. Then there was a burst of laughter and giggles. "You could have said that in here," Mabel said. "Almost everyone in this house has been rejected by Franklin at least once."

"Hallelujah to that!" Jessie Mae added. "Franklin can do better. He just need to stay away from that drug-dealing Raymond."

"I remember when Franklin did…," said one cousin.

"And I remember when…," said another.

The stories continued throughout the house about being rejected by Franklin. Bryce was now laughing. He was beginning to feel less guilty about his failure. "Well, it was nice to have met you all," Bryce said.

"Brenda, why don't you show your Mr. Wright to the door. We see that you can't keep your eyes off of him," said one of Martha's sisters, causing the laughter to continue.

Bryce didn't mind this ribbing at all. His eyes had been drawn to Brenda's. He found himself captivated by her charming appearance. He noticed, too, that her eyes seemed to light up whenever he spoke.

Brenda was reaching for the door when it opened and Monique walked in. "Hello, Mr. Wright," was her greeting. Her voice was quavering, and her face had a stricken look. She immediately rushed through the crowd to her mother in the kitchen.

Bryce closed the door. He felt he needed to tell her about his failure with Franklin, and he wanted to make sure she was okay. He reached the kitchen in time to hear her say, "Momma, when I came out of the library, I had a flat tire. That man that I've been seeing here and there, well, he came over and offered to change it for me. He seemed polite, but I got a glimpse of his face, and it was heinous. I almost started to run off, but he had already started to change it."

"Is that man still following you?" Mrs. Brown questioned.

"What man is this?" asked Mabel.

"Martha, how come you didn't tell us this?" queried Jessie. She, too, used a pointer, but hers was a chicken drumstick. "We can't have our niece being stalked."

"It not like he's stalking me," Monique said, "but he has turned up most everywhere I've been lately. Usually his face is hidden under a hood. Today I got to see it. He has a long scar on the right side that runs from his forehead across his eye to under his chin. It's pretty scary looking. Yet, he was very pleasant, and afterward he suddenly disappeared."

"What do you mean he suddenly disappeared?" asked Jessie Mae. "You sure you haven't been in your mother's vodka?"

"No, Aunt Jessie. When he was finished I reached to get him some money, and when I turned back, he was gone. He seemed kind of shy. I sort of feel sorry for him, the way he looks and all."

"Well, it's very dangerous out there today. You had better be careful," spoke one of neighboring ladies. "When we were little, our parents would let us run all over this neighborhood. Now, there's too many creeps out there." Everyone agreed.

Monique turned to Bryce and asked, "Why are you here, Mr. Wright? Is Franklin alright?"

"He's here to see Brenda," joked one of the ladies.

"And how was your date?" teased Mabel.

"I went to the library," Monique shot back.

"Martha, when are you gonna let this girl date?" one went on.

Monique asked Bryce to follow her back to the front part of the house, after noticing that she wasn't getting anywhere in that conversation. "Is Franklin alright?" she asked again.

"I was confident that I would be able to help your brother. But he didn't want anything to do with me," Bryce said. "My supervisor asked me to stop by and tell you and your mother the outcome of my visit. We're going to discharge Franklin from our services and move on to other clients."

"Please have a seat for a minute, Mr. Wright," Monique requested. "Do you know what's going on here today?"

"No, not really."

"Well, I'll tell you. My mother is in this club, or association I may say, with some of my aunts, cousins, and neighbors. Every Friday and sometimes on Saturday, they gather at one person's home to play cards. They have some kind of rotating schedule. They put up quarters to play. This fee is mostly given to the hostess who provides the food and drinks. The games are mostly for the association of friends and family. They have fun. In addition to the vodka, this is my mother's thing."

"I see," Bryce acknowledged.

"Now, me," Monique continued, "as you probably just heard, I came from the library. I write poems. I hope one day to have them published. I read a lot of poetry, and when I go to college, I plan to study creative writing. I can really get wrapped up in my poetry. And that's my thing."

Bryce started to comment but Monique continued. "Now my brother, Franklin, he has had a tough go of it all his life. He won't listen to me, because I'm his baby sister, as he puts it. He keep making bad choices. And he has an illness that keeps him going all the time and acting like a wild man. The next few months he doesn't want to be bothered by anyone. Not even me or Mama. He can do better if he stays away from those street drugs. We have seen him do good with help. He was doing good with Allison, but everybody always quits on him. I been hoping and praying that God would send someone along to help him. I thought my prayers were answered when you came around. Now you're quitting on him, too. I was sure that once he got his shoe box, he would open up to you."

"Shoe box!" Bryce said. He banged his fist into his open hand. "I didn't give him the shoe box. Actually, I forgot it and left it in the car. It's still in the car on the back seat. How could I forget the shoe box?"

"Anyway," Monique continued, "Franklin has a strange attachment to that shoe box. It used to always seem to comfort and cheer him up. He never opened it in front of us or anyone else for that matter. So you see, along with vodka, these card parties are my mother's thing. For me, poetry is my thing. That shoe box is Franklin's thing."

At that moment, Bryce felt an urgency to get back to see Franklin. Monique's admonition, along with the fact that Franklin was accustomed to rejecting people, kindled his determination. However, it was the beginning of the weekend, and Tuesday was the day for case managers to visit the Eagles' Nest. Besides, Nick had asked Bryce to wrap up this case.

All the way home, Bryce's mind drifted back and forth on two matters. One was Brenda. Bryce felt an overwhelming attraction to her. She had the looks that Bryce had been searching for in a woman. He was hoping that he would be able to see her again.

The other matter that clogged his mind was Monique's words. Those words dogged and nagged Bryce. "Everybody always quits on him," she had said of Franklin.

Bryce had been a quitter after his discharge from the Army. It caused him a great deal of loss. Once he became sober, he vowed never to quit on anything that he started and felt was important.

When Bryce reached his front door, he remembered the guys he used to hang out with. They spent time drinking and wasting their lives. Over half of them were dead. The others are suffering from some infirmity to the point that they can't enjoy life. They seem to have given up on themselves. Bryce was determined not to quit like they had. He tried to stop drinking for his former wife. He tried to stop drinking for his children. He tried to stop drinking for his employer. It was only when he decided to stop for himself that he became successful. This, he felt, was a lesson he could pass on to Franklin.

CHAPTER 5

There was no staying up late for Bryce on the computer this Friday night. He wanted to get to bed early. He had already resolved that he was going back to the Eagles' Nest. Bryce fluffed his pillow, and twice he almost had it right. Before falling asleep, he felt himself rotating like a log racing down the rapids on its way to the grinding mill. His dreams were haunted by Monique's words and his own guilt for not delivering the shoe box.

Early Saturday morning, Bryce gave thought to what he was about to do. He knew the work rules, and normally he abided by them. Besides the state's rule of not visiting clients on personal time, the Eagles' Nest had specific visiting arrangements with the state. Yet Bryce didn't feel that he could wait until Tuesday to give Franklin the shoe box.

Route 272 is a winding road, and its scenic beauty was a distraction for Bryce today. He wished that it was straight, like a drag strip. Even though he had seen no cops on his previous visit, Bryce valued his life, and he only drove the speed limit.

With the administrative staff off for the weekend, Bryce encountered only a roaming security vehicle. He entered the grounds undetected. He remembered his way back to Franklin's cottage but didn't find him in his room. The same sleepy-eyed, yawning young woman came out of her room and asked, "Are you looking for Franklin? He's in the dining hall with everyone else."

Bryce thought, "This is not how I planned to do this."

He had such a hard time with Franklin on his first visit, and he didn't want to repeat that scene, especially in front of a crowd of people. That would make his informal visit even more noticeable. Yet he had not come this far for nothing. With the shoe box clutched tightly in his hand, he followed the young woman's directions to the dining hall.

The smell of fresh coffee and breakfast foods led Bryce to the dining hall. He remembered that the Eagles' Nest had a reputation for serving delicious food.

Bryce paused before he entered the dining hall. The sound coming from inside was cheerful and noisy. He took a deep breath and stepped in. He observed a lot of activity. There was a man in a white cap and apron taking orders, and there was another man filling those orders on a large grill. A variety of other food was spread along a counter, and people lined up to help themselves. There were about fifty men and women of different races throughout the dining area. They were eating and stopped from time to time to chat. Some of the younger people gathered off to one side. Bryce was surprised to see Franklin sitting in the middle of that group. He seemed to be taking the lead in the conversation. This shouldn't have surprised Bryce. Monique had told him that Franklin always kept a lot of people around him when he was well. There was something about him that attracted people. He appeared to be a good leader. He knew how to entertain people and make them laugh. He probably got that trait from his mother.

At any rate, they were having so much fun that Franklin failed to recognize Bryce standing there. Suddenly, though, his gaze became fixed as his eyes zoomed in on the shoe box. An eerie hush fell upon those who had been listening to his jokes. They seemed to be waiting quietly for him to snap out of the trance and conclude with the punch line. Instead, Franklin stood up, excused himself, and walked over to Bryce.

It was an intense moment for Bryce, too. The butterflies had gathered in his stomach. Franklin stepped right up to him. "Why don't you get in line for breakfast, Mr. Wright. I'll take the box and meet you at the table over there," Franklin said, pointing to a secluded spot.

Somewhat startled by Franklin's actions, Bryce ordered breakfast, but he didn't get all that he would have liked to. He was anxious to get over to the table. "Is this the same Franklin?" he asked himself.

For the first time, Franklin seemed agreeable and on the same wave length with Bryce.

"Have a seat, Mr. Wright," Franklin said. "It was kind of you to drive all the way up here to bring me my shoe box. Why didn't you bring it the other day?"

"Well, actually I did, but I forgot to give it to you."

"Oh! What you mean is that I was so rude that I made you forget to leave it. I can be pretty rude at times. I want to apologize for acting that way. You see, I wasn't feeling well. I get so down at times that I don't want to be bothered by anyone. I don't understand what's wrong with me," Franklin explained.

Bryce was unsure what Franklin meant. Did this mean that he was finally accepted by Franklin? Or was his friendliness due to the recovery of the shoe box? In either case, Bryce realized that Franklin 's mood may not be so accepting for long. He had to get some answers quickly.

"You did come here to bring the shoe box, didn't you?" Franklin asked.

"Well, yes and no," Bryce replied.

"Yes and no? What does that mean?" Franklin returned.

"Yes, I wanted you to have your shoe box. But I am also here to offer you our services."

"Listen," Franklin started, "I repeat. I do appreciate you bringing me my shoe box. But you cannot help me. No one can help me. I've been this way for a long time. I've had people from your agency trying to help me for years. It's become a game to them. I can play my own game. The only person up there who really cares about helping people is Allison, and you see what they did to her."

"I didn't get to meet her," Bryce said. "I've only heard Monique talk about her."

"Oh! So you met my little sister?" Franklin inquired.

"Yes. She's a smart young woman. I also met with your mother and some of your other relatives. You have a nice family and lot of support."

"Yeah, right! That's why I can't go to their houses," Franklin said with a bit of sarcasm.

"You know Franklin, according to what I've read in your charts, you've never needed a lot of psychotropic medications. For most of your life you've been treated with Prozac and Risperdal. The charts show that when you've been compliant with taking them and stay away from street drugs, you've been able to live a relatively normal life. Your bouts of depression seem to occur less when you take your medication. If you could kick your cocaine habit, you might be able to recover from your illness or at least put it in remission."

"I really don't want to live like this. I'm tired of these kind of places. But when I get down, cocaine is the only thing that helps."

"I see how you're thinking," Bryce said, "But you only get down when you stop taking your medication."

"So how can you help me? You don't know what it's like."

"Why do you say that?"

"Well, look at yourself. You don't look like you've ever done a bad thing in your life."

"That's not true," Bryce replied. "I've been clean and sober for ten years. But before that, I suffered just like you. I've been in and out of institutions like this one. I've even been in mental hospitals."

"What for?" Franklin asked. He was beginning to show some interest.

"I'm a recovering alcoholic. I did crack cocaine and everything else that the crowd did. I've been diagnosed with depression. I've been homeless twice. Everything you've done, I've done way before you thought about doing it. Well, except for getting into trouble with the judicial system," Bryce related.

"Oh, yeah, that court thing. I'm going to have to face up to that one of these days," Franklin admitted.

"There, you see. I do know what you're going through. That's why I believe I can help you. But only if you want and accept help." Bryce continued, "My problems started when I was young, like you. I tried to escape them by enlisting in the Army. I was doing good until they shipped me off to Vietnam. It was in Nam that I became exposed to drugs."

Bryce noticed that whenever he said the word Vietnam, Franklin's eyes widened. Bryce now had Franklin's full attention.

"Wow! You were in Vietnam!" Franklin mused.

"Yes. After that experience, I had a hard time adjusting to stateside. I became very confused, rebellious, and irresponsible. I just couldn't seem to get it together."

"My father was in Vietnam."

"Oh, yeah. I remember your mother telling me that. I also remember both your mother and Monique telling me that the two things that you cared the most for was your father and that shoe box. What's with that shoe box anyway?"

"This shoe box has always brought me comfort. My father gave it to me, and I have never let anyone look inside, not even Mama and Monique. But today, because you drove all the way up here to bring it to me, I'm going to show you what's inside. Not here though. Let's go over to my cottage," Franklin said in a secretive voice.

Bryce felt exalted to have this honor. He was thinking that the drive had been well worth it. Franklin was about to reveal something to him that none of his family had seen.

With this new kindling relationship, Bryce thought he could take the opportunity to gather more information from Franklin. "When I went to your apartment for the shoe box, I surprised someone who was rummaging through your stuff. He ran away through the back as I entered. I got to the window just in time to see a silver-colored BMW speed off. The car's window was tinted, and the license plate was lettered. They couldn't have wanted the shoe box. I easily found it sitting on the closet shelf."

Franklin didn't respond immediately. After a minute or so he said, "Don't worry about it. It was probably my friend Ray-Man."

Franklin's happy mood was changing, and Bryce realized it. He had put Franklin on the spot. Something sounded fishy about Franklin's explanation, but Bryce didn't want to push the issue and blow the opportunity he had. Franklin was opening up to him and was giving him the privilege of looking into the shoe box.

At the cottage, Franklin sat on his bed and offered Bryce a chair he had pulled close. Franklin sat the box between the two of them, and Bryce thought of Pandora's Box. He wondered if it had been this exciting. This was better than any mystery movie he had seen in a long time. Bryce licked his dry lips. Franklin slowly untaped the box, and Bryce thought back to Nam. He remembered how the troops would sit around, dry-mouthed from anticipation, as someone opened a Care package from home. It had become a common practice for everyone to share the contents of their packages.

Franklin reached into the box, pulled out a set of metal wings, and handed them to Bryce. "Um, your father was a paratrooper, I see. I was a paratrooper, too," Bryce mumbled. He then gave them a slow appraising glance.

Next Franklin handed Bryce six medals and said, "The contents of this box are the only connection I have with my father now."

Bryce recognized the medals. He said, "A Good Conduct Medal, a Vietnam Service Medal, a Vietnam Campaign Medal, and an Army Accomodation Medal."

Bryce had also been awarded these medals. However, the next two medals he didn't recognize right away. Then he gawked in disbelief and shouted, "Hey! This is a Bronze Star, and this one is a Silver Star! Wow!"

"What does that mean?" Franklin asked, reacting to Bryce's excitement. His breath got caught in his throat as he tried to rush his words.

"Are you sure these are your father's?" Bryce asked. A sudden course of adrenaline had rushed through his body.

"Yes. My mother told me that before my father died he put all of this together for me. So what do they mean?" Franklin repeated.

"Your father was hero. Only heroes get medals like these," Bryce informed him.

"Wait, there's more in here," Franklin said. He pulled out two shoulder patches and handed them to Bryce.

Bryce opened his mouth, but no words came out. He leaned back into his seat. He gaped in stunned silence as he stared wide-eyed at the patches.

"What do they mean? What do they mean?" Franklin pressed.

"Your father and I served in the same Army divisions. See this one with the eagle. This is the 101st Airborne Division. I was with this unit in Nam. And this one, with the double A's, this is the 82nd Airborne Division. They're America's honor guard. I was with this unit here in the states. What else is in the box?" Bryce asked.

"Not much," Franklin replied, as he handed Bryce four saving bonds. "I don't know what to do with these. How long do I have to save them?"

"Wow! These are $100 bonds. You've had these since your father died?" Bryce asked.

"Yeah," Franklin answered.

"You should continue to save them," said a quick-thinking Bryce. He hoped Franklin would not cash them in. This might put his treatment in jeopardy. "They're hard to cash anyway," he added for insurance.

"Is that all that's in the box?" Bryce inquired. He was feeling the excitement slipping away.

"Only some old pictures of my father and some of his friends in Vietnam." He handed a couple of them to Bryce. The pictures had begun to fade awfully. They were taken with an old black and white Polaroid. They were called Swinger, the first camera to develop film instantly. Being shut up in the box probably did the most damage to the pictures, though.

Bryce examined the pictures closely. He recognized the scene as being the monsoon season in the highlands of Nam. He was able to make out faces and some of them were familiar. Bryce asked Franklin for more pictures. He stared at the next one for awhile. He then placed that picture face down on the bed. He looked up at the ceiling and shook his head in disbelief. Franklin was silent. He realized that Bryce had seen something very important.

Bryce picked up the picture again. Again he studied it acutely. Then he asked, "Which one of these guys is your father?"

Franklin pointed to the big guy holding the machine gun.

"I know that guy!" Bryce said. "As a matter of fact, I know all of these guys. Let me see the rest of those pictures."

The next picture Bryce looked at caused him to jump reflexively. He leaned so far back in his chair that he almost flipped backwards. Franklin reached out and caught him. He asked, "What's the matter?"

"See this picture! See this guy standing next to your father. That's me! That's me! I knew your father! Your father was my buddy! T.C., that's what we called him. That's T.C., and that's me standing next to him. I've been looking for your father ever since I left the Army."

Bryce suddenly realized that his carrying on was affecting Franklin. Franklin eyes were starting to mist over. "I'm sorry," Bryce said. "I got a little carried away."

They both stood up. Tears dripped from their eyes. They hugged. Franklin had found a connection to his father, and Bryce had found the son of his lost friend from Nam.

Bryce was still floating on cloud nine. He said, "Wow! That's me in the picture. You know, I never made the connection: T.C., Tyrone Cooper. In Nam everyone had a nickname. That's why I had a hard time finding your father. All I could remember was T.C."

"Well, Mr. Wright, maybe you can help me after all. I sure would like to hear all you can tell me about my father and Vietnam. I have hundreds of books and magazines with stories about Vietnam. They give me a picture but I would like to hear about it from a person who has been there. Most of all, I want to know what it was about Nam that caused my father to drink so much that it killed him. My mother said that he didn't even drink before he went to war."

"Listen, Franklin," Bryce started, "You can call me Bryce. Your father just called me Doc. If he had to find me, he probably wouldn't recall my real name either. Anyway, I understand why you have those medals now. Your father was a hero. He was a real American hero. Long before the movie "Rambo", your father carried his M-60 machine gun in one arm, and he used to fire it from that position with accuracy. Mind you now, this type of gun was designed to be fired from a tripod on the ground. Your father saved my butt several times. Had it not been for your father's courageous fighting ability, I might not have made it home. He saved our whole company, not just once, but several times. One day I'll go into details about the things he did."

"If he was a hero in Nam, why did he give up and turn to the bottle here at home?" Franklin asked sadly . His face became twisted with pain.

"From what I've learned from your mother, he died from something that's killed a lot of veterans and almost killed me. In Nam, we gave it a name. Your father died "fighting the elements". In Nam, we came to recognize all the elements that could cause us harm, but we underestimated the elements that waited for us back home."

"Alcoholism is one of those elements?" Franklin inquired.

"Yes. There are a few more, though. I don't have time to explain it all now. In time I'll tell you. The most important thing for us to work on is keeping you drug-free. I must go. I'm not supposed to be up here. I could get into trouble, but I'm really glad I came back. If I can convince my supervisor to put me back on your case, I'll be back on Tuesday. Then you'll have to sign some releases."

"You mean they almost took you off as my case manager?"

"That's right. I took a chance so you could have the shoe box."

"See how the shoe box looks out for me. I'm really glad you came back. I need to know about my father."

CHAPTER 6

Bryce was riding high when he pulled into the parking lot Monday morning. The only available space was next to John. He, too, had just arrived. After such a positive weekend, John was the last person Bryce wanted to see. He had successfully avoided him for most of last week. "What's up Bryce?" John asked. "How was your weekend?"

"Weekends are always good," Bryce replied. "How was yours?"

"Not bad. Not bad at all. By the way, Bryce, I heard you had a hard time with Franklin last week. I told you he was no good. Guys like him are nothing but trouble. You're better off working with someone else. He's a waste of your time."

"Well things have changed now, John. Franklin is cooperative and willing to accept our services."

"When did all this happen? The last I heard on Friday was that he had shot you down," John said, sounding angry and surprised.

"I forgot to give him his shoe box when I first went there. I went back Saturday, and he was more agreeable then."

"You did what? Don't you know that's against the rules? Look, I'm supposed to be training you. How's that gonna look on my behalf? Besides, we can't help this guy. He's gonna suck you in just like he did Allison," John shouted.

John was quite adamant by his remarks. Bryce was thinking of putting up a defense. After all, this was his lost friend's son. Instead, as they reached the building, John headed for the stairs. Bryce turned to the elevator, avoiding a confrontation. The elevator opened on the third floor, and Bryce practically stumbled into his supervisor.

"Bryce," Nick said, "your timing is perfect. I need to see you in my office as soon as you put your things away."

"Boy!" Bryce thought, "How did he learn so quickly? Did John run up the stairs to tell him?"

Monday was off to a bad start for Bryce. He never liked it whenever he was summoned to the office. He always thought the worst would happen. This time he couldn't deny that he was guilty. Bryce started to build his defense as he made his way to Nick's office.

"Have a seat, Bryce," Nick suggested. "How was your weekend?"

"Listen Nick, I know you asked me to close Franklin's case. I know it was wrong for me to go there on my own time, but I forgot to leave his shoe box. That shoe box is the most important thing in that young man's life. However, when I got there, he was very receptive. He's agreed to our services. He's ready to sign releases and all. We can work with him now."

"Well now, that's very interesting to know but that wasn't why I called you. Over the weekend I got a call from the medical director of the Eagles' Nest. He would like to talk to you, which means, you will be going there tomorrow. It seems that Franklin has been seeing three different doctors and getting three prescriptions filled at three pharmacies. All of the prescriptions are for Prozac. We want to know why he needs so much Prozac, especially when there's none showing up in his blood."

"Oh!" Bryce said. "I thought maybe John had run up here and told you about my weekend."

"No, I haven't seen John, but I already know what you did on Saturday. Listen, Bryce, not all the rules around here are written in stone. I personally like an aggressive case manager. But, you have to play by my rules. All you had to do the other day was beep me and make me aware of your plans. You remember that in the future."

"I understand," Bryce said.

"Another thing that's working in your favor is that someone's pulling strings for Franklin. The commissioner's office also called me over the weekend. They want us to continue trying to reach Franklin. All of a sudden this Franklin has become important to someone. So you're back on the case."

"That's great! I really think I can help him. You won't believe this Nick, but I knew his father while we were in Nam," Bryce said just before being interrupted by a knock at the door. Nick turned to open the door, and John seemed surprised to see Bryce sitting there. "Oh, it's not that important. I'll talk to you later," John said to Nick before walking away.

"I don't understand why John gets so upset with my working with Franklin," Bryce commented. "And the name Allison seems to spark anger in him."

"Allison used to work here. She was Franklin's case manager at one time. She was making good progress with him. Then it was alleged that she had become too emotionally involved with him," Nick conveyed.

"What does that have to do with John?" Bryce asked.

"They were engaged. When the rumors started to spread around here, John became outraged. Finally, they broke off the engagement. I guess Allison felt uncomfortable working here. She transferred to the Department of Children and Families. We lost a good case worker when we lost her," Nick offered.

"Well that explains a lot," Bryce noted.

Bryce went off to start his normal Monday's tasks. His plans were to visit Mrs. Brown and Monique after work. He was anxious to tell them the good news. Bryce now felt good about working on this case. Because he had known Tyrone, Bryce was beginning to feel a sense of obligation toward his family.

When Bryce arrived at Mrs. Brown's house, he heard shouting coming from inside. He rang the doorbell and was greeted by Monique, who was crying. "Hello, Mr. Wright, come in," she managed to get out. "Maybe you can talk to my mother."

"What's the matter?"

"I can't get her to stop drinking. She's been in the bathroom throwing up. She's been throwing up for two days, but she won't stop drinking. Everything she tries to eat comes back up. Now she's walking around bent over holding her stomach. Maybe she will listen to you."

When Mrs. Brown came out of the bathroom, she immediately resumed her screaming. "Where's my vodka? I thought I told you to find my bottle. Where did you hide it this time?"

"Mrs. Brown, Mrs. Brown," Bryce called.

She recognized his voice and tried to straighten up. She was barely able to look up and reach out to him. Bryce understood that as a gesture for help. He could clearly see that she wasn't well. The whites of her eyes and the palms of her hands were yellow. Again she made an effort to straighten herself but became very unsteady.

"Listen, Monique," Bryce whispered. "I need you to call an ambulance right away."

"I heard that!" reacted Mrs. Brown. " I don't need no ambulance. Just find my vodka. She hid it on me, Brian. Can you image that! After all I've done for her, she go and hide my vodka. She need to be out of here. You need to be out on a date. You hear me? She need a boyfriend. Right, Brian."

The shouting tired her, and she lost her balance and began to fall. Bryce was able to catch her and ease her to the floor. She slipped into unconsciousness but was still breathing. The ambulance arrived quickly. Without resistance, the crew had her on broad and off to the hospital in a matter of minutes.

Monique was sobbing outright when Bryce asked her to call her aunts. Then they left for the hospital in Bryce's car. Bryce tried to distract

Monique from her mothers situation by informing her that he was working with Franklin again.

"I'm glad you're able to work with Franklin, Mr. Wright." Monique's concerns for her family were many, and she began to verbalize them. "I don't know what's going to become of my family. We have so many problems. We've had so many losses. Mama's slowly killing herself with her drinking. Franklin is away all the time. When he's not, I rarely can talk to him anymore because he's always high on something. Why can't people see what alcohol and drugs do to a family?"

Bryce did not answer right away. He thought it would be best to let her vent her frustrations.

"All Mama talks about lately is me going out on a date. It's like she's trying to get rid of me or something. I'm not interested in dating. Besides, who will take care of her when I'm out? Who's gonna clean and keep our house together? Why do you think she is doing this to me?" she asked.

"Well," Bryce answered, while searching for the right words, "maybe she's concerned about your safety and you being alone. Having suffered many losses, she's probably worried about losing you. You do go out to the library alone, don't you?"

"Yes, that's true," Monique replied.

"I recall how upset you were when you spoke about some guy following you around," Bryce reminded her.

"Yeah, that's true, and I've seen him three times this week. He's beginning to show up more and more, especially since I let him change my tire."

"Do you have any idea who he might be?"

"No, I don't recognize him. He wears a hood year round to hide his face. It's strange, but I really don't feel threatened by him. It's like having your own guardian angel. Do you know what I mean?"

"I guess I do. But you shouldn't go out alone," Bryce warned.

"Well maybe I should date. What do you think?"

"It's not for me to make that decision for you. Besides, that's not quite what I meant. I meant maybe you should spend more time with one of your cousins or aunts."

"Oh, I see," Monique conceded.

"Speaking of your cousins," Bryce continued, "how's Brenda?"

"She's just fine," Monique replied. "She'll be accompanying my Aunt Jessie. They should meet us at the hospital."

Bryce and Monique rushed into the emergency room at the hospital and asked to see Mrs. Brown. They were told that they would have to go back into the waiting room because the doctor was performing tests on Mrs. Brown to determine the cause of her ailment. The nurse would let them know when they could come in. This only rekindled Monique's concerns for her mother. She started to cry. Again Bryce tried to distract her.

"I see that you've been holding onto that folder pretty tight. Do you have some of your poems in there?" He calmly asked.

"What?" Monique responded.

"Poems. Do you have poems in your folder?" Bryce repeated.

"Oh, yes," Monique answered as her crying subsided. "I brought these along because they relax me."

"I've been doing some writing myself," Bryce commented. "I have a sixteen chapter novel about recovering from Nam that I've completed. But I haven't had any success in getting it published."

"Oh, is that right? I didn't know you were a writer."

"Well, I wouldn't say that I'm a writer. I haven't had any training. I'm more of a storyteller. I have to send my work out to be rewritten for me," confessed Bryce.

"I think I need to learn more about writing, too. That's why I've enrolled in a school that offers writing classes. I start the fall session," Monique stated.

"I think you'll do good."

"I 've written poems for every member of my family," Monique revealed, "even for my father, who I don't remember, and Franklin's father, who I never even met."

"Oh! I forgot to tell you," Bryce remembered, "I knew Franklin's father. We were together in Vietnam. He's a main character in my book, and I've been looking for him for years."

"It seems so strange. You were with Franklin's father in Vietnam and now you are his case manager. It's like you are Franklin's guardian angel or something."

"It's more like something than angel," Bryce returned.

They both laughed.

"I didn't know about his father until he opened up the shoe box. And I wouldn't have had that opportunity if you didn't encourage me to go back," he said.

Feeling slightly embarrassed by the compliment, Monique asked, "Would you like to read some of my poetry?"

"Of course," Bryce replied. "I thought you would never ask."

They both leaned back in their seats, getting more comfortable as Bryce started to read her first poem.

MY DREAM
By Monique Brown
> *I'm having a dream, you can share it with me.*
> *Equality and peace is all that I see.*
> *I see no violence or crime on the street,*
> *Just happy faces and tranquility.*
> *My dream can be your dream, come enjoy it with me*
> *No thoughts of superiority from one race or the other,*
> *Just happy people together as brothers.*
> *No more poverty, no disease on our planet.*
> *Beauty's so prevalent, it's taken for granted.*

My dream can be your dream, come enjoy it with me. No more pollu-
tion of water or air,
In my dream there's only people who care
My dream can be your dream, I'll share it with you,
Cause if everyone dreams it, it's bound to come true.

"That's very good!" Bryce said.

"Do you really think so?" Monique responded while handing him another one. "Here, read this one."

Let us Spread Love
by Monique Brown
I've an abundance of love I can share
with people who want to be loved everywhere.
I don't care who you are, what you have, love is free
Take a chance, give yourself, you can share it with me.
Love your man when you can,
Love your child for a while,
Love a friend from within,
Let us spread love.
All the world that we see is filled with hate,
cause on sadness they all concentrate.
Forget the lie that was told and the evil that was done.
Look around, give a smile, search out people just for fun.
Throw a kiss, hug a neck,
Do what one won't expect.
Watch and see, thrilled you'll be!
Let us spread love
Think, we're different, I'm white and you're black.
Color's small, as a matter of fact.
We both think, can agree, I'll love you, you love me,

And together we'll live peacefully.
Let a child see you smile,
Let him know why you glow,
Cause at least you've let prejudice pass.
Let us spread love

"Boy! You really have talent," Bryce commented.

Before Monique could respond, she spotted Brenda and Aunt Jessie Mae entering through the emergency room door.

"How is she?" they both asked.

"Lord, I don't know what to do with my sister. I thought I told her to get her butt up here yesterday," Jessie Mae preached. "Lord, one day that drinking is going to kill her."

Monique tried to explain why they were waiting outside the examination room, but Jessie Mae was fixed on seeing her sister. With Brenda in tow, she stormed through the double doors. They had hardly gotten in when they began backing out. They saw the doctor, and two nurses and Mrs. Brown on a stretcher. Monique burst into tears when she saw her mother with an oxygen mask covering her face and IV tubes coming out of her arms.

"She'll be admitted to the third floor ICU for the time being," the doctor said. "The tests show that she has acute pancreatitis."

Jessie Mae comforted Monique and whispered to Bryce, "Brenda needs to get back home. She's gonna call the family. Would you mind giving her a ride? I'll drive Monique home after we see that her mother is okay and in her room."

Even though it wasn't a pleasant situation, Bryce and Brenda got to learn a little about each other. Bryce learned that Brenda worked as a telephone operator for the local phone company. She was once married and had a daughter who was living with Brenda's mother and father in New Jersey. Brenda felt comfortable in blue jeans and this is what she preferred to wear most of the time. They learned that they did have some things in common. They both liked the same kind of food and enjoyed listening to the same type of music. They found out that their attraction was mutual. They made plans for a dinner date.

CHAPTER 7

It was raining cats and dogs Tuesday morning. Bryce concluded this when he ventured outside to start his car and stepped in a "poodle". This was a silly joke that Bryce used to tell around the office whenever there were torrential downfalls.

This was the type of day Bryce faced for his trip. Outbursts of echoing thunder with lightning were followed by long periods of downpour. The storm awakened him before the alarm could ring. He thought about the mission that lay ahead and was unable to fall back to sleep. He decided to get started.

Bryce headed up Route 272, and the rain started to subside. He now encountered a heavy fog as he climbed the elevation going up to the Eagles' Nest. Bryce was not familiar with the curves he faced, and this made driving difficult. He would be alright, though, if he took his time. He turned down the volume to the dancing classics on the radio to give his full attention to the road.

However, it wasn't the fog that weighed the heaviest on his mind. He was mulling over what he perceived as a difficult decision. Should he tell Franklin about his mother's ailment? Was it his responsibility to do so? If he didn't tell Franklin, could he maintain a good conscience about the matter? He reasoned that if he did tell Franklin the bad news, he might become depressed, and that would jeopardize his treatment. On the other hand, if Mrs. Brown became gravely ill, and Bryce did not tell him, would Franklin continue to trust him?

Contemplating these things, Bryce hardly realized that he had gone more than half the way with no problem with the fog. Suddenly, he came to a sharp bend in the road and encountered a car coming directly toward him. It was not handling the curve well. It was well over the yellow lines. Bryce swerved hard to the right. He ran off the road and came to a stop in front of a fence. The other car kept going.

Bryce replayed the incident in his mind and realized that it was a silver BMW with tinted windows. It was the same car he had seen at Franklin's apartment. Bryce felt his stomach flutter and his heart was thumping. He managed to gather himself together and continued up the road to the Eagles' Nest.

Bryce informed the receptionist at the Eagles' Nest that he was there to see the medical director. After her husband's death, Ms. Langdon had hired a close friend of the family to direct the medical program. This was Dr. Andrew. However, to Bryce's disappointment, the receptionist told him that Dr. Andrew was there only on Monday and Thursday mornings til noon. She related how the doctor had expected to hear from him the day before.

Bryce did not spend a great deal of time trying to figure out whose fault it was. Nick had told him that Tuesday was the earliest he could come. Neither one of them thought to call for an appointment. For the time being, Bryce's concern was for Franklin's well-being. Bryce realized that the BMW may have been bringing illegal drugs to him.

Bryce rushed to Franklin's cottage and found his room empty. The shoe box was on the bed. Bryce paused and stared at the shoe box as his worst thought came, "Franklin has sold the saving bonds to get high."

Frantically, Bryce tore the loose tape from the box. Everything seemed to be there, including all of the bonds. He sat on the bed and breathed a sigh of relief. He picked out the picture of himself and Franklin's dad. His mind drifted back to Nam, and he clearly recalled the day they took the pictures. He smiled and got up to leave. "Franklin's probably entertaining people in the dining hall," he thought.

Bryce closed the door behind him and turned to face the now familiar sleepy-eyed, yawning young woman. Her words were devastating to Bryce. "If you're looking for Franklin, he left in a silver car."

Bryce sat down on the edge of the couch in the lounge and shook his head. The stress that comes with this type of work was beginning to get to him. Since being assigned to Franklin, he had been riding an emotional roller coaster. Up and down. Up and down. Battle after battle. Crisis after crisis. Now he faced another tough decision. "What should I do?" he thought. "I'm gonna have to inform Ms. Langdon that Franklin has left the grounds. He'll probably get dismissed from the program."

"Good morning, Mr. Wright." Ms. Langdon greeted.

"Good morning, Ms. Langdon."

"Now exactly what is your problem, today young man?" she calmly asked.

"I have bad news. It appears that Franklin has left the grounds," Bryce said.

Bryce was surprised by her reaction. She remained calm. He was sure she would flip into a rage, screaming about how they didn't tolerate such behavior. But no, she reclined back in her chair, interlocking her fingers. She gently removed her glasses and said in a rather confident voice, "Well, you just go, find him, and bring him back here."

"Pardon me!" Bryce spoke.

"That's what I said, young man. You go and find him and bring him back," she repeated.

"Okay, I'll be glad to do that, Ms. Langdon," Bryce assured.

"Before you go running off, Mr. Wright," she continued, "I need to tell you that it took my husband forty years to build the fine reputation this place has established. Other than me, the only other person that was dear to him was his little niece Allison. He did love his Allison. On his dying bed, he asked me to make sure she got whatever she asked for. She never asked for anything until she came to me for help with this young man, Franklin. I asked her if she was in love with him. She said no. She said that despite all his problems, she believed that he was a good kid. However, she did say that she was fond of his mother and little sister."

"I understand," Bryce said.

"So I want you to go, find him, and bring him back to me. Because he's been sick, I have not had a good talk with him yet. Another thing, Mr. Wright, listen carefully, and you must keep this to yourself. I have not revealed this to anyone else, but my feelings tell me that I can trust you. Since my husband's death, the Eagles' Nest has been having financial problems. As you can see, more and more treatment centers are popping up. The competition is beginning to affect us. We still have an extensive waiting list, and we have established a good record with the state. They assured me that if we maintain a high rate of recovery, the state will grant us a good deal of money for our operations. I need this money, because I plan to leave this place to Allison. She is the kind of person that can make this place work. First, we need to show that we can handle tough cases like Franklin's. Mind you, now, I've only told this to you, and it must remain that way for now. Now go, find Franklin, and bring him back."

"Thank you, Ms. Langdon."

"Oh, Mr. Wright, remember our policy. If he has taken any drugs, he must be detoxed before returning here. Good luck," she concluded.

Bryce thought of Torrington as a nice family town. When it was his turn to work the late shift, he saw people out late. They regularly visited the downtown park where a variety of concerts were held. Couples could be seen strolling at night, holding hands. There was plenty of activity to keep kids busy and out of trouble. It was unlike Waterbury, where it seemed that only those interested in crime walked the streets at night. Yet like most towns today, drugs had found their way into Torrington. Bryce didn't know where to look for Franklin, though, because Torrington was fairly new to him. "Maybe he went home to get high," he thought.

Then, again, that would be too easy. Who could show him where people in that area went for drugs? Bryce thought of John and his many years of experience, and he did live in the area. But Bryce definitely didn't want John to know the situation. He was already too negative about Franklin.

Bryce didn't want to leave any stones unturned. His first stop was Franklin's apartment. There was no evidence that anyone had been there since he last saw the place. Bryce wondered how long the landlord would continue to honor Franklin's lease.

After driving around, and searching without any success, Bryce thought to ask Monique where he might find Franklin.

Monique was busying herself peeling potatoes when Bryce arrived. She answered the door with the peeling knife still in her hand. She reminded Bryce of her mother. She, too, liked to talk while waving the knife around. "Hello, Bryce," she greeted him. "We're expecting family members, and you've probably seen how my family loves to eat."

Bryce explained what had happened with Franklin, and Monique hurriedly got herself ready. They left in Bryce's car.

Unable to locate Franklin at his local hangouts, Monique thought of a place he might be in Waterbury. Monique had overheard some of Franklin's friends speak of that hangout in school. She knew the name of the place, and that was all that Bryce needed. Waterbury was Bryce's city, and he was familiar with that tough section not far from his own apartment. Two years ago he had to go there to rescue his own son from a bunch of hoodlums. It was a gang-infested section, and a person put his life at risk going there.

In Waterbury, Bryce tried to persuade Monique to wait in a fast-food store. She insisted on continuing. She was determined to go with him to search for her brother.

Monique's hunch about Franklin's whereabouts was fruitful. Bryce drove up Willow Street and spotted the silver BMW. It was parked in front of a restaurant known for drug trafficking. Bryce pulled up behind the car, and for the first time he was able to clearly see the license plate. Ray-Man was the name it beared.

"I don't think you should go in there," Monique said.

"The sooner I get Franklin back, the better it will be for him. Besides, this place doesn't scare me. I've been through Vietnam, remember," Bryce said boldly. He was trying to show Monique that he was courageous but he could feel a wave of terror welling up from his belly.

"Yeah, but this isn't Vietnam. Talk in Torrington is that it's worst," Monique said. She was more sensible.

Bryce left Monique in the car and went inside. He heard people rushing out the back as he pushed open the door. He wondered why they would abandon the place on his entrance. He looked down and noticed he was wearing his state badge over his jacket pocket. The state car he was driving was the newer black Dodge Stratus. It didn't have the usual state seal on the side of the door. After putting these two together, Bryce concluded that they must have thought he was the police.

Franklin remained seated at a table toward the back. He must have sensed it was Bryce, because without looking up, he shouted,"What are you doing here? Are you crazy or something? Don't you know you could get killed coming in here? These people are dangerous. They don't play. I was coming back to the program. I only came here to pay Ray-Man the debt I owed."

"Oh, yeah," Bryce said. "Then how come you have that cocaine residue in front of you?"

"This? Oh this is what I get when I make a deal. Forget this. How did you find me anyway?" Franklin asked. He then peered up at Bryce with an incriminating look.

"Monique had heard of this place," Bryce answered.

"So, she told you where to come?"

"No, she came with me," Bryce said. "She's outside."

"She's where?" Franklin belted. He slammed his fist on the table and jumped to his feet. "Are you crazy? She doesn't belong up here. These guys are like vultures. Come on, let's go."

Franklin stormed out the door. Bryce was at his heels.

Outside there were nine guys that had gathered around Bryce's car. They must have realized that he wasn't a cop after observing "State Vehicle" on the license plate. The one called Ray-Man was bending over the window, talking to Monique. He turned when he heard Franklin coming out of the restaurant. "Franklin, Franklin," he said. "What are you doing bringing the man to my place?"

"Who? This guy?" Franklin answered. "He ain't the man. He's a friend of my father. That's all he is."

"Franklin, Franklin, you mean to tell me that you have a father. You didn't tell me that you had a father. I thought I was your father. And you didn't tell me that you had a pretty little sister either," Ray-Man sniffed haughtily.

"You stay away from my sister," Franklin said sharply. He gritted his teeth and moved to face Ray-Man. Bryce moved in and was able to steer Franklin toward the back door of the car. They managed to get seated, and Bryce fumbled to get the key into the ignition. Ray-Man stood in front of his gang. He was still taunting Franklin.

Ray-Man's appearance was typical of gang leader. He had a clean-shaven face that matched his bald-head. He was short in statue, about five feet six inches. He was shorter than anyone else standing on the sidewalk, but he certainly was the one commanding. He was dressed in a black T-shirt and black pants, and he wore black Army boots. He was weighed down with gold. He had a ring on every finger, a row of gold bracelets around each wrist, and a heavy gold chain around his neck. With his skin almost as dark as the clothes he wore, his glitter was blinding. He perfected his image with two gold teeth that reflected the light every time he spoke. He was definitely showing off for Monique.

"We'll see you in one month, Franklin," he said as the car sped off.

This was the first time Bryce had been in the company of Franklin and Monique together. He listened as Franklin sat through a thorough tongue-lashing from his little sister. When it was Franklin's turn, he tried to chastise her for coming to that neighborhood. They went back and forth for a while at each other. All the while, Bryce drove and listened. Through all the arguing, he sensed the closeness and affection they had for one another. Soon they were hugging. It was Franklin's turn to cry when Monique told him about their mother's ailment. He began to make all kinds of promises to Monique. He promised to clean up his act. He promised that he would do his best to kick the drugs. He admitted that he had been smoking and snorting cocaine all morning.

"Do you think we can stop by the hospital so I can see Mama before we go back?" Franklin asked.

"It doesn't work that way, Franklin," Bryce answered. "You have to go to detox first. Ms. Langdon wants you back at the Eagles' Nest, but you have to go through another detox. Then you can visit your mother."

Franklin's mood was still positive even after experiencing the setback. Bryce decided to ask him some questions that had been puzzling him.

"Why have you been seeing three doctors for Prozac prescriptions? How did you get money for the cocaine? What did Ray-Man mean when he said he would see you in one month?"

"Hey, hey, slow down, man. My head can't handle all that at one time," Franklin complained.

"Okay, one at a time," Bryce agreed. "What's with the three prescriptions for Prozac?"

"Hey, that's a strange question," Franklin said with intentions to stall the conversation.

"I thought you promised to be truthful," Monique interjected.

"Okay, okay. It's like this. I have this deal with Ray-Man, you see. We've been doing it this way for a long time. He brings me to these doctors, and they write my prescriptions. Then we go to these different pharmacies and get them filled. Sometimes my Title XIX benefits cover them. Sometimes Ray-Man just pays for them. He keeps the Prozac. I get crack for nothing," Franklin revealed.

"Then Ray-Man sells the Prozac. Right?" Bryce concluded.

"No, man. You got it all wrong. Ray-Man ain't selling no pills. He takes just a little of the Prozac and mixes it into his cocaine or crack. Prozac enhances cocaine. It makes the high last twice as long. Ray-Man is the only dealer that does this. He can sell his cocaine for almost twice as much as they do on the other side of town," Franklin explained.

"Wow!" Bryce cried out. "What will they think of next?"

"So you have to continue to do the same thing each month?" Monique inquired.

"Yeah, except I'm not making anymore deals. Ray-Man will not like that, but I can't get clean if I keep dealing. It's not like he'll be out of business if I quit," Franklin said.

"What do you mean by that?" Bryce wanted to know.

"Well, this thing with Prozac is getting bigger and bigger. I don't know who all is involved. The doctors don't really see me. They just write the prescriptions. The pharmacies never question me. They just continue to fill the prescriptions. One of my prescriptions is for a one-month supply. The other two are for a three-month supply. Ray-Man has a list of people who have prescriptions for Prozac. He preys on the mentally ill population. Not all of them get crack or cocaine. Most of them get cigarettes in exchange for their prescriptions. Ray-Man gets the name of everyone who's put on Prozac from someone up there at the Mental Health Center. That's why it was hard for me to trust you. Your agency is crooked," Franklin revealed.

They arrived at the hospital just as Bryce was thinking that this mess was getting more and more complicated as Franklin talked.

Bryce explained Franklin's situation to the nurse in the Emergency Room. She stated that the hospital would keep him for detox for three days, but they could not do another placement. Bryce assured her that he could handle things from there.

After a relatively short stay in the ER, Franklin was admitted to the 7th floor. Bryce drove Monique home. She wanted to check and see if any relatives from out of town had arrived. She was going to return later with her aunts and Brenda. Bryce planned to join them after work.

CHAPTER 8

Nick was about to leave for the day when Bryce entered his office. Bryce told him all the things that he had learned from Franklin earlier. Bryce was surprised when Nick's facial expression did not change, even when informed about the role Prozac played in the whole thing.

"Don't you understand!" Bryce explained. "There might be some kind of conspiracy going on in this matter. There could be doctors and pharmacies and employees of this agency involved."

"Slow down your horse, Bryce," Nick said. "There's no conspiracy going on with doctors and pharmacies. All that conspiracy stuff that Franklin's spouting is only the grandiose thinking of a small-time drug dealer. This Ray-Man is starting to feel the heat. So, he's trying to make it look like more people than just him are involved."

"You know about Ray-Man?" Bryce asked. His eyebrows shot up in surprise.

"Of course we do. He's been victimizing our clients for years. First it was that food stamp scam. Now it's Prozac he's after. Up until now, we haven't had anything on him," Nick revealed.

"Well, I'll be," Bryce said. He threw up his hands in disgusted resignation and came to his feet. "How come I'm the last to find out anything around here? If you knew all this, how come you've been feeding it to me a little at a time? I feel that this agency is only using me to get information from Franklin. I thought I was supposed to be helping people who had mental problems. This agency is using Franklin, too. This young man could get killed. I could get killed. Guess what? I came pretty darn close to that today. What's really going on here, Nick?" Bryce's eyes narrowed with suspicion.

"Sit down, Bryce," Nick said. He reached into his desk drawer and pulled out three newspaper clippings. He placed them in front of Bryce. "Don't you read the news?" he asked.

Bryce picked up the articles and read that in the past month alone, five people died from a new form of crack cocaine. It was reported to be more potent than any ever used in this area. It is extremely dangerous to first-time users, but three of the people who died recently were regular users. This new drug could offset the rhythm of the heartbeat, sending the user into cardiac arrest.

"Wow! I didn't know about this," Bryce confessed. His eyes widened with alarm.

"We know that it's Ray-Man who's selling these drugs, but we haven't been able to get enough solid evidence on him. Other than Franklin, the ones that he's been getting Prozac from have profound mental illness and are afraid of him. They couldn't testify anyway because of their mental status," Nick said. "It was the doctors and the pharmacies who alerted us to this buying scheme. It was their reports that brought in the federal agents. The Drug Enforcement Agency is monitoring this case. They have been allowing Franklin to continue to buy as much as he could in order to trap Ray-Man."

"Yes, but at the same time, they're trapping Franklin," Bryce barked.

"Not exactly. They don't have anything on Franklin. He's not doing anything illegal. He's only doctor shopping. A lot of our clients do that. They keep switching doctors until they get what they want," Nick said.

"It's not going to work. Franklin has decided not to deal with Ray-Man anymore," Bryce informed Nick.

"That's too bad, " Nick returned. "At least he would have had the protection of the DEA."

"This boy needs to get clean and stay clean. When he's not using crack and is taking his medicine, his episodes of depression are fewer. Besides that, his family needs him. I think he made the right decision. I'll protect him if need be," Bryce said.

Bryce turned to leave, and Nick said, "Oh, you were right on one thing. We do suspect that someone here is giving information to Ray-Man. So be careful."

"Thanks, Nick," Bryce said. "What about the Eagles' Nest people like Ms. Langdon, are they in on this, too?"

"No, not to my knowledge. That old lady is genuine and as straight as an arrow," Nick laughed mockingly.

Bryce folded the newspaper articles, tucked them under his arm, and went to his desk. Bryce thought about the risk Franklin had taken by using such strong cocaine. "When will it all end?" he wondered. "The drug dealers are constantly coming up with new ways to get people hooked."

At the hospital, Mrs. Brown was moved from the ICU to a private room on the fifth floor. She hadn't suffered any further setbacks, but her condition remained guarded. Bryce decided to stop by to see her before going up to see Franklin. However, there was a sign on her door that read, "Please stop at the nurse's station before visiting." "What's this all about?" Bryce wondered.

It wasn't as bad as Bryce initially thought. The nurses simply redirected him to a large family room at the end of the corridor. Mrs. Brown was having so many visitors that they were wearing her out. There were too many people for the small room. It seemed as though the whole card party was there. Bryce recognized some of the neighbors.

"Hey! There's your Mr. Right, Brenda," one of them yelled.

Brenda tried to conceal her embarrassment, but her caramel-colored skin flushed as she excused herself through the crowd to welcome

Bryce. They quickly slipped out into the hallway for quietness. Bryce inquired about Monique. He hadn't seen her there.

"She went to the library to complete something she's been working on," Brenda related. "I'll be picking her up later."

Franklin was asleep when Bryce entered his room. Bryce pulled one of the chairs near the bed and reclined back to watch television. It had been another emotional day for him. Within minutes, he too was asleep.

The two men woke up at the same time. They eyed each other skeptically. "What are you doing here, Bryce?" Franklin asked, breaking the stare.

"I stopped by to see you and your mother," Bryce answered.

"Yeah, mom. Did you see her? She has tubes coming out everywhere. I stayed with her until the room got crowded. What's wrong with her, Bryce?"

"Well, the doctor said she has pancreatitis," Bryce answered.

"Oookay. Like I suppose to know what pancreatitis is?" Franklin's face had an ironic expression.

"Her pancreas is inflamed. The major cause of pancreatitis is alcoholism," Bryce explained.

"Probably all that vodka she drinks. I don't know why she has to drink so much. Don't she remember how it killed my father."

"She's probably worried about you a lot," Bryce said.

"Yeah, maybe. I thought you were going to tell me about my father," Franklin suggested, obviously trying to change the subject.

"Yeah, your father; my friend TC," Bryce began. "He was a real American hero. Your father was our John Wayne in Nam. He was tall like you, except he was huskier than you. He had a lot of arm muscle. Probably came from the way he carried his machine gun. Remember, I told you that he was the first person we saw that carried an M-60 machine gun in one arm and fired it from that position. Anyway, your father was a gritty country boy when he came out to us in the boonies. Right away, though, he became a leader with his fearless fighting ability.

As Bryce recalled these things about TC, Franklin became very attentive. He sat up in the bed and his eyes beamed eagerly as he waited for the next words.

"Because your father was a machine gunner," Bryce continued, "he had two guys with him all the time. One was an assistant gunner, and the other, was his ammo barrier. I was the medic for the platoon, but I spent most of my time with your father. I also volunteered to carry ammo for the machine gun. The way he could shoot, I had no problem helping. Whenever we got into a firefight, the three of us were right on his butt. Literally."

"How did he get the medals?" Franklin asked.

"Up in the Central Highlands, in the jungle and rain forest, we got into a big firefight. We had been following a trail for two days. In the jungle, trails or paths were like super highways. As a matter of fact, some were traveled so much that they didn't need to be paved. Well, on the third day, we made contact. The fight went on for four days. During that time, we lost all of our leaders. The Company Commander, the platoon leaders, and all the sergeants were killed. At that time your father was a Spec-4, same as a corporal. Out of sixty men, we were down to thirty-one with no leader. Your father took command. He was constantly on the radio with the commanders back at the firebase. He had to read the map, something he had never done, and lead us to an area where helicopters could come to pick us up. He did this while we were still fighting off the Viet Cong. It was a scary and nervous time for us, especially while waiting for the helicopters. We weren't sure we were in the right place, and it was a major goal of the Viet Cong to shoot down as many helicopters as possible."

"Wow! My father did all that," Franklin said.

"Yes. He took charge and saved our lives. When we got back to the firebase," Bryce continued, "each one of us was asked to give a detailed account of the things your father had done. I believe this is how he got at least one of his medals. I do know that he got promoted to sergeant after that ordeal. His heroics became so well-known that the commanders offered him the opportunity to go to West Point to become an officer after his stay in Nam. This was just the beginning of the heroic things your father did. He was a special kind of guy and was fun to be around."

Bryce was able to talk about Vietnam without being interrupted by questions because of Franklin's keen interest in the subject. Franklin had read many books and saw practically every movie made about Nam. He even understood some of the terminology that Bryce used. Bryce seldom talked to anyone about Vietnam, but whenever he did get the opportunity, he could go on for days. With Franklin, he was getting what every Vietnam veteran needed when they returned from that awful place; a listening ear.

Neither of the two realized how late it had gotten until the nurses came around during the shift change. Bryce was politely asked to leave so that Franklin could get his rest.

There were two messages on his answering machine when Bryce arrived home. Both were from Brenda. The first message alerted him to possible trouble. Brenda had gone to the library to pick up Monique. The library had closed, and Monique was nowhere to be found. Brenda sounded frantic as she mentioned the man that had been stalking Monique. This was exactly what was on Bryce's mind, too. He quickly turned his attention to the second message. It had come just minutes before Bryce came in. Brenda now sounded relieved. She was at Monique's home when a car pulled into the driveway to let Monique out. In the message, Brenda said that Monique told her that a male friend picked her up at the library and took her for a ride.

This sounded strange. Neither Brenda nor Bryce knew of any male friend that Monique had, especially one that she trusted enough to ride around with.

CHAPTER 9

The following night the nurses reported that Mrs. Brown's condition had improved. She no longer needed oxygen to assist her breathing. They had removed her nasogastric tube, and X-ray results showed that the inflamation was subsiding. She still maintained a low-grade fever, however. Her diet was now clear liquids. If she continued to improve to the point of eating solid foods, she should be able to go home in a week.

There was still a large supporting group of relatives and friends, visiting in the family room. Many of them were from the church that Mabel and Jessie Mae attended. Mrs. Brown was not a regular at any church, but many of them had tried to persuade her to come.

Bryce only popped in to say hello before going up to see Franklin. Again he noticed that Monique was not there.

Even though he had been encouraged by the things he learned about his father the previous night, Franklin was down in the dumps. The effects of the cocaine was wearing off. His eyes looked haunted by pain. The glum hang-dog expression on his face suggested that he was nearing a depressive episode.

"How do you feel?" Bryce asked.

"I feel terrible. I never had a detox like this one," Franklin said in a lifeless monotone. "What did they give me. There's a dull, empty ache gnawing away at my soul. My stomach is contracted in a tight ball. I keep having a feeling to throw up, but nothing will come up."

Bryce knew that the side effects of Librium, the medicine taken for detoxification, could also be the cause of his sour mood. Bryce had wanted to talk to Franklin about Ray-Man and show him the news articles. Instead, he decided to not risk exasperating him. He made his visit brief.

The following day, back at the office, Bryce reviewed Franklin's treatment plan. He came across another reference to VA FILE #362034. He had the same reaction as when he first encountered this information. "What could this mean?" he wondered. He remembered Mrs. Brown speaking about TC doing some investigating with Army doctors. Who would know the meaning of this? How could he find out the results of TC's investigation?

When Bryce enlisted into the Army in 1966, many of the friends with whom he had grown up had left Virginia to go to school in the Washington, DC, area. Some later got jobs with the government. One of Bryce's friends, Willie Johnson, worked for the Pentagon. Bryce had heard that he last worked in personnel records and decided to give him a call to start his search.

Franklin was due back at the Eagles' Nest on Friday. Bryce went to pick him up at the hospital and found that he was less depressed and in a more talkative mood. He wanted to stop by to say goodbye to his mother before making the trip back. Bryce waited in the hall so that they would have some time alone. Inadvertently, Bryce overheard Mrs. Brown ask Franklin to take care of his baby sister in the event that she passed away. Bryce could hear Franklin crying as he made promises to his mother. He promised to try his best to stay away from drugs and to always be there for Monique.

As they headed north on Route 272, Bryce reached into the glove compartment and handed Franklin the newspaper articles he had gotten from Nick. After reading them, Franklin said, "This is bad. The way I felt trying to detox, I may have had some of that stuff. I did feel something tugging at my heart. This is bad."

"Yes it is. You see, your friend Ray-Man is responsible for these deaths. If you continue to deal with him, you may be considered an accessory," Bryce informed him.

"No way man," Franklin remarked. "I don't want anything else to do with Ray-Man. I certainly don't want to have anything to do with killing people. I want to help people, to save lives like my father did. I was really inspired by the things you told me about my father. I want to be like him."

"First, you must help yourself. You can't help others until you get your own act together. You can do that up here. Take time and work on yourself," Bryce instructed.

"What about Vietnam, the country?" Franklin asked. "What was it like to live over there? What did you all do all day? I need to get a picture of what my father experienced."

"Well," Bryce began, "you see how this area around here looks. I mean, with the mountains. We spent most of our time in a place much like this, except that the mountains were higher and the forest was thicker. We were either up on the mountain side or down in a valley. There was a huge basin called the Ashau Valley."

"Wow! I've read about the Ashau Valley. That's where the Ho Chi Ming Trail is, isn't it?" Franklin inquired, becoming intensely animated.

"That's right," Bryce acknowledged, "but let me start from the beginning. You can get a better picture of Nam by checking out the elements we fought. By the way, it was your father who first coined the term 'fighting the elements.' The very first element we had to deal with was the heat. The temperature hovered around the 100 degree mark all the time. In the jungle, it could get a little cooler. Sometimes we could walk for days without seeing the sun. This was because of the jungle's thick canopy. Along with the heat, the amount of equipment we had to carry contributed to our exhaustion. Television and movies portray GI's running around in Nam with barely no equipment and wearing berets. That's not quite how it was. We were required to wear our helmets. We called them steel pots. They were heavy, but they could save your life. We also carried a backpack, which was called a rut sack. In these we carried five days worth of food. Canned food, remind you, plus whatever else we decided we wanted. Next, we had to carry the equipment for whatever job we did. For example, being the medic, I had to carry my medical supplies, which I mounted on the rut sack."

"Man, that was a lot to be carrying around in that heat," Franklin commented.

"Wait, that's not all," Bryce continued. "We needed water. Mostly everyone carried at least four canteens of water. Then there was the ammo that we needed for our weapons. The more ammo we carried, the more protected we felt. In your father's situation, he needed a lot of ammo because we all depended on his machine gun as a main source of firepower. That's why he had an ammo barrier, and that's why I carried some ammo for the machine gun. Besides, I only carried one clip of ammo for my M-16. I didn't have to get in the thick of the fighting. My job was to help those that got wounded. Anyway, we loaded all of this stuff onto our rut sacks. Then we would sit, put our arms through the straps, and wait for someone to come to pull us to our feet. Then off we'd go in the 100 degree heat, straight into another element. This one we called a wait-a-minute bush."

"What's a wait-a-minute bush?" Franklin asked before Bryce could explain.

"These were the thick vines of the jungle. With a heavy load on your back, it was very frustrating to be caught in them. Most guys would struggle trying to get free. The more they struggled with the vines, the more entangled they became, all the way to the point of becoming over-heated in the already hot climate. The solution was to do nothing, to stay still. Take a minute and wait for someone help you get out. The GI's had a name for everything and those vines became known as wait-a-minute bushes."

Franklin was sitting gaped pop-eyed from what he was hearing. He was reeling with excitement. "These are the things you don't read about or see in movies," he stated. "Go on. What's next?"

"Another element, one we fought against on a daily basis were mosquitoes. We didn't have to travel to the jungle to fight mosquitoes. They greeted us as we got off the plane in Nam. Rain or shine, night or day, the mosquitoes were always there. Our only protection from mosquito bites was insect repellent. We literally had to bathe ourselves in insect repellent three to four times a day. Every part of our body that was exposed had to be rubbed down with insect repellent, and we still got bit. One specific job I had as a medic was to pass out malaria tablets. I also had to keep a record, and anyone who refused to take the pill had to sign off on it. Apparently, many of our guys were getting malaria after leaving Nam. Just by asking guys to sign off on the record got me into a lot fights. Most of them refused to take the pill and refused to sign off. It got to the point where my obligations ended after just offering it. I got resistance even doing that."

"Why?" Franklin asked. "Didn't they want protection from malaria?"

"The reason for the resistance," Bryce continued, "was that these guys weren't taking any chances of biting down into one of those big orange pills. The awful taste would stay in your mouth for days. You couldn't flush away the taste with water, and no one wanted to waste water trying. It was an awful-tasting experience, one you would not want to repeat. I know, I accidently bit down into one one day."

Bryce was about to detail another element, but they arrived at the Eagles' Nest. He and Franklin went directly to Ms. Langdon's office. There he turned Franklin back over to her care.

"Will you tell me more about the elements on your next visit?" Franklin humbly asked. "Oh, and keep me up to date on Mama's condition."

"I'll see you on Tuesday," Bryce replied, heading for the door.

Saturday evening, Bryce was lathered and refreshed. He had been looking forward to his dinner date with Brenda. Bryce had made reservations at the Café Pyramid, a restaurant that was quickly becoming popular because it offered dancing sponsored by the dancing classic radio station that he favored. Brenda had mentioned that she hadn't been dancing in a long while.

After a fun night of food and dancing, they both expressed their concerns about Monique. It was late, but they decided to stop by to see if she was okay. It was one o'clock and Monique was not home. They convinced themselves not to worry or to look any further for her. She had been going out lately with a friend. Bryce bought Brenda to her apartment, and they made plans to meet at the hospital later in the day. Brenda was anxious for Bryce to meet more of her family. They were driving up to visit Mrs. Brown.

Mrs. Brown was doing remarkably better. She was sitting up and sipping a clear soup. Not satisfied with that, she was demanding solid food. Unfortunately, the nurses were unable to fulfill her demand. The doctor wanted her to ease into solid food. It would be a couple more days before her diet would be upgraded.

Mrs. Brown's visitors filled the large family room and flooded over into an adjacent unoccupied room. Her relatives had come from as far away as South Carolina. These were the ones that were staying at Mrs. Brown's house.

Brenda introduced Bryce to her father and uncles. They were stocky and tough looking, towering like football linemen. Brenda's father was the tallest of the three. His bulldog face was intimidating and he held out a callused, stubby fingered hand to Bryce. At first, they made Bryce a little nervous. He wasn't sure how they would react to his dating Brenda. Bryce was older than her, and he noticed that they treated her like a precious vase. After talking to them, he learned that they were truck drivers and knew a lot of people from Bryce's hometown, Suffolk, Virginia. They also gave Bryce the feeling that they were pleased that

Brenda was now dating someone who was mature. As a matter of fact, if Brenda had not interrupted, her father would have told Bryce her life history, including about every man she had ever dated.

Brenda escorted Bryce to the adjacent room, where a large group of her relatives from Hoboken, New Jersey were seated. They brought along a bunch of little rowdy ones. They seemed to be getting into everything. Among them was Brenda's daughter Shawana.

She was introduced to Bryce and he turned to Brenda and said, "Your daughter is taller than you are. And you say she's only fourteen?"

"Yes, you see how tall my father and uncles are. Well, she's going to be like them. Franklin's tall like them, and I have some first cousins that are bigger and taller than my father and uncles. I must have taken after my mother's side of the family. They're all short."

"Where is your mother? I didn't meet her."

"She didn't come. She only travels with my father when it's necessary. She's afraid of traveling in a car."

The family brought a lot of food to the hospital. They had a table placed in the middle of the family room and put a variety of southern dishes on it. Actually, that floor of the hospital smelled more like a restaurant than a ward. Even the patients in the other rooms inquired about the whereabouts of the food. It was the smell and knowledge of her family's good cooking that made Mrs. Brown crave solid foods.

After learning that only a small portion of Mrs. Brown's family had come to visit, Bryce wondered what it would be like to attend one of her family's reunions. Again he noticed that Monique was not there.

It was around six o'clock when the nurse announced that all of Mrs. Brown's relatives and visitors would have to leave. The head nurse came to the family room and informed that Mrs. Brown was suffering a setback. She was vomiting convulsively. They were going to re-insert the NG tube and was putting back on her feeding tube. It seemed that someone had slipped her a plate of food.

Brenda said goodbye to her family. She then asked Bryce if he would accompany her to check on Monique. Bryce had expressed his concerns.

Monique was home when they arrived, but she didn't look like herself. She looked as though she had been up all night. Her usually neatly brushed hair looked uncared for. She was dressed provocatively in clothes that were unchanged and wrinkled. Monique had always impressed people with her well-groomed look. She peered about wide-eyed and didn't say much either. She didn't even inquire about her mother's condition. When Brenda tried subtle ways to find out about her friend, Monique became withdrawn and gave a look of uneasy puzzlement.

Bryce made his visit brief. He left Brenda there to care for Monique. They were genuinely concerned and agreed that something was not right in Monique's life.

Chapter 10

Mrs. Brown soon recovered from her temporary setback. She was scheduled to be discharged from the hospital the coming Friday. She would have to follow a strict dietary plan if she wanted to avoid suffering another attack.

Franklin was pleased to hear of his mother's improved condition. He told Bryce that Mrs. Langdon had given him a stinging tongue lashing. He said that, as strange as it sounded, it made him feel loved, wanted, and cared about. It really contributed to him wanting to become a productive member of society.

Bryce reminded Franklin of an important date approaching: the day Franklin was to appear in court to answer the arson charge, but Franklin wanted to hear more about fighting the elements. Bryce insisted that he needed to know more about the facts surrounding the arson incident. Bryce assured Franklin that with the treatment plan he had written to present in court, the judge would grant probation. It would be important for him to promise to follow that plan, or he would probably go to jail.

Franklin began to tell Bryce what happened the night of the fire. "I had been hanging out with these white kids that I knew since school. They were home from college. They weren't familiar with my side of town but would come to me whenever they wanted to buy cocaine.

They wouldn't dare go into that section without an escort. After buying crack and powdered cocaine, they wanted me to go back with them to New Milford. That's where one kid had moved to. We spent two days getting high in this vacant house. After the crack, the beer, and all of their money was gone, we went to the kid's house. His mother was very nice to us. She fed us and made a place for us to sleep for the night. There was four of us left over from the partying. However, I couldn't sleep. I kept hearing voices telling me to kill myself. I was feeling very depressed. I got up and went back to the empty house. I was really feeling bad, and the voices were even more persistent. I found a can of lighter fluid in the closet of the kitchen. I stood in the big room and poured the lighter fluid in a circle around me. I figured that if I was in the middle after lighting it, I wouldn't be able to get out, and I would succeed in killing myself. But as soon as the flame rose around me and I began to feel the heat, I became afraid of dying. I ran back to the kid's home and slipped back into the bed. The screaming fire trucks woke everyone up. It wasn't long before the police were knocking at the door. They knew that the kids sometimes hung out there. They took all of us downtown. They were gonna charge all of us until I told them that I alone had set the fire. It turned out worse than I had imagined. I almost burned down the library next to the house. Well, anyway, it was the kid's parents who got together and put up bail money for me to get out."

"Wow! That was some ordeal," Bryce said. "Had you ever done anything like that before?"

'Well, when I was younger, I used to set fires to get attention. I set fires in school for the kids to get out early. They paid me to do that. That one in New Milford was a big one, though. I almost burned some buildings down," Franklin confessed.

"Do you still have the compulsion to set fires?" Bryce asked. "I'm asking you this because I'm sure it's going to be asked in court. And what about Ms. Langdon, does she know about your setting fires?"

"I don't think I have a compulsion to set fires. Sometimes the voices are strong, and they urge me on. I explained everything to Ms. Langdon, and she still wanted to help me. That's why I feel like I've found a home here. I feel safe here. I wish I didn't have to go back into this cruel world, but I know I will soon."

Bryce asked Franklin a few more questions about his past and the fire. Then he gathered his things and left.

There was a message for Bryce on his voice mail back at the office. It was Willie Johnson. He was unable to access the information that Bryce needed. However, he was also interested in finding out what is was about. He recalled that it had been a big secret project years ago. Since then the project had gone cold. Also, he knew another one of Bryce's hometown friends, James White. He had worked on the project. Willie promised that he would contact James and get back to Bryce.

On Friday Mrs. Brown was discharged from the hospital as scheduled. Along with the strict dietary plan, the doctors gave specific orders for her to not drink any alcoholic beverages: no dinner wine or anything that had the slightest amount of alcohol in it. They advised her to not even smell alcohol. Her pancreas was now allergic to alcohol, and the next attack could be fatal.

This would be difficult for Mrs. Brown. The two things that she loved best after her children were her food and alcoholic drinks. However, she had promised Franklin that she would give up drinking. And he had promised her that he would stay clear of drugs.

The newly blooming couple were the first to visit Mrs. Brown at home. Bryce was a bit stunned to see Mrs. Brown's home so out of order. It was not the same neat place he had become accustomed to seeing. Clothes were thrown everywhere. Dirty dishes were piled up in the sink. The mess seemed to be Monique's doing. It looked as though she had been living on the run.

Brenda was outraged that Mrs. Brown had to return to her place in that condition. She asked her aunt about Monique's whereabouts.

"She picked me up at the hospital and immediately we had an argument. You should have seen how she was dressed. That skirt on her was so short that I could see her butt. She never used to wear clothes like that. And she was in such a big hurry. Where was she going? Did she get a job or something? This house never looked like this. Before she could get me into bed, the phone rang, and she was out the door. I couldn't get to the window fast enough to see who picked her up. But I could hear the car as it sped away. I'm really worried about her. She's not acting like my little girl. She usually makes a fuss over me when I'm sick. This time she barely said two words," Mrs. Brown related.

"I believe she's starting to date," Brenda said while handing Bryce an apron.

"Date!" Mrs. Brown screamed. "Who told her she could date. She's too young to be out dating. Besides, whose gonna be here to take care of me. After all I've tried to do for these kids, they treat me like this."

Mrs. Brown began to cry and had to catch herself as she started to ask Brenda to fix her a drink. Brenda comforted her aunt and tried to reassure her that Monique would be alright. Brenda told her that she'd make arrangements for herself and other family members to come to care for her. She then escorted Mrs. Brown back upstairs and helped her into bed. After a short while, Mrs. Brown was able to fall asleep.

Bryce was in the kitchen washing dishes. Whenever Brenda passed by he would shoot a knowing wink. Brenda went about dusting and polishing furniture. She stopped often to gaze at Bryce candidly. While moving things around, she found empty liquor bottles stashed away in some of the strangest places.

The pair took advantage of their time together alone. While continuing to clean, they made dinner, played music and stopped for an occasional dance. Bryce said that cleaning had never been so much fun.

By ten o'clock Bryce decided to leave. Brenda had made plans to stay the night and care for Martha. Monique had not come home, and they both were not sure that she would.

CHAPTER 11

Bryce looked toward the coming weekend with mixed emotions. This ambivalence caused him anxiety. Until he met Brenda, he had spent most of his weekends with his daughter Tanya, her husband, and their two boys. Tanya had grown especially close to him. He treated her much like Brenda's father and uncles had treated her at the hospital. Those weekends together were special to her. Now Bryce wanted to include Brenda, of whom he had become particularly fond.

However, from the moment they were introduced, Bryce could sense an uneasy, icy atmosphere arising. Even though Brenda made an effort to make the occasion go well, Tanya disagreed with her on every issue. Finally, the tension erupted into an argument about absolutely nothing. Bryce decided to cut the visit short, and he drove Brenda home.

Bryce wasn't exactly on Cloud Nine when he pulled into the parking lot Monday morning. To make matters worse, John had spotted him and was waiting to speak with him.

"Good morning, John."

"Yeah, right. Good morning," John retorted. "Listen, Bryce, we gotta talk."

"No problem. What's up?"

"It's about your boy, Franklin. Are you still working with him?"

"Yes, why?" Bryce wanted to know.

"Well, I told you that Franklin was scum. Now he's caused an investigation of our agency because of his big mouth. They even came to my house over the weekend. Everyone here is being questioned. If you had left him alone like I suggested, none of this would be happening," John said. His face was lit up with bitter anger.

Bryce felt this accusation was unjustified. He also felt that he was making too much progress with Franklin to go on taking this abuse from John. The heated argument that erupted between the two had been long in coming. They became so loud that people from other agencies in the building started looking out of their windows. The argument also caught Nick's attention. He had just come into the parking lot. The two of them were summoned to Nick's office.

By the time Bryce and John reached Nick's office, he had already taken out two copies of the general work rules. He handed each one a copy and said, "You both should have a copy of these rules somewhere in your files. But it's evident that you haven't read them. Don't you know you could get fired for having an outburst like that here at work. What is this all about anyway? And don't tell me it was about Allison again."

"Allison! What does he know about Allison?" John asked. His face became hot and pinched with resentment.

"Calm down, John. I told Bryce all about you and Allison. Now, what's this all about?" Nick repeated.

"Franklin is making up allegations and reporting them to the Drug Enforcement Agency. They questioned me at my home over the weekend. My poor, sick mother is frightened, and worried that I might lose my job. Everyone here is under suspicion because of him. I warned Bryce that Franklin was trouble," John continued to barked.

"I want you two guys to listen good," Nick started. "This investigation was pending long before Bryce started to work with Franklin. We asked for this investigation. If no one here has done anything wrong, there won't be anything to worry about. Now this time you guys are getting off with a verbal warning. Do not let this kind of outburst happen again. Now go to work."

Even though Bryce had no part in prompting the investigation, he was treated like he had by his peers. This was probably because John, who had worked there much longer, told them his version of the story.

When Tuesday came, Bryce was eager to leave for his trip to the Eagles' Nest. It was late in May and flowers and trees were in full bloom. The scene on Route 272 had changed. It was more beautiful than ever. The blue sign on the side of the road that read "Scenic Road" had survived another New England winter.

Franklin was waiting outside of his cottage. The often sleepy-eyed, yawning young lady that Bryce had become accustomed to seeing was sitting with him. In the sunlight and fully awake, she was quite a pretty girl. Her hair was cut short. It was wavy and black with a gold tint that crowned the top. For an Afro-American, she had a very light complexion and her smooth skin was arrayed with freckles. She greeted Bryce by name with a large incriminating smile. She evidently was becoming close to Franklin. He introduced her as his friend Korianne.

Franklin handed Bryce a manilla folder. "This is a letter for the court from Ms. Langdon," he said.

"I have a letter from our agency and a recommended treatment plan also," Bryce said. "Are you nervous about going to court?"

"Yes," Franklin acknowledged. "I don't trust the courts. Anything can happen."

"Maybe if you were going in alone, without these letters and without being in treatment, you would have reason to be afraid. Our recommendations should help," Bryce encouraged.

Korianne accompanied them to the car. She wished Franklin well as the two headed out of the compound and south onto Route 272. "How's Mama?" Franklin asked. "Usually I get calls from Monique, but lately I haven't heard from her. Is everything alright?"

"It's going to be a while before your mother fully recovers. Right now she's doing good," Bryce answered. He made his remarks short, not knowing what to say about Monique.

After traveling about a quarter of a mile in silence, Bryce said, "I'm beginning to become too familiar with you."

"What do you mean?" Franklin asked. He then gave Bryce a side-long glance.

"Well, by the look in your eyes, I can tell that you want me to tell you more about 'fighting the elements.' Am I right?"

"You're right," Franklin confessed. "I've been replaying those things you told over and over in my mind. I try to picture my father in that scene."

"Okay, so where did I end?"

"Let me see. You talked about the heat, the mosquitoes, the heavy equipment, and the wait-a-minute bushes," Franklin reminded.

"Oh yeah," Bryce laughed. "Those were some major elements. But, there were a lot more. Ground leeches were a real problem for us."

"Ground leeches! What could they do to you?"

"Well, let me continue," Bryce said. "Ground leeches in the jungle used to come at us by the hundreds. They were mostly on the ground, but sometimes they could be found up on branches. They were called ground leeches because down in the southern part of Nam, they were found mostly in the water of rice paddies. Well, at least that's where I encountered my first one. It attached itself to my leg. I thought it was a little snake because of its color and length. The ones up in the northern jungles were about the size of a paper match. First, they made their way up your boot, and from there they would crawl to a suitable sucking spot. From that paper match size, they got as big as your thumb from sucking your blood. Normally, after feeding undetected, they would simply fall off. Sometimes they would cause a stinging sensation. This was the only way you would know that they were there."

"Man! That was awful. It gives me the willies just imaging it," Franklin commented. He clamped his eyes shut and his face contorted with disgust.

"But that wasn't the worst part," Bryce continued. "If you found a leech on you sucking your blood, you couldn't just pull it off. What I mean is that it was difficult to pull it off, because it was attached to you. While sucking, it's head was embedded under your skin. If you did succeed in pulling it off, you risked breaking off the head. This happened a lot, and it was a serious problem out in the boonies."

"Why?" Franklin inquired.

"The head left under the skin could cause an infection. Mostly all infections in the jungle never healed. They would lead to what is called jungle rot. The sore would keep getting bigger and bigger. Eventually, the person would have to be evacuated back to the main camp for treatment," Bryce explained.

"Then how did you deal with the leeches?" Franklin asked.

"We dealt with them the same way we did with the mosquitoes. We used insect repellant. Leeches sprayed with insect repellant would shrivel up and die. So we sprayed insect repellant on our boots to stop them from initially getting on us. This seemed to work, but we would still pick them up whenever we sat down or while we slept. It was nothing for us to wake up in the morning and discover leeches on our faces. Guys would find leeches on almost every part of their body. We also used hot matches, lit cigarettes, or a cigarette lighter to make the leeches withdraw their heads from under our skin," Bryce related.

"Man! You wouldn't think that all those things could happen. I thought that fighting the Viet Cong was all that the Vietnam War was about," Franklin revealed.

"I believe that is what most people think. We had to contend with a lot. That is why I wrote Fighting the Elements, my sixteen chapter manuscript. In it, I detail all the elements. You probably would enjoy reading it. It tells more things about your father than I can think of now."

That was all Franklin needed to hear. He practically begged Bryce to bring him the manuscript.

Bryce watched Franklin's facial expression change from a cheerful one to a pitiful look of appeal as they pulled into the courtyard. Listening to Bryce, he had become so excited that his mind was visualizing the things he said. However, the sight of the courthouse brought him back to reality. He began to squirm and chew on his lip. His face grew pensive.

"Don't be afraid. You should be alright with these letters," Bryce encouraged.

"Maybe. You never know how things are going to go," Franklin said.

They entered the security check station, and several of the officers spoke to Franklin. Walking down the hallway, another group of men, dressed in business suits, also recognized Franklin and greeted him. "How come all these people know you?" Bryce asked.

"I know the security officers from school and around town. The heavy-set man in the blue suit is the prosecutor. The others are lawyers. They all know me from these court rooms," Franklin answered.

"You're very popular. I don't know if that's good or bad. Do you also know the judge?"

"I know several of them. That's why I'm afraid. I was told by one not to show my face in his court again."

Bryce and Franklin took a seat in the back of the crowded courtroom. They watched case after case come before a seemingly cranky judge, one that was new to the circuit. He had periodic spasms of irritation across his face as his eyes raked the courtroom. This didn't do much for Franklin's morale. He couldn't find a comfortable position on the hard seat, and he went back and forth to the men's room.

Around midday, the court clerk summoned Franklin forward. Bryce went in front of the judge with him. Although Bryce wore his state badge over his jacket pocket, the judge asked Bryce his name and the agency he represented. Bryce then handed the letters to the judge, and the charges were read against Franklin. Franklin attempted to plead guilty, but the judge interrupted him. "These are serious charges against you, young man. Before you make a plea, have you consulted an attorney?" the judge asked.

"I don't want to waste any time with an attorney. I'm guilty, and I just want to get this over with," Franklin said.

"Well, if you're going to wave your right to an attorney, I'd like to hear what exactly took place that night," the judge requested.

Bryce was impressed by Franklin's calmness and honesty, as he told the judge the same story he had told him earlier. Bryce could sense that all attention throughout the courthouse was on Franklin. He looked over his shoulder and saw that even the security guards had left their stations to hear what Franklin had to say. Franklin concluded his confession, and the courthouse remained silent as the judge read the letters.

"I see that you are now in treatment. Is that right?" the judge asked.

"That's right, Your Honor," Franklin answered.

"From what the prosecutor tells me, you are very familiar with us. Actually, it seems that you have spent much of your life in and out of these rooms. However, I'm not going to make a quick decision on this matter. It's been a long morning. We're going to lunch. I'll give you my decision when we return. Court is recessed until 1:30 pm."

"That's just great," both Bryce and Franklin agreed, as they walked to the diner across the street. "Now we have a little longer to sweat this out." Bryce had a little to eat, but poor Franklin was too nervous to eat anything. He complained that his stomach was contracting into tight balls. His mouth was white from him licking his lips dry. He only had a small soda.

Standing again before the judge, they heard the charges read aloud. "I've read these letters, and it seems that you do have some people willing to support you," the judge stated. "However, there was a considerable amount of damage done. I can't dismiss that. Here's my decision. I'm going to sentence you to five years in prison, suspended. I'll place you on probation for five years with the condition that you continue your treatment with the Eagles' Nest and the mental health agency. Also, I'm fining you $5,000. Your release today will be based on how much of the fine you can come up with."

Franklin's eyes widen and he turned to Bryce and asked, "What am I going to do? I don't have any money. I knew this was going to turn out bad. I'm gonna have to go to jail."

"What about your mother or your aunts? Do you think they can help?" Bryce asked.

"They don't have that kind of money to spend on me. Besides, they wouldn't lend any to me. I've stolen too many things from them."

"What about the shoe box?" Bryce remembered.

"Okay, what about the shoe box?"

"The shoe box! The bonds! Your have those United States saving bonds in it."

"I thought you said they were no good."

"Forget what I said. They're worth something now. Do you want me to cash them in for you?"

"Of course I do," Franklin said. "Go. I want to get out of this place."

Bryce approached the judge and explained Franklin's money situation. He told the judge of their plan to cash in the bonds. Franklin, would have to be detained. Bryce looked on heavy-chested as Franklin was put into handcuffs and led away to lockup.

Bryce drove cautiously up Route 272. He didn't want to get stopped by the police and be detained any longer than necessary. All the way he tried to figure out how much money Franklin could get for the bonds.

At the Eagles' Nest, Bryce went to see Ms. Langdon. She had asked him to keep her updated on the court proceeding. However, she had left for the day. The receptionist explained how she had suddenly become ill. Bryce used the phone to call Nick. He remembered the warning his supervisor had given him about keeping him informed of what he was doing. Bryce simply wanted to cover his butt.

Bryce opened the shoe box and carefully removed all the items until he came to the bonds. There were only four of them. Each one cost $100 at the time of purchase. Bryce noticed something different about these bonds. TC must have made sure that only Franklin could benefit from them. The bonds had Franklin's name typed on them. Bryce realized he would have to take the bonds to Franklin to be signed and then try to make the bank before it closed. It was already getting late. Time was running out. It was impossible to get back to Franklin and make it to the bank. Certainly it would take time to calculate the value of the bonds. It seemed that Franklin would have to spend the night in jail.

Chapter 12

The next morning Bryce was at the bank with the bonds. He was surprised when he was told the value of the matured bonds. Each of the $100 bonds was now worth $540. Franklin had been holding $2,160 in his shoe box without knowing it.

Bryce presented $2,000 to the judge and explained where the money came from. When the judge learned that Franklin was the son of a war hero, he was somewhat sympathetic. He, too, was a Vietnam veteran. However, he accepted the money, but he ordered Franklin's immediate release. Franklin would still have to pay the balance of his fine. The judge informed him that the clerk would set up a payment agreement for him. Also, he would have to abide by the stipulations of probation and continue to follow the treatment plan of both the Eagles' Nest and the mental health agency. Franklin's eyes danced and his face brightened, as he realized that he was free to return to the retreat.

On the way back to the Eagles' Nest, Bryce gave Franklin $160-the amount that was left over. He tried to explain to Franklin how his saving bonds had matured, but Franklin was distracted counting his dollars over and over.

"Wow! I had that much money in my shoe box all along?" Franklin asked.

Bryce was about to explain a second time how the bonds had matured when he noticed that Franklin was crying. "What's the matter?" he asked. "Why are you crying? You should be happy that you're free and that you got out using your own money."

"That's just what's the matter. I was thinking how after all these years my father is still looking out for me. He made sure I would have this money when I needed it. He's responsible for my freedom. I also believe that he sent you here to help me get over my illness. That's why that shoe box is so dear to me. I believe his spirit is connected to it."

"Your father was a good man," was all that Bryce said. He didn't want to discourage Franklin, but he didn't want to agree that a spirit was in the shoe box either. "I didn't forget to bring the manuscript. It's on the back seat if you want to take a look at it. In it you'll find a lot more about your father."

The rest of the ride was quiet. Franklin barely said a word. Bryce could hear him reading softly. He would read. Look up at Bryce with his eyes glinting with pleasure. He would cast a broad smile, lower his eyes and continue to read. He really seemed to be enjoying the things he was reading.

At the Eagles' Nest, the two went directly to Ms. Langdon's office. Bryce explained everything that had taken place, including Franklin's probation and its conditions. Ms. Langdon was pleased with the outcome. She asked Franklin to give her the money. It was against the retreat's policy for residents to keep more than $5. The receptionist would place the money in the safe, and he could draw from it as needed.

Franklin handed her the money. Bryce noticed that she was having difficulty in reaching out for it. She wasn't her normally perky self. Her swan-like neck disappeared as her head sunk into drooping shoulders. She tried but her left hand fell lifeless on the table. Bryce took the money from Franklin and sat it before her. He then asked her about her health and she simply confessed: "I've been feeling pretty lousy lately. As I was talking to my doctor on the telephone, I felt I suffered some kind of setback. He said that what I described to him sounded like a mild stroke. He wanted me to be taken to a hospital, but I believe I can manage it. Besides, I need to be here. I convinced him to come here."

"Is there anything we can do to help you?" Bryce asked.

"No, not you, Bryce. But I'm going to need Franklin's service. As you can see, I'm having trouble with one side of my body. Driving is becoming difficult for me, but I need to be here. My days here are numbered. I need to get all my affairs in order so that Allison won't suffer trying to figure out the finances. Now Franklin, you'll have to stay out of trouble. I'm going to need your help until I get better. Do you have a driver's license that I can see?" she asked.

"Yes, Ma'am," Franklin answered. He reached into his wallet and handed it to her.

After looking it over, Ms. Langdon turned to Franklin and said, "Okay, this is what I have planned for you. I need a driver: someone to pick me up from my home and drive me here, and then bring me back home when I'm tired. Do you think you can do that?"

Franklin's eyes blinked, his face glazed, and his breath got caught in his throat as tried to answer. He had to stand in order to get the "Yes" out. No one had ever trusted him enough to offer him a job. Franklin was reeling with excitement.

"Now I don't want you doing this for nothing. I'm going to be putting wages into your account here with your other money. I'll arrange for the receptionist to send monthly payments toward your restitution. How does that sound?" she asked.

Franklin's felt his heart leaping. There was a surge of elation that passed through his body and he became speechless. He just nodded. He was willing to do it for nothing. Getting paid hadn't even crossed his mind.

Bryce walked Franklin back to his cottage. Franklin's moments of joy had started to fade. Bryce listened as he began to express self-doubt. "What if I become depressed and don't want to be bothered by anyone?"

"You shouldn't worry so much about your depression as long as you keep taking your medicine. Street drugs are what causes you to slip into depression. Stay away from them, and you'll be alright. Everyone suffers some kind of depression from time to time, but it goes away. One common kind that a lot of people suffer from is seasonal affective disorder. This form of depression is brought on by diminishing sunlight, like during the fall or winter season. Sometimes people need medication to get through it, but more commonly it goes away when spring comes. So don't worry. You'll do just fine," Bryce encouraged.

The words sounded good to Franklin. He was even more determined now to stay clean. Things were beginning to shape up and make sense to him. Furthermore, he was beginning to feel good about himself. He was feeling a sense of belonging. The hope he had been praying for from the shoe box was becoming a reality.

It had been another emotional and exhausting two days for Bryce. He was looking forward to taking it easy for a while. He was relieved to have Franklin heading in the right direction. "Tonight I will sleep good," he thought. Then he remembered the other problem he had: Brenda and Tanya. "What am I going to do about that situation? I really like Brenda, and I hope I didn't damage our relationship by bringing her along to meet Tanya. I think Tanya is being selfish. I should be able to have a female companion. I shouldn't be forced to choose between the two," he thought.

Bryce entered his apartment, and the flashing light on his answering machine caught his attention. His thought was, "What's wrong with the kids this time?"

It wasn't that at all. There were two messages, and they both were from Brenda. They both said practically the same thing. "Please come to Aunt Martha's house when you get home from work. Brenda."

Bryce raced to Mrs. Brown's place. He wondered what could make Brenda's message sound so urgent. Was Mrs. Brown sick again?

"It's Monique," Brenda said after greeting Bryce. "She hasn't been home for two nights. Auntie says she's been away from home a lot lately, but never all night. Now it's two nights in a row. This is strange. She hasn't called anyone either. And there's that stalker guy out there. Oh, my God! What if the stalker has gotten her?"

"Calm down, calm down," Bryce said. "Did anyone call the police?"

"I don't know ," Brenda said. "Let's go upstairs and ask Aunt Martha. My aunts Jessie Mae and Mabel are with her."

"Hello everyone," Bryce greeted.

"Hello, Brian. I'm glad you're here," Martha said. Her eyes were bloodshot from crying.

"My Lord, Martha, the man's name is Bryce," Mabel corrected.

"That's okay," Bryce said.

"Listen Brian," Mrs. Brown continued, "please find my little girl and bring her home."

"Did anyone call the police?" Bryce asked again.

"No. It's too soon. She's only been gone two days," Jessie Mae stated.

"That's right. They're not gonna do anything until after seventy-two hours," Mabel added.

"That's not true," Bryce informed them. "That's only on television. They will start immediately in certain situations. Especially since there's a stalker involved. Why don't one of you call and make a report? Brenda and I will drive around town to see if we can find her."

"If we knew who her friend was it would help," Brenda mentioned.

"Yeah, you're right. Hopefully she's with that mystery friend of hers, and everything is alright," Bryce said.

It seemed that the couple had drove up and down every street in town. Monique was nowhere to be found. Finally, Bryce pulled up to a phone booth. Brenda got out and made a call to her aunt's house. Mabel answered the phone. She informed them that the police were now helping in the search for Monique. They were starting at the library first, something neither Brenda nor Bryce had thought of. Mabel said that the police also mentioned that it would help if anyone knew the name of the friend or even what type of vehicle he drove.

Bryce and Brenda were beginning to tire. They agreed to take one more ride through the roughest section of town, even though they didn't expect to find Monique there. Monique loathed drugs and dealers. She often stated that they were bloodsuckers. She felt that they mostly preyed on poor people, people who already didn't have much.

"Pull over!" Brenda shouted. "Pull over!"

"What?" Bryce asked, not knowing what she meant.

"Pull over behind that car," she said. "I recognize that car."

"I recognize that car, too," Bryce said. "That car belongs to Ray-Man. You don't think Monique is here, do you?"

Before Bryce could finish his words, Ray-Man came out of the pool parlor, one rumored to be his drug drop-off spot for this area. He held open the passenger side door. In stunned silence, Bryce and Brenda watched as Monique walked out and got into the front seat of the car.

A sudden spurt of adrenaline shot through Bryce's veins, and he jumped out of his car. Brenda was immediately by his side. Quick-thinking Bryce let Brenda do the talking, since she was a family member. "Monique, what are you doing here? Your mother has been worried sick about you. why didn't you call?"

While Brenda talked, Bryce took the opportunity to observe Monique. This was not the young lady he had come to know. This was not the same woman whose face had radiated with good cheer, when she greeted him at the door of Mrs. Brown's house. She looked up at Bryce as if she had never seen him before. The look in her eyes were distant, as if she was in a trance or something. The words she spoke seemed to be by command or practiced. "Why is my mother looking for me all of a sudden? She is the one that's been insisting that I go out on a date. So that's what I'm doing. I'm out on a date. I'm out with my friend, Ray-Man," she said.

As Brenda continued to appeal to Monique to come home, Bryce eyed Ray-Man. He assumed a posture of superiority, puffed up with self-importance. But alone without his gang, his cowardness began to show. The longer Bryce stared at him, the more his eyes narrowed with suspicion. Bryce looked at him the way one would look at a cockroach needing to be stepped on.

"Don't you think you should come home with us?" Brenda pleaded.

"No. I'm not going back there yet. I'm not finished with my date. I'm staying with my friend, Ray-Man. Let's go, Ray-Man," she said.

Monique's words further angered Bryce. He realized that she was not herself and that Ray-Man was controlling her. He made a lunge for the car door but had to let go as the car sped off. Bryce stood on the sidewalk, his face etched with helplessness. He was dumbfounded by what he had witnessed.

When the two returned to Mrs. Brown's house, the police were there. Bryce explained how they had seen Monique. Even though she spoke freely, she seemed to be captive. They explained that there wasn't much that they could do if she was willing to go with him. Being that she was only sixteen, if they caught them together, and if she made a complaint, the police could act on that.

Days passed and Monique continued to refuse to come home. To no avail, Mrs. Brown sent several family members to persuade her to come back. Monique spent her days hanging out with Ray-Man. Ray-Man avoided the police by constantly switching the cars he drove.

At night, Monique slept at the house of a friend of Ray-Man's. The middle-aged woman had five children of her own. The filthy, bug-infested apartment was small and crowded. Yet Monique continued to stay there without any complaint. After seeing the woman, it was difficult for Bryce to understand the connection between her and Ray-Man.

Monique being away from home did not help Mrs. Brown's recovery process. She spent most of her time up in her bedroom. Her sorrowful face was a study of desolation. With no other plan working, she called for Bryce. When Bryce arrived, Mrs. Brown put $50 in his hand and asked him to give it to the lady at the apartment where Monique was staying. She said it would make her feel better if she knew that Monique was eating well and paying her own way. She didn't want her to be a burden on anyone. She also handed Bryce a bag of Monique's clothes for him to deliver.

"Maybe she'll need these things," she said, as her voice degenerated to a childish whimper.

For the next few weeks, Bryce collected money from Mrs. Brown and gave it to the woman. On today's visit, he had the rare opportunity of seeing Monique there during the day. She sat at a table, saucer-eyed, staring catatonically up toward the ceiling. It was apparent to Bryce that she was being controlled. Seeing her that way, Bryce realized that the longer she stayed there, the more at risk her life became. His face hardened with determination to do something. "There's gotta be a way to break Ray-Man's hold on her," he thought.

Bryce went to Nick to ask if he could speak with the Drug Enforcement Agency investigating Ray-Man. The meeting was soon arranged, and they informed Bryce that they were making substantial progress in their investigation. They knew that he was an illegal alien, but they wanted more evidence on drug violations or possible murder charges. They informed Bryce that Franklin played a key role in helping them bring the case to a close.

All the while Bryce had withheld what was happening to Monique from Franklin. He was doing well, driving Ms. Langdon to and from work. He hadn't had any depressive setbacks. But Bryce knew how Franklin loved his little sister. He would probably kill Ray-Man if he knew what was going on.

Later that week, Bryce was visiting Brenda when Mrs. Brown said that a thought had come to her that might help in getting Monique to come home. "Remember that social worker that Monique liked so much. She might be the one who can convince Monique to come home.

Monique would do anything she asked. Brian, you know who I'm talking about. That pretty blonde girl. The one that works with you. Ally, Alice, you know. The one that liked Franklin, " she said.

"You mean Allison," Bryce responded. "She doesn't work with us anymore."

"That's too bad. She could get my baby girl home," Mrs. Brown said, sounding hopeless.

"Where is she?" Brenda asked.

"She now works for the Department of Children and Families," Bryce informed. "I've been wanting to talk to her myself, Mrs. Brown. I'll see if I can contact her tomorrow."

That seemed to satisfy Mrs. Brown. Soon after, she fell asleep. There was a broad smile across her face.

CHAPTER 13

After only getting her voice mail on his initial attempts, Bryce finally reached Allison on the phone. The news about Monique was disturbing to her. But she was even more upset to learn that Mrs. Brown had become ill and no one had notified her. She agreed to meet Bryce at Mrs. Brown's house after work.

Later, while Brenda sat inside with Mrs. Brown, Bryce paced the front porch. He was continuously jangling the change he had in his pocket. A wave of acid had built up in his stomach. "Why am I so nervous?" he asked himself. "I already know more about her than she knows of me."

Then, a late-model candy-apple Volkswagen Jetta with a white convertible top pulled into the driveway. A young woman stepped out, and Bryce hurried over to introduce himself. "Hello, I'm Bryce. It's a pleasure to meet you."

"Hello, I'm Allison."

"I feel like I already know you. I've met a lot of people that you know. Nick, John, Franklin and, of course, Ms. Langdon."

"I hope they all had good things to say about me."

Bryce observed her as she walked toward the porch. He could see why John had fallen for her. However, he could not see how he could let her get away. She was an attractive lady. Bryce recalled that Mrs. Brown had said that she was blond. But actually her hair was golden. Dollishly golden and pulled back. The style was similar to the way Monique wore hers. Her large dewdrop eyes reminded Bryce of the Virginia bluebells that grew wild around his home. Her face was sweetly expressive. Bryce sensed that she was self-conscious, because she blushed easily. But it was her modest dress and style that impressed Bryce the most. She wore a long cotton dress with a sweetheart neckline that covered her sleek, leggy frame. She sort of sauntered up the stairs to the door where Brenda was waiting. Brenda also had heard of Allison but had never met her.

Allison and Mrs. Brown embraced. Mrs. Brown started to cry as she appealed to Allison to assist in getting Monique back home. Allison, too, began to cry as she tried to console Mrs. Brown. Bryce could now see why everyone viewed her as special. Even though she presented herself as a person who was well-bred and knowing what to do in every social situation, she was earthy and had the gift of making people feel good about themselves.

Brenda stayed behind with Mrs. Brown. Bryce and Allison set out to find Monique. "We'll be going into some pretty tough territory. It's best if we go in my car. Yours will attract too much attention. Are you afraid?" Bryce asked.

"Of course I'm afraid. Will that stop me from going? No way!" Allison responded. "Working for the Department of children and Families, we go into a lot of rough places. And we see a lot of terrible things. You should see some of the things people do to children."

"I can imagine they are pretty bad," Bryce said.

"It's funny that you mentioned John and Franklin in the same sentence. How are they doing?" Allison asked.

"Well Franklin is out at the Eagles' Nest with your aunt ,or is she your cousin? I'm talking about Ms. Langdon."

"Auntie Lou. That's what I call her. She's my father's brother's wife. Uncle Vince was my favorite uncle. I practically grew up at the Eagles' Nest. So Franklin finally got in."

"Franklin is working for her. He's driving her around since she had a stroke," Bryce said.

"Stroke! What stroke?" Allison asked with her eyebrows shooting up in surprise.

"Ooh! You didn't know? She had a mild stroke and lost some of the strength to her left side. She said that driving was difficult for her. So she hired Franklin. I took it for granted that you knew. She speaks about you all the time."

"No, I didn't know. No one in my family keeps me informed of things that happen. I did get messages from her saying that she wanted to speak with me, but I've been procrastinating about getting out there. I'd better call her tonight."

"I really didn't mean to surprise you," Bryce said.

"Oh that's okay. Thanks for telling me. Now, how's John doing?"

"Well, I've sort of been avoiding John. We had a big argument a few weeks ago. He's kind of on edge these days. I don't want to push him. He gets very upset whenever he hears your name," Bryce revealed.

"That's too bad," Allison said. "John is going through some rough times right now. I believe it started when his father died and his mother had to move in with him. She's a diabetic, and she has a lot of problems with her lungs but still insists on smoking. John had to give up his free lifestyle to be home to give her insulin twice a day. He's become short tempered and bitter. He says that if he could win the lotto, he'd be able to put her into a home. He's become obsessed with winning, and he's spending more money than he's winning. I offered to help, but then this thing about my work with Franklin happened."

"Do I detect that you still care for John?" Bryce remarked.

"Care for him? I still love John very much. It was unfortunate what happened to us. I believe that John was coerced by some of our coworkers. He had never been jealous like that before. John knows that I really get involved with the people I work with. But it wasn't the jealousy that drove us apart. It was the lack of trust that he had in me."

"So do you think you and John can get over this?" Bryce asked.

"Sure. I'm just waiting for him to come to his senses."

"I really don't think that John realizes this," Bryce said, as he pulled in front of the house where Monique was sleeping.

"Where are we?" Allison asked.

"This is where Monique has been staying at night. The woman here is a friend of Ray-Man. Have you heard of Ray-Man, the drug-dealer?"

"Yes. I tried to get Franklin away from him."

"I'm almost embarrassed to bring you here but this is where Monique has chosen to stay," Bryce said.

"Have you forgotten that I go to places similar to this everyday?" Allison corrected.

"Well, anyway, be careful. This is a strange woman, and I don't understand the connection between her and Ray-Man."

This time the woman did not let Bryce into her house. She held the door ajar and peered out venomously at Allison with eyes narrowing in contempt. In a voice as cold as death, she said that Monique had not come in yet. She then put her hand out for the money that Mrs. Brown had sent and slammed the door.

"Boy, that was scary," Allison said as they rushed back to the car.

"It sure was," Bryce agreed. "I've never seen her quite like that. Most be a full moon or something."

Bryce drove by the pool hall where he and Brenda had once spotted Monique, but the BMW was not there. He didn't want to risk bringing Allison inside, and he didn't want to leave her outside alone either. It was getting dark, so they both agreed to continue their search the next day.

Bryce pulled into the parking lot the next day and spotted John leaning against his car. Usually his hands were busy with scratch-off's, but this time he was wringing them excessively. Bryce sensed that something was wrong. "Oh no! How could he have learned overnight that I talked to Allison. I gotta stay calm this time. I'm not going to let him upset me," Bryce said to himself, remembering Nick's warning.

Bryce noticed that John's face was pale and that beads of sweat formed on his forehead. His voice strained as he spoke. "Good morning, Bryce. I need to talk to you. It's important, and it must be in privacy."

"Okay, John," Bryce said. "Let's go to the picnic tables at the back of the parking lot. It's pretty private down there."

"I'm in deep trouble, and I don't have anyone to turn to for advice other than you," John started. He was blinking uncontrollably.

"What's the problem?"

"First, you know how sensitive I am about people finding out things about me. You have to promise me that you won't tell anyone until I can get this straightened out," John implored.

"You must trust me a little or you wouldn't have come to me. So what's the problem?" Bryce repeated.

"You know about the big investigation. How the DEA is trying to trap Ray-Man and how they suspect someone here of feeding him information about our clients. Well that someone is me," John revealed.

"Oh no, John!" Bryce gawked in disbelief.

"Believe me Bryce, this is the dumbest thing I've ever done. I let Ray-Man suck me into his scheme. I needed the money. My mother is going to put me in the poor house. I didn't know what else to do. But I can't afford to go to jail. My mother will die. There's no one else to care for her. This is absolutely the dumbest thing I have ever done," John cried.

"I don't think you'll be going to jail, John. The only wrong you've done is to break confidentiality. They don't send people to jail for that," Bryce said, trying to be encouraging.

"You don't get it. It's more than that. The money I was getting for the names looked good but went away fast. Anyway, there's only so many names you can give. So I got this so-called brilliant idea to sell Ray-Man the Prozac that I stole from our medication room. Man! Was that dumb or what?" John disclosed.

"Wow!," Bryce said, his eyebrows shooting up. "John, you could lose your nursing license for that."

"Nursing license? I could go to jail," John paused as his breath kept getting stuck in is his throat. "I don't know what to do. I thought about doing what Franklin was trying to do when you first met him. Franklin, Franklin, Franklin.!I blamed him for my mistake. I thought if he stayed away from our agency, this mess would go away. Then he came back into the picture. I blamed you for that. And that Ray-Man. Ray-Man is a bloodsucker. He keeps coming back for more. I thought about killing him. Either way, if I kill myself or Ray-Man, my mother would be left alone with no one to care for her."

"There's only one thing to do John. You have to stop here. You have to turn yourself in. You have to go to Nick and tell him before the DEA approachs you. It's better to turn yourself in than to get busted. This way it will look like you were bothered by what had happened. Then they would see that you were trapped into this by Ray-Man. Things will turn out in your favor. Ray-Man is the real target and cause of all of this mess. This is not the end of your life, John. I've been in deeper holes than this. Besides, most people here know about your situation with your mother. Allison told me about her last night," Bryce made the mistake of saying.

"Allison? Last night? Where did you see Allison last night?" John questioned.

"She has been helping me find Franklin's sister, who ran away from home. She, too, has been caught up in Ray-Man's schemes."

"You're sure she's not doing this just for Franklin?" John again questioned. This time his voice was thick with insinuation.

"What does that supposed to mean? Allison is a God-send, and you don't even realize it. She's a beautiful young lady, and she's loyal to her clients. Now what's wrong with that?"

"You just met her. You don't know her. You talk about her as if she was an angel. Well, she's no angel. She has bad habits like everyone else. For example, she uhh, she uhh. She checks herself in the mirror too much, and sometimes she wears too much perfume."

"Come on, John, all women do that," Bryce said, as it dawned on him how John really felt. "You know, Allison is still very much in love with you. She told me so. She's just waiting for you to come to your senses and see that. She thinks you two can still make it as a couple."

"Really! She said that?" John asked with regenerated enthusiasm which quickly evaporated as he thought. "She'll never take me back now. Boy! What have I done? Am I not the dumbest man in the world or what?"

"You need to go talk to Nick as soon as possible. I believe you can work through this," Bryce encouraged.

"You're right. Thanks for the advice," John said, as they headed for the building.

"You know you guys are late," Nick spoke, waiting at the entrance.

"Oh, I'm sorry. It's my fault we're late. I needed to talk to Bryce," John said.

"Well, it's good to see that you two guys can talk without the whole world hearing you," Nick said jokingly.

"Nick, I need to speak to you alone," John requested.

"There's never a dull moment on this job," Bryce thought as he made his way to his desk.

Chapter 14

Bryce remembered that he had to meet Allison at Mrs. Brown's house after work. They had planned to use as much daylight as possible to continue their search for Monique. However, about 4pm, he received a call from security at the Eagles' Nest. There had been an altercation on the grounds, and somehow Franklin was involved. That was all that security was instructed to tell Bryce over the phone. They needed him there as soon as possible.

Bryce called to Mrs. Brown's house. He explained to Brenda why he would not be there. He then asked her if she would meet with Allison and ride around the neighborhood to see if they could spot Monique. He told Brenda not to do anything risky, but to call the police if they saw her.

Bryce raced up Route 272. Today he was not interested in the scenery. His familiarity with the road allowed his mind to speculate on what was happening. He wondered what could have happened to make security's call sound so urgent. Did Franklin wreck Ms. Langdon's car? How bad was he hurt? Or did he get into a fight? They did say "altercation." What was their meaning of altercation? How serious was the altercation? Did Franklin violate his probation?

Pondering these questions, Bryce found himself at the retreat. He drove right up to Franklin's cottage and ran inside. Bryce felt a sickening wave of terror churning in his belly. A pained expression masked his face and he began to worry even more when he didn't find Franklin in his room. He encountered Korianne in the hallway as he was about to leave. "If you're looking for Franklin, they brought him to the medical building. It's next to the administration office. I hope he'll be alright. It was a terrible sight to watch."

Bryce didn't bother to ask her what exactly happened. He raced immediately to the medical building. The situation was bad, but not as bad as Bryce had imagined. Franklin was badly beaten, but he hadn't broken his probation. The doctor treating him explained that as bad as it looked, Franklin had only a few lacerations and a lot of bruises. It was nothing life-threatening. A snarl of agony spread over Franklin's face. Both of his eyes were swollen, and his cut lip still dripped blood. He was holding his right side and grimacing in pain.

Ms. Langdon showed thoughtful insight when she asked the doctor to come there instead of having Franklin taken to the hospital's emergency room. There he would have had to make a report to the police.

The doctor finished bandaging Franklin, and he and Ms. Langdon left Bryce alone with him. The doctor instructed Bryce not to stay too long.

"What happened?" Bryce asked, even though Ms. Langdon had already told him.

Franklin, still writhing in pain, cleared a lump from his throat and spoke. "It was Ray-Man and his boys. They came up to make a deal. I refused to cooperate, and they attacked me."

"You must have put up a pretty good fight for them to do this to you," Bryce stated. "Did I do the right thing?" Franklin asked. "Whether I did or not, I feel good about myself. Ouch! Boy does my lip hurt."

"You did the right thing. Your father would have been proud of you. Ms. Langdon seems especially proud of you. Looks like you're determined to keep your promise to your mother and Monique. You keep doing good, and you'll become a hero like your father," Bryce said encouragingly.

"What about those drug agents? Did I blow the trap they're trying to set ?" Franklin inquired.

"Don't worry about them. You did the right thing. I think it's best for you to get out of this mess while you can. They have other people they can use. Besides, with all the things Ray-Man is doing, they should be ready to close in on him."

"Listen, Bryce," Franklin started, but he stopped to take a breath. "There was something that Ray-Man said as he was leaving that I didn't understand. He said, 'Your sister will help you change your mind.' What did he mean by that? He don't know my sister. He's only seen her one time. Is she okay, Bryce? What did he mean?"

Bryce had anticipated Franklin asking him that. Until now, he didn't know how he would answer. Considering what Ray-Man had done to Franklin, if Bryce lied to Franklin, he would never forgive or trust him again. Bryce reasoned that he should tell him the truth.

"Okay, I need you to listen and stay calm," Bryce began. His voice began to constrict. "Monique has run away from home. She's been seen with Ray-Man. Even though she refuses to come home, she seems to be captive. She's been spending her nights at the house of one of Ray-Man's friends. Some lady on Hill Street who has five kids of her own."

Franklin swelled with anger. The veins in his temples throbbed, and his nostrils flared. The muscles of his jaw twitched, and his voice ascended to a murderous falsetto as he fumed, "What? Oh no! I swore I would kill him if he went after my sister. And that lady. In the neighborhood they call her Mrs. Rudolph, the witch doctor. She's Ray-Man's voodoo connection. How did this happen?"

"Calm down, calm down. Allison and Brenda are out looking for her right now."

"Allison and Brenda? They can't do anything against Ray-Man and his gang. He's got girls that will eat them alive," Franklin said as he struggled to get dressed.

"What are you doing?" Bryce asked.

"What do you think I'm doing? I'm going after my sister. That's what I'm doing."

"Wait, wait, you can't go. I'll go get your sister. This time I promise I'll bring her home. You can't go. Look at yourself. You can barely see through those swollen eyes. The way you're holding your side, you may have a cracked rib. You could puncture your lung. The doctor should have ordered an X-ray. So sit down and calm down. Think for a moment. You've come a long way. You could lose everything if you go."

"My sister is everything," Franklin returned.

"I understand that," Bryce replied, "but trust me. I've helped you get this far, haven't I? Listen to me. Allison, Brenda, the police, and DEA agents are all looking to save Monique. We'll find her. Now just stay calm. I'll find her and bring her home," Bryce said with determination.

Franklin's body stiffened in apprehension, and he doubled over in agony. He started to calm down after realizing that Bryce was right about his bodily condition. Bryce got up to leave. He said, "I'll stop and let the doctor know about your side. He'll probably arrange for you to have an X-ray.

Bryce tried to give Franklin a reason to stay put. He also knew that with Franklin's compulsive behavior, he might review the situation, change his mind, and go after Ray-Man. Bryce thought about how to outsmart him. He stopped at the security station and asked them not to give Franklin the car keys. "Not under any circumstances," he said. Franklin had to turn the keys in to security after bringing Ms. Langdon home. That was the rule.

Bryce raced south on Route 272. His face was tight and pinched with determination to rescue Monique. Bryce was willing to put everything on the line, and work rules did not matter. He thought about Nick's words to call if he was doing something against the rules. He dismissed that thought. He didn't want anyone to talk him out of doing what he had promised Franklin. He also felt that he had watched this mess go on too long without anyone taking action. He shuttered as he remembered what Franklin had said about the voodoo lady. He now understood why Monique's face looked unexpressive. Bryce's face grew haggard with worry as he thought about the dangerous situation he had put Brenda and Allison in by sending them out alone.

Bryce was beeped before he reached town. He didn't recognize the number, and this worried him. He reached for his cellular phone but couldn't find it. He couldn't recall if he had checked one out in his haste to leave the office. His initial thoughts were that it might be Allison or Brenda beeping him from their personal phones. He turned off Route 272 to look for a gas station with a pay phone. His search took him further away from the main road than he had planned. He finally spotted a booth at a roadside rest area. Bryce felt that something had gone terribly wrong. Chills ran up his spine and his arms were blossoming with goosebumps as he dialed the number. His anxiety briefly lifted when security at the Eagles' Nest answered the phone. The anxiety quickly returned as a knot in his throat when security told him that Franklin had taken the car and was heading for town. It seemed that Franklin had outsmarted them all. He had made an extra set of keys and did not turn them in.

In the meantime John, after confessing his involvement to Nick, was brought to the DEA agents. The agents asked John if he would cooperate in trapping Ray-Man and his gang. In return, they would not press charges against him. They wanted to set up one final deal with John to bring Ray-Man a large amount of Prozac. With that evidence in hand, they might be able to connect Ray-Man with murder.

It was getting dark. So Brenda and Allison decided to make one more drive through the Willow Street area. This time they spotted Monique and Ray-Man standing outside the restaurant. They kept driving by but stopped down the street to call the police like Bryce had instructed them. They then parked the car where they would be undetected but could still keep an eye on Monique. They didn't know that DEA agents were positioned nearby, staking out Ray-Man and his gang and waiting for John to arrive.

Allison gaped in stunned silence as she watched John pull up, get out of his car, and walk directly to Ray-Man. He had a large bag in his possession. "What in the world is he doing here?" Allison said, breaking the silence.

"Who is he?" Brenda asked.

Before Allison could answer, another car came speeding up. It almost crashed into the crowd. Everyone was stunned to see Franklin jump out. He stormed straight toward Ray-Man. His fists were clenched with suppressed rage, and he was gesturing furiously.

At the same time, the police that the women had called used poor judgment and came up the street with their siren screaming. The gang panicked and took off in different directions. Monique slipped back into the diner. Ray-Man went down the alley by himself. Franklin, still bellowing ferociously, went after him.

Finally, Bryce came rushing up. The scene was chaotic. Brenda pointed Bryce toward the alley where Franklin had gone after Ray-Man. With their lights glaring, the agents, the police, and John followed Bryce into the alley. Midway down the alley they came upon Franklin trying to shade the lights from his already swollen eyes. In his hand was a six inch knife with blood dripping from it. On the ground near his feet, lying in a puddle of blood, was Ray-Man. It seemed apparent that he was dead by his motionless body and that huge amount of blood that surrounded him.

Bryce stood dumbstruck. He felt like he had been shot and was waiting to fall. His heart leaped in his chest. "How could Franklin do this? If only I had spent more time with him, I might have prevented this tragedy. Now his whole life will be put on hold. How will this affect Mrs. Brown and Monique? It doesn't matter that Ray-Man was scum. It doesn't matter that he deserved to die. Here in America, a person is given a trial before they are executed." Bryce thought about these things as he stood staring at the horrific scene.

CHAPTER 15

Allison and Brenda took advantage of the opportunity to go after Monique. Normally, they wouldn't dare enter the diner alone, but they had seen the gang scatter. They went searching through the place as far as the back door, which opened up to an alley. Monique was not there. She seemingly had disappeared. The two women turned to leave and heard water running in a nearby bathroom. The door was ajar. They pushed the door open and found Monique standing at the sink. She was studying herself profoundly in the mirror and splashing water on her face.

"Brenda! Allison! What are you two doing here?" she asked, as she jumped reflexively. She raised one eyebrow in a questioning slant and asked, "What am I doing here? Why am I dressed like this?"

The police cruiser left the alley, and Monique spotted Franklin seated in the back. Franklin saw her and slumped back into his seat. He had a pitiful look of appeal on his face. His eyes widened innocently as they exchanged glances.

"Why is Franklin in the police car? Monique asked explosively.

Brenda and Allison were equally shocked to see Franklin in the cruiser. They had no answer to her question. They had no knowledge of the tragedy that had just occurred.

Soon Bryce and John emerged from the alley. They informed the women that Franklin had been accused of killing Ray-Man. "Why would Franklin want to kill Ray-Man?" Monique asked.

Bryce had had a bleak, wintry feeling, but his face quickly brightened when he heard Monique's response. She sounded like she had returned to her old self. They all agreed that it was best to get her home right away.

"I'm going down to police headquarters to see if I can help Franklin," Bryce said. He turned to the group and started giving instructions. "Brenda, you take Monique home. John, maybe you can give Allison a ride home."

Allison insisted on staying with Monique until she was safely home. She brushed her hair back, turned to John, and in a gregarious manner asked, "What were you doing out there? We need to talk. I will call you at home later."

Her words sounded a little motherly, but they were like sweet music to John's ears. It had been awhile since Allison had said anything to him. His eyes danced, and he smiled broadly as he nodded okay.

"Who's going to tell Aunt Martha about Franklin?" Brenda asked. "She's going to take this very hard."

"Don't mention anything about Franklin until I return from the police station," Bryce suggested.

Before they could make it home, Monique fell asleep. She had complained about how tired she felt and how it felt like she hadn't slept for several days. She stretched out on the back seat of the car.

Mrs. Brown was waiting and peering out the front door. Her eyes brimmed with joy at the sight of her daughter being steadied as she climbed the steps. She started to cry as she embraced Monique. "Oh, thank you God! Thank you God for bringing my baby home. Never again will I push her out there in those streets," she testified.

"I'm okay, Mama. I'm just tired and sleepy. I feel dirty. Who put me into these clothes? They're not even mine," Monique said, as she climbed the stairs like a person scaling a ledge. She stopped at the top, turned, and said, "Look at this house! What happened to it? It'll just have to wait until tomorrow."

"Yeah. She's back," Brenda acknowledged.

"Thank you, thank you," Mrs. Brown said. This time directing her appreciation to Allison and Brenda. "Where did you find her?"

The two women eyed each other with the obvious thought of which one was clever enough to explain how they saved Monique without having to reveal what happened to Franklin. Allison, her features remarkably composed and angelic, was about to speak when the door-bell rang. It was Bryce. He hadn't been allowed to see Franklin but was told that his arraignment would be the following morning.

"Hello, Mrs. Brown," Bryce greeted. He tried to maintain a straight face, but his features had fallen. "Why don't you have a seat. I have something to tell you."

"What is it, Brian?" she asked. "I have my little girl home, so what could be the problem?"

"It's Franklin, Mrs. Brown. He's being held for the stabbing death of Ray-Man."

"What?" she screamed. "How can that be? Franklin would never kill anyone. That can't be true. The person that said he did it is lying. It just can't be true. Besides, Franklin is way up there in that Eagle place. Why do they say that Franklin did it, Brian?"

Allison and Brenda were quickly at her side, trying to comfort her. Bryce told about all the things that had happened, including the details that led up to the stabbing.

"You see there. They pushed him to do it. I knew for a long time that Raymond was a bad seed. He was a bad influence on Franklin. I always thought that someday he would get himself killed and maybe get Franklin killed, too. I never thought it would turn out like this," Mrs. Brown said. Her bottom lip curled, and her long face showed immense sadness. She suddenly complained of feeling ill and asked for assistance in getting upstairs to bed.

Bryce assured her that he would be with Franklin in court for his arraignment before saying goodnight. Allison and Bryce departed for home, leaving Brenda behind to care for Mrs. Brown and Monique.

Allison remembered to call John when she got home. John had been waiting eagerly for the call. He answered the phone on the first ring.

"Hello, John."

"Hello, Allison."

"First of all, John," Allison started, "what were you doing out there with that Ray-Man gang? Don't you know that they are a dangerous group?"

Having to tell Allison all the trouble he had gotten into was very distressing to John. But he told her everything, not leaving out one detail.

"I wish you had come to me for help," Allison said. "Did you think I would turn my back to you? I love you."

"It seemed so overwhelming. My mother needs a lot of supplies," John said. "I saw no way out. I only meant for it to be a one-time deal. There're no one-time deals with Ray-Man. He looks for the opportunity to trap people."

'Well, that's for sure. We saw that with Monique," Allison agreed. "What happens now?"

"Well, as for the criminal charges, I believe there is no case now that Ray-Man is dead. I still have to face the nurses license review board. I could lose my license, which means I could lose my job. So you see, I'm still in hot water that's getting hotter and hotter," John confessed.

"Well, at least you won't be going to jail, and that's a good thing. No?" Allison remarked. "And there are other places you can work. Look at me, for example. I'll be going to my third job within a year's time.'

"What do you mean by that? I heard you loved your job at DCF. Everyone says you are a natural at working with kids. Why would you leave?"

"It's a matter of a family obligation. I promised my Uncle Vince that I would help my Auntie Lou if she needed me. She called to ask me to take over at the Eagles' Nest. She suffered a mild stroke and doesn't want to risk having another one. Besides, I would still be helping people there. I can work with kids in my spare time."

"That's great, Allison," John said. "I have no doubt that you'll be good at that, too."

"That's it, John!" Allison said, her voice raised to a delightful pitch. "That's the answer. You can come to work at the Eagles' Nest."

"I don't know about that. I love you, and I hope to marry you one day. But I think I would have trouble working for you."

"But you won't be working *for* me. You'll be working *with* me."

"Who's going to inherit the place?"

"I am."

"Well then, I will be working for you. You know how I am, Allison. I can't have you supporting me. It would be like a handout. Then there's my mother to worry about."

"Listen, John," Allison interrupted. "If you plan to marry me, you better let me start getting involved in your life. I understand the problems you face. They're too much for one person, but together we can do it. That was a proposal that you made, wasn't it?"

"Of course," John answered. "But we'll have to wait on that job offer. Maybe I won't lose my job after all."

Bryce was seated in the courtroom when Franklin was escorted in. He was handcuffed at the waist and wore leg shackles. He held his head high, trying to look brave, but from his seat, Bryce could see Franklin's facial muscles twitch nervously.

The court officer positioned Franklin in front of the judge's bench. Bryce pinned his ID on his shirt pocket and stood next to Franklin. The stern-faced judge looked unforgiving. He peered down his nose imperiously at the two men. "Who are you?" he asked, flashing a superior grin.

"I'm Franklin's caseworker from the Department of Mental Health," Bryce answered.

The clerk read the charges aloud. The judge asked Franklin if he understood the charges filed against him. Franklin said yes. The judge then asked Franklin if he had an attorney and if he could he afford one. Franklin answered no. The judge instructed the court officers to take Franklin down the hall to the Public Defender's Office, where he could apply for representation. Bryce followed. After qualifying, Franklin was assigned an attorney. The man introduced himself as Peter Silverman. He was a young and thoughtful-looking lawyer. He wore a light blue chalk-striped suit with the same color bow tie. His shoes were polished black as if he had spent much time on them. His crew-cut hair style gave him a military look. To Bryce this was good. This indicated to him that the lawyer was probably unaffected by peer pressure and that he would work in Franklin's behalf, not just routinely.

Franklin stood before the judge again. This time only his lawyer was at his side. Again the charges were read, and again the judge asked Franklin if he understood them. Franklin answered yes. The judge asked Franklin to give his plea to the charges.

"I plead innocent, Your Honor," Franklin answered.

The judge asked the clerk to schedule Franklin and his lawyer for a pre-trial date. Attorney Silverman then argued for a low bond to be set for Franklin. He mentioned how Franklin was compliant with his treatment program set up by the state and the Eagles' Nest. He also related some of the details leading up to the stabbing, including how Franklin had been savagely attacked and how the gang had held his sister.

The judge wasn't sympathetic. He set Franklin's bail at $100,000. Bryce watched the blood drain from Franklin's face as he was taken back to the lock up.

Silverman asked Bryce if Franklin's family had enough money to bail him out. Bryce said he would go and talk to Mrs. Brown about the situation.

Bryce headed for Mrs. Brown's house and thought about how surprised he was to hear Franklin say that he was innocent. All that Bryce had seen seemed to prove Franklin's guilt. Why was he denying that he did it? There had been something else at the crime scene that made Bryce positive that Franklin had done it. It kept nagging away at Bryce, but for the life of him, he couldn't quite piece it together.

Brenda answered the door at Mrs. Brown's house. She had come over to check on Monique. Monique was sound asleep and appeared undisturbed about the night before. Strangely, though, Mrs. Brown was not home. She had not been there when Brenda arrived. They both thought it was odd for her to go out and leave Monique alone. Within minutes, Mrs. Brown came walking in. She claimed that she had been out shopping, but she had no bags with her. She was holding tight to a large purse. Bryce told her about the arraignment and how Franklin had pleaded innocent.

"I told you he didn't do it. I knew it, I knew it!" she said.

"Unfortunately, though, for him to get out on bail is going to take a lot of money," Bryce informed.

"How much money?" Martha asked.

"His bail is set at $100,000. I believe a person has to put up ten percent of that, which is $10,000," Bryce answered.

"What about my house? Don't people put up property for bail?" she asked.

"I believe so. Let me call Franklin's lawyer to check on that."

The public defender informed Bryce that property was accepted for surety. He explained how it was risky, because a person could lose their home if the bonded person failed to show for court. Bryce explained this to Mrs. Brown.

"I want my son out of jail," she argued. "He didn't do this. Besides, I've always asked him to protect his sister. Three or four years ago I might not have done this. Franklin was wild and out of control then.

Since you've been working with him, he has calmed down a lot. He looks up to you like a father."

Mrs. Brown and Bryce left Brenda with Monique and headed downtown to free Franklin.

CHAPTER 16

Franklin was glad to see that his mother was recovering and that she was up and about. He also was glad to be set free from jail. He spoke about a sleepless night on a cold, hard, metal bench. His thoughts had been on the Eagles' Nest and how he had taken his comfortable bed there for granted. Bryce had called Ms. Langdon to update her on what was happening. She still supported Franklin. She said that the Eagles' Nest was his home and that's where he belonged.

Bryce listened quietly as Franklin tried to explain to Mrs. Brown what actually happened in the alley. Regardless of what Bryce had seen, Franklin told her the same story as he had originally. That was all Mrs. Brown needed to hear. She and Franklin renewed the promises they made to each other in the hospital.

At the house, Bryce gave Franklin time to visit his sister. Monique was still sound asleep. Franklin sat on the edge of the bed. He gazed down tenderly at her and gently brushed her hair to one side. He remembered when she was just a little baby. Even then she had a full head of silky black hair. He remembered her cute little round face and how bubbles would come from her mouth when she tried to talk. "She was probably trying to recite poetry," he thought. He remembered how she used to try to climb out of the crib after him. Then he remembered how he wanted to tip her crib over. He wanted her to go away. She was getting all of the attention and affection that had once been his alone.

He remembered walking her to school. She was no longer the little brat he wanted to lose. She had become his private possession. He was proud of her. Even at that young age, her personality was different from her peers. She always wanted to stop and read something. She was a quick learner. Franklin remembered seeing her grow into an attractive young lady. He thought he would have to fight to keep the boys away from her but, unlike him, she didn't like to be in the spotlight. She would rather be home reading a book than out attending a party. They became very protective of each other. Now she lay there motionless, dead tired, almost losing her life because of the problems he had caused. Franklin gently kissed her forehead: his way of saying thanks.

The ride north on Route 272 took longer today. Bryce had decided to take his time. There was a lot of sun glare affecting his vision. He looked over at Franklin, who was completely relaxed. He was nodding in and out of sleep. "Why are you sticking to that story?" Bryce asked. "I was the first to enter the alley after you and Ray-Man, and I didn't see anyone else."

Franklin yawned and stretched. He rubbed the sleep from his eyes and said, "I am innocent. Someone came out of the dark and attacked Ray-Man. I was just pulling the knife out of his side when everyone showed up with the lights. I realize now that that was a dumb thing to do."

"I don't know. You looked very guilty to me. Not only did you get caught holding the knife, but your eyes were blazing murderously, and you had a wicked smile on your face. We can discount your facial expression because you did go there mad as hell, but there was something else I saw that connected you. I keep getting a blank when I try to recall what it was. That really bothers me."

"Listen, I didn't do it, and it doesn't feel good being accused of killing someone," Franklin confessed. "But even though I didn't do it, I probably can't prove that I didn't. I'll probably have to go to jail anyway."

"I really want to believe you, and you do sound sincere, but the evidence won't go away. It can't be good for your conscience, being accused of murder," Bryce noted.

"What about you and my dad? Did you two have to kill many people in Nam? How did it feel to you?" Franklin asked.

"Well, first of all, in Nam we were fighting for our lives. And, yes, your father did kill a lot of enemy troops. At the time, I was glad that he did. They were trying their best to harm us. Most of us, including your father, didn't have anything personal against them. We just wanted to come home alive. Therefore, we had no choice but to defend ourselves. Besides, we weren't sure about the ones we did kill or wound," Bryce related.

"Why was that?" Franklin asked.

"All of our enemies, the Viet Cong and the North Vietnamese Army, used to drag away their wounded and dead. They didn't want us to see how many we had hit. It was very frustrating to fight for days and never know if you hit anything. It was equally frustrating to be shot at and never see anyone to shoot back at."

"And why was that?" Franklin asked again.

"They lived underground in bunkers or were hidden just below the ground in spider holes. They were always heavily camouflaged. In the thickness of the jungle, very seldom did we see the enemy. One of their tricks was to try to cause trouble between the black and the white soldiers," Bryce explained.

"How did they do that?"

"They knew about the racial problems that we had back in the States. They knew about Dr. Martin Luther King Jr. and that he had been assassinated while we were there. So at night, some would come up to our camp and say, "Hey soul brothers, what are you guys doing over here fighting against us. We don't have anything against you guys. The White Man in your camp is the enemy. Why don't you guys go home? What do you say, soul brothers?"

"Did that trick work?" Franklin wanted to know.

"No. We were a tight group in Nam. They failed to realize that in Nam, we were all soul brothers. Black, white, Spanish, and some Native Americans. It was only when we came home that we divided. Anyway, the propaganda brought us closer together. We knew that the Viet Cong's main objective was to get someone to answer back so that they could zero in on their position. They would do anything to get an opportunity to shoot at us. No matter what race we were, we all realized one thing. And that was that big, strong, brave guys like your father were our ticket back home."

At the administration building, Ms. Langdon welcomed Franklin home. He had a lost expression on his face when he saw that she now was supporting herself with a cane. Her careworn face with rheumy eyes made her look weathered. Her voice quavered when she politely asked Bryce to wait outside her office. She wanted to talk to Franklin alone.

A short time later, the door opened, and Ms. Langdon asked Bryce to come in. She informed him that Allison would soon be managing the Eagles' Nest. She then reclined in her seat the way she always did when she was about to give one of her famous speeches. "Regardless of the situation surrounding this murder mess or what you think you saw, everyone in America accused of a crime is innocent until proven guilty. That includes Franklin. Franklin will continue to call the Eagles' Nest his home, and he will continue to have our support. Even when I'm no longer able to come here. I hope your agency feels the same way."

Bryce got up to leave. On his way out, he thought, "Franklin is very fortunate to have the support of such a strong-minded woman as Ms. Langdon."

Before he could close the door behind him, she called out, "Oh, Bryce, Franklin is indeed innocent. I know there's strong evidence that says otherwise, but he's innocent. I have that feeling."

Even though Franklin had been proclaiming his innocence all along, and Mrs. Brown was staking her house that her son did not commit the crime, it was Ms. Langdon's speech and stern conviction that started Bryce questioning himself.

Allison, Brenda, and Bryce had made plans to meet at Mrs. Brown's house to talk to Monique. They were curious to see if she could recall any of the details of her nightmarish ordeal.

The two ladies were there ahead of Bryce. They told him that when they got there, Monique was still sleeping. They were concerned because it was now two days and she hadn't awakened even to eat, according to Mrs. Brown. They sat around and chatted for a few minutes. Then Brenda went upstairs to check on Monique. She came down wearing a big smile. She said in a whisper, "She's awake now. She'll be down after she gets dressed."

Allison and Brenda had brought food. They started setting up the table, and Allison said, "We picked up this great meal for Mrs. Brown and Monique. There's more than enough for everybody. You'll have to join us, Bryce."

Monique came down the stairs yawning and smacking her lips. She was still a little unsteady on her feet, but she moved as if she was drawn by the smell of food. She took a seat and immediately started to eat. Mrs. Brown, though, insisted that she wasn't hungry and stated that she'd rather go upstairs and lay down. Brenda persuaded her to stay and try to eat something.

"I had a bad dream that woke me up," Monique began. "I kept seeing Franklin in the back seat of a police car."

"That wasn't a dream," Brenda explained. "That was the last thing you saw before we brought you home. Franklin was arrested on suspicion of killing Ray-Man."

"Killing Ray-Man? Why would Franklin want to kill Ray-Man? He calls Ray-Man his friend," Monique questioned, as her eyes widened with shock.

"How much do you remember about the past few weeks?" Bryce asked.

"I can't say. When I try to think back, everything becomes foggy. The last clear thing I remember is that Mama was in the hospital. Oh, and I remember coming home from the hospital and discovering something strange had happened," Monique said.

"What was that?" Brenda asked, shooting upright in her chair.

"I found the back door partly opened, and the refrigerator door had been left open. I didn't know if I left it like that or not. I left home in a hurry, and I was worried about Mama. Then again, very seldom do we use our back door. It was just strange."

"So you don't remember being with Ray-Man at all?" Allison asked.

"Ray-Man? Me with Ray-Man? Are you crazy? Why would I want to be with Ray-Man? He's scum. He's a predator. A predator that feeds on poor people by making them buy his drugs. The only reason I would even mention his name is because Franklin thinks he is his friend."

"For the past few weeks you were held captive by Ray-Man. That's why Franklin went after him," Bryce told her.

They all thought that Mrs. Brown would want to hear about Monique's mysterious adventure. Instead she kept squirming in her seat. She kept clearing her throat and began to drum her fingers on the table. Finally, she stood up, excused herself, and went upstairs to her room.

"What else can you remember?" Allison asked.

"Well, I thought it was strange how after finding the refrigerator door open, everything that we had to drink was either open or loosely capped. I didn't think much about that at first. I drank some milk and felt weird afterward. I love milk, and I drink it all the time. I went to bed and my head started to spin. I couldn't sleep, so I warmed more milk. But then I became suspicious of the milk. I began to hear a distant ringing in my ears. It wouldn't go away, and when I closed my eyes to try to sleep, it kept getting louder. Soon I began to hear the beating of drums, as if some festive ritual was going on in my head. Finally, I got up and got dressed. It was very scary, and I didn't know what to do. I looked out of the window, and someone was standing in the driveway, calling me to come out. I looked around in the kitchen for something to protect myself with. That's all I remember until I saw Franklin in the back seat of the police car." Monique was about to conclude, but then she remembered. "Oh! I remember having a recurring dream about being in a strange place. A man and woman with dark piecing eyes were standing over me."

There was a hush in the room, and the three adults sat exchanging questioning glances. The silence continued as they tried to process the incredible story. Monique got up and cleared the table. She began to serve coffee.

"I think it is a blessing that you don't remember all that happened," Bryce said. "No coffee for me. If I drink that, I'll be up all night, and I have a busy day tomorrow."

Bryce got up to leave. Allison and Brenda went upstairs to say goodnight to Mrs. Brown. Bryce had gotten as far as the porch when the two women were suddenly on his heels. Mrs. Brown had refused to let them into her room. She told them that she was tired and wanted to sleep.

Bryce was sitting at his desk the next day. He looked over to the empty chair where John usually sat. Bryce got up and walked over to John's desk. It was littered with papers and scratched lotto tickets. Bryce picked up one of the losers. His eyebrows raised in a questioning slant, and he thought, "What is it about these things that get people hooked? They're just as bad as alcohol or drugs. With my addictive personality, if I played, I would most likely be hooked on to them, too. Poor John thinks that these tickets are the answer to all his problems. That might well be if he got the money back that he put into them."

Bryce's thought was broken when the phone rang and his beeper sounded its alarm. He shut off the beeper and answered the phone. It was Monique. Her voice shrilled with horror as she pleaded for him to come over. "It's Mama!" she said with a strangling cry.

The number on the beeper was Brenda's. Bryce called, and she told him that she had just gotten a call from Monique asking her to come.

Bryce rushed toward Mrs. Brown's house. His thoughts raced. "We made a mistake leaving her last night. She was acting suspiciously. She was probably having a pancreatic attack and didn't want to tell anyone. I should have insisted on seeing her. I wonder if Monique called for an ambulance. She's a smart young lady. She probably did that first."

Bryce breathed a sigh of relief when he saw the ambulance and police there. However, it seemed odd to him that the paramedics where standing around outside chatting and smoking. "There must be others inside," Bryce reasoned.

Bryce was met on the porch by Monique and Brenda. Monique's face was haggard, and her eyes were swollen from crying. Brenda was glum. Her faced was etched with sorrow. Bryce took them both into his arms. "How is she?" he asked. "Is it a bad attack?"

"She's dead," Brenda whimpered.

"Dead? That can't be!" Bryce said as he pulled away from the women and ran upstairs. He stopped at the bedroom door and peered in. He crept closer and saw Mrs. Brown sprawled out on the floor. Next to her body was an empty bottle of liquor. Bryce's eyes transfixed with shock and grief. The sight of her lifeless body lying there struck him like a hammer blow. Bryce's chin sunk dejectedly into his chest.

CHAPTER 17

Everyone who knew Mrs. Brown was devastated by the news of her death. Especially disturbing was the manner in which she had succumbed. Mrs. Brown was a fun-loving, friendly woman. She entertained because she enjoyed having people around her. Her taste for alcohol caused her to dwell too much on the negative things that were happening to her children. She turned back to the bottle and became the tragic victim of alcoholism.

Mrs. Brown's relatives were concerned about Monique living at the house alone. Aunt Jessie Mae and Mabel put together a schedule for family members to stay with her in shifts. Allison heard about the schedule and insisted that her name be added to the list.

Monique had just recovered from one traumatic experience and was now in the middle of another one. She didn't sleep. She was constantly washing, mopping floors, rearranging furniture, ironing clothes and folding them. She even did her mother's clothes. It was Allison who came to her aid with a sedative that Monique's doctor ordered. Not only was she grief-stricken, but she began to blame herself for her mother's death.

"I should have taken better care of her," she would say repeatedly.

Family members asked Bryce to take the arduous task of telling Franklin the sad news. Bryce thought it was strange how the scene driving up Route 272 always seemed to blend with his mood. Today it was a long gloomy drive. The sky was overcast, and the dark clouds added to his depression. He had a deep feeling of sorrow and regret. It was grief growing inside him like a cancer. His sadness was for the family he had come to know. Bryce wondered if it would have been different if he had come to know them earlier. Would he have been able to help them overcome some of the problems that caused this turmoil? He recalled similar experiences in his life. He remembered how alcohol and drugs had brought him to the brink of suicide. He recalled the repeated visits to mental health clinics and hospitals for depression. He remembered his own brush with demonism and that he, too, had almost died from pancreatitis. It seemed as though, through this family, he was living his life over again. Each time he got the same feeling of navigating through an emotional minefield.

Bryce found Franklin in the dining hall. He was surrounded by peers. Franklin had been clowning around and telling jokes. When Bryce popped in, Franklin was attempting impressions of some popular people. "He isn't bad at it," Bryce thought. Franklin had a unique quality. In the face of all his problems, he still knew how to make people laugh and feel at ease.

Korianne was sitting next to Franklin. She was the first to notice Bryce and made Franklin aware that he was there. "What's up with that hang-dog expression on your face?" Franklin asked.

"Mind if we go somewhere private? I need to talk to you alone."

Bryce walked with Franklin back to his cottage. "Franklin, today the ride here reminded me of someone traveling through time. I was sent back many years to when I used to walk around under the shadow of a dark and dismal cloud. This cloud was there because I carried the weight of the world on my shoulders. The things that I saw happening in this world really got me down. People were being mistreated. People were starving while others had more than they needed. I saw people dying from all sorts of ailments at an early age. The worse thing I saw was the hatred that is so prevalent in the world. There's little love of

neighbor or natural affection. I saw bad people getting away with murder, while good people were getting hurt. So I turned to God for
answers, and I learned from the Bible that God does not hurt people.
It's not even God that causes them to die. I read that unforeseen occur-
rences will befall some of us. Do you know what that means?"

"Yes. Probably that no matter how good a person may be, sometimes
bad things will happen even to him."

"Exactly. I don't believe I could have said it better. Hopefully, now
you will understand what I have to tell you. You wouldn't believe how
much I wish I had a shoe box like yours so that I could reach in and pull
out the right words."

"You don't even have to tell me," Franklin responded. "I already
know. The moment I spotted you, I knew what you came to tell me. You
see, I've had the same dream for the past three nights. It was as vivid as
any dream could get. I have this thing about dreams, you know. It's like
I can see things before they happen. My mother has that same ability,
but she tells me that there is nothing to it. It's just a down south super-
stition, she says."

Franklin paused to catch his breath. He then continued, "It's
Monique, right? She's pregnant with Ray-Man's baby, isn't she?"

"No, Franklin," Bryce regretted to say. "I'm sorry to have to tell you
that it's your mother. Your mother has died."

Franklin flinched. Bryce watched the blood drain from his face.
Franklin opened his mouth to speak, but his words seemed stuck in his
throat. He looked up to the sky and then gave a startling gasp that
sounded like "No." He repeated it over and over until a shattering clash
of thunder and lightning came, as though on Franklin's command. A
strong gust of wind blew them off balance. The cloud above them burst,
and a torrential downpour caught them before they could reach the
door. Franklin's face grew dark with pain. His eyes took on a wounded
look. Bryce put his arms around Franklin and led him to his room.
Franklin laid across his bed and wailed with grief. The sight of Franklin

laying there, almost delirious with grief, caused a tugging at Bryce's heart, but he did not interrupt him.

An hour passed, and Bryce was still sitting there. Other Bible verses came to his mind: "For everything there is an appointed time, even a time for every affair under the heavens. A time for birth and a time to die. A time to plant and a time to uproot what is planted. A time to weep and a time to laugh. A time to wail and a time to skip about." Bryce realized that this was Franklin's time to weep.

Just when Bryce thought that Franklin had finally fallen asleep, he sat up and moaned. "Why did she have to die?" His voice dissolved in tears. "Why couldn't I have been there to save her? Why am I losing all of my family? Why does my family have to suffer so much pain?"

Bryce did not answer him. He knew that venting his frustrations would be good for Franklin's healing.

Franklin reached for and held onto his shoe box. With the shoe box close to his chest, he started to talk to his father. Bryce quietly got up and walked out, unnoticed by Franklin.

Ms. Langdon was alone in the administration office. She was surprised to see Bryce, but his presence brought a cheerful smile to her face. He regretted to have to tell her about Mrs. Brown's death. Ms. Langdon's smile disappeared, and her eyes misted over. Bryce respected Ms. Langdon for her being a person that had good insight and used good judgment. She always seemed to be in control of her emotions. Even though saddened by the news, her immediate focus was on Franklin's well-being. "This is going to put Franklin in a very difficult spot. We'll have to put him under watch for the time being. He is very vulnerable at this time. How was he when you left him?" she asked, while drying her eyes.

"He was crying and talking to his shoe box."

"When he stops talking is the time we have to watch him closely. We'll do half hour checks on him through the night." she said.

The next couple of days Franklin was in a depressive state. He didn't even leave his room to eat. This concerned everyone at the Eagles' Nest. They came by his room to extend their sympathy but still gave him plenty of room to grieve. Some brought food along. Ms. Langdon canceled his classes for the week. The watch was continued because of the severity of his depression. Most of the time Franklin's body slouched across the bed, but his spirit sunk to the floor.

Monique appeared to be doing much better than Franklin. She was now engaging in conversation and greeting relatives she hadn't seen in a long time. Mrs. Brown's large family was pouring in from Hoboken, New Jersey, down to South Carolina. One of Mrs. Brown's grandmothers had eleven children, and the other had thirteen, giving her twenty-four aunts and uncles. The aunts and uncles had many children of their own. Mrs. Brown's cousins numbered in the hundreds. Franklin's father had a large family, too. All of them were planning to be at Mrs. Brown's funeral.

Bryce was busy assisting the family. He made several trips to the airport and helped those arriving find motels and hotels.

Besides showing the family around town, Bryce also cared for Franklin's needs. Franklin had withdrawn money from his account and asked Bryce to buy him a suit and tie. Franklin showed a little light in his recovery when he joked about how this would be the first suit and tie he ever owned. Bryce asked Franklin if he wanted to meet some of his relatives. Franklin decided to wait until the funeral before going into Torrington.

The funeral was set for Saturday morning. Thursday and Friday night the family held a "sitting up." This is the term they used down South for what people in the North called a "wake." They decided on that because most of Mrs. Brown's older relatives lived in the South. The sitting up differed from the wake in that the wake lasted only a few hours, which the sitting up lasted all night. People brought food and consoled family members.

Bryce got the opportunity to meet Brenda's mother at the sitting up. Brenda was right about her height. She was a little woman, but charmingly friendly. Bryce felt more comfortable talking to her than he did to her father. She spent most of the night pointing out to Bryce who was who in the family.

Saturday morning started out as a bright day. Everyone moved about preparing themselves for the funeral. Brenda and Allison were helping Monique, while Bryce took a ride up Route 272 to assist Franklin.

By ten o'clock Franklin was hand in hand with Monique, and they were escorted to the long black family car belonging to the funeral service. Outside the church, hundreds of family members and friends had gathered. The church bells rang three times, signaling the start of the funeral. Franklin, Monique, and Mrs. Brown's sisters and brothers were led to the front row seats. The rest of the family followed them. Bryce took a seat off to the side and watched as the church quickly filled. There were so many people that the church was not big enough to seat them all. People stood in every available spot.

Bryce spotted Brenda sitting behind Franklin and Monique. She searched the room for Bryce, and for a moment they eyed each other adoringly. Bryce was glad to see that Allison had made it in. He smiled again when he saw John sitting next to her.

Bryce thought that the church was uniquely built. It slanted toward the front and began to rise at the podium. It had the appearance of a concert hall. Bryce had never seen anything quite like it before.

Bryce recognized those in the choir section. Brenda's mother had pointed them out as Mrs. Brown's relatives from Philadelphia. They made up the whole choir themselves.

A one-legged man, propped up on a crutch, positioned himself as if he was the conductor of the choir. Brenda's mother identified him as both the family's pastor and Mrs. Brown's uncle.

Bryce thought the way the funeral was conducted was unusual. After an opening prayer by the church's regular pastor, Mrs. Brown's uncle, the one-legged pastor, stood and began to sing a solo. The song started out sad, and then quickly jumped to a more upbeat tempo. The song caused people to act differently. Some began to cry, while others stood and clapped to the music. At first Bryce was confused. He looked over at Brenda. She was caught up in the music and was standing and clapping. It seemed like everyone in the church knew the words to the song except Bryce, Allison, and John. But even they stood and clapped to the music. Bryce watched as the grieving family was comforted by a performance from other family members. "There's a lot of talent in this family," Bryce thought. He found himself clapping his hands and stumping his feet.

After the one-legged pastor preached the eulogy, a heart-wrenching crest came to the session with Mabel and Jessie Mae coming forth to sing. They started with the song, "Oh, When the Saints Come Marching In." They sang the opening line, and everyone who knew the song joined in with the chorus. It was really a wonder to behold. After the first time through, everyone stood and was singing and clapping. The two aunts had angelic voices. They lifted everyone's spirits to soaring heights. Bryce was very impressed. Never in his life had he seen anything like this. They did not mock the dead. Rather, they changed a sad occasion into a reflection on happier times.

Finally, Mrs. Brown was put to rest. The effect of the sermon had strengthened Franklin and Monique enough to go through that part. Bryce stood off to the side. He knew that later, when everyone had gone their way, Mrs. Brown's departure from them would resurface like a haunting chill. When they lowered her body, Bryce felt a cold fist close over his heart.

The family gathered back at the church to have a meal and to say goodbye to each other. Like most families, they only got to see each other at weddings and funerals. Bryce wondered what it would be like to see all of Brenda's family together. Here, at the funeral, he saw a part of the family, and that was an impressive number. Bryce was surprised to see that Franklin knew as many of his family members as he did. Franklin was a moody person because of his illness, and Bryce thought that he would prefer to be alone, but he went around talking to his cousins close to his age. Everyone commented him on well he looked and how how well he appeared to be doing.

After the funeral, Franklin and Monique spent hours together. They promised to continue to look after each other. Monique expressed her fear of being alone if Franklin had to go to prison.

On the ride back to the Eagles' Nest, Franklin had a lot of questions about death. Bryce tried his best to give Franklin satisfying answers.

"Have you ever lost anyone close?" Franklin asked.

"Yes, I lost my sister to a disease, and my father had a heart attack."

"How were you able to cope with those deaths?"

"My sister's death was very difficult for me to accept. Mostly because she had cancer of the bones and had suffered tremendously. Dying was a relief for her but it was very saddening to our family. During her illness, I watched my mother's hair go from black to gray. My sister was young and pretty. She left her young son behind."

"That was sad. What happened to your father?" Franklin wanted to know.

"It was a little different with my father's death. He drank a lot when we were growing up. There were many nights when we didn't know if he would make it home alive or not. This was because of how much he drank and where he did his drinking. Toward his later years, though, he decided to quit. I guess it was too late for his body. He suffered a lot of ailments. One night, while watching a Muhammad Ali/Joe Frazier fight on television, he had a heart attack and died. The excitement was too much for him. The one thing that eased our grieving was the big smile he had on his face. We don't know if it was because he had picked the winner or that he attained death without pain or agony. At any rate, that smile on his face helped us to accept his death a little better than my sister's."

"Yes, I know what you mean. I felt the same way when I saw Mom. She seemed to be smiling and at peace. It made a difference to me to see her that way. She looked like she met something wonderful in the course of dying," Franklin added.

CHAPTER 18

Franklin suffered a great deal of loss throughout his short life. Those that he became close to were the ones that he lost. First there was the tragic death of his father. Then came the death of both his paternal grandparents, with whom he lived. Franklin had been in relationships with girl after girl, only to lose them because of his unpredictable mood swings. After years of fighting with his mother, he finally made peace with her. She too, had now been taken away from him.

The one favorable thing he had to look forward to was the new relationship he had formed with Ms. Langdon. She became like a grandmother to Franklin. Often when he was haunted by the desire to run away to get drugs, it was her that he feared to have to face.

Franklin had always looked to Allison with the utmost respect. Her recent involvement with his family made her like an aunt to him. Franklin could sense her caring nature and compelling attachment to him and Monique.

Bryce had searched a long time for his hero-buddy and found Franklin instead. To Franklin it was not mere chance that Bryce was assigned to him. He believed that through his shoe box, his father arranged for Bryce to be there for him.

Franklin's most precious possession was still his baby sister Monique. Franklin knew that he would have to be strong for her now that they were alone. Yet it was her strength that he envied. She had been able to stay clear of the alcohol and drugs that had destroyed their family. Franklin was proud of her for that.

The days passed, and Franklin's depression lifted. He returned to class and began to interact with his peers. Franklin began to bring the shoe box along with him everywhere he went. It was never out of his sight. The manuscript Bryce had given him was also always in his possession. He read from it religiously and at every opportunity. The things that he was learning about his father were causing a rising tide of joy to wash over his body. He could not wait for Bryce to visit to answer the many questions he had.

Ms. Langdon's health finally caused her to retire. She quietly turned the Eagles' Nest over to her niece Allison. Franklin was no longer needed as her driver, but Allison hired him to do other chores on the grounds, no doubt at Ms. Langdon's request. The Eagles' Nest had become a home away from home for Franklin. He readily accepted his duties and went about them like a person feeling whole and with a purpose.

Allison tried to settle down into her new role at the Eagles' Nest. Growing up there, she had always roamed around the retreat as a free spirit. Now the challenge of managing the place caused her to see it differently. She worked late nights studying the financial records. Ms. Langdon had told Allison that the Eagles' Nest records were a little behind, but Allison felt her skin grow clammy and her arms blossomed with goosebumps at what she discovered. The facility had been operating in the red for a long time. It appeared that neither her Uncle Vince nor her Auntie Lou were good at management. Not only were their records a shamble, but they had been taking loans in order to keep the place open. In a few months the Eagles' Nest would be getting ninety new residents. The fee for the eighteen month program was $12,000. Most of those on the waiting list were from family that had insurance money to pay for their stay. Those on state welfare had theirs paid by the state. Therefore, it was the immediate threat of the loans that cause

Allison concern. The Langdon's had risked everything on getting a grant from the state to clear their credit. For years, because of their generosity, they took in too many people who didn't have the means to pay. The approval of the grant now rested upon the outcome of Franklin's murder case. If Franklin was to go to prison, it would show that the program was not strong enough to produce a ninety-percent recovery rate. This was a criterion of the grant. This is what Allison had to face. It was a difficult situation, but she was determined to make the program work. There were ninety people at the retreat who needed it to stay open.

Allison had been contemplating this matter and had a plan in mind. Unfortunately, her plan would mean the lay-off of many of the paid staff. She wanted to replace them with volunteer residents who were qualified and were willing to do the job. Franklin was already helping by doing a variety of odd jobs around the retreat. He would now have to do them without pay.

John's world seemed to be collapsing around him. He realized that he would not be a winner, regardless of the outcome of the hearing. "If only I could scratch off the right numbers or hit the big power-ball lotto, I could get away from this mess. You know what, Bryce? I would march right in there and tell them all where to go," John said bitterly. John's face hardened, and his eyes took on a crazed look. He reached for one of the magazines on the table and fanned through it as though it was a deck of cards. He slammed that one back on the table and grabbed another. He read the cover aloud, "Fortune Magazine, great! That's all I need: a fortune."

Bryce had taken a seat outside the personnel office with John. He wanted to be there to encourage him. It was his advice that got John to confess his role in the Prozac scam. Bryce felt that the least he could do was support him, but with John venting, he didn't get a word in.

It was a short meeting, and John came out muttering peevishly under his breath. His lips curled up with disgust. His eyes narrowed with contempt, and he gave Bryce that-keep-your-mouth-shut look. Bryce tried to soften his stand. He asked, "Well, how did it go in there?"

"It didn't go well, that's for sure. I don't understand why I'm having so much bad luck. Ever since my father died and my mother moved in, its been like hell," John whined. "The Nursing Review Board suspended my license for two years. Those bastards don't care if I live or die. They probably don't have mothers to feed. I can't hold my position here without my license. I don't know what to do. I have over fifteen years in this darn place. You'd think that would count for something."

"That's too bad," Bryce said. "Maybe you can work in another position, one that's not nursing."

"No, it's over for me here. Someone wants me out and this is their chance. You don't know how political this place is. Someone in administration probably wants my position for their daughter or son."

"What about Nick? Maybe he can help."

"Nick? Are you kidding? He sat there the whole time and didn't say one word in my defense. I've worked with him for ten years. I showed him some things when he first came. You'll learn one day, Bryce. Everyone here is for themselves, and that's it. Nick doesn't have that much authority around here. He's trying to keep his own job. Besides, they want to replace all of us nurses with social workers. If you stay here long enough, you'll see."

"What do you think you'll do, John?" Bryce asked.

"Well, I have money in a pension plan, and I have tons of sick and vacation time that I will get paid for. That should hold me until I find another job. Without my nurse's license, it'll be hard to find anything that pays the same. Maybe I'll go back to selling shoes," John said, flashing a false smile.

"I'm sorry this all happened," Bryce said. "I still feel you did the right thing by confessing. You could have ended up in jail."

"Oh, I'm quite sure I did the right thing. That was a heavy burden I was carrying. I may be jobless, but I now have a clean conscience."

"I'm sure Allison will be glad for you," Bryce mentioned.

"Oh yeah. Thanks for your support and advice. You helped open my eyes to see Allison as she really is. She's a real special person. It's going to be hard facing her after this. How can she continue to accept me after I keep digging a hole for myself? You know, we're practically engaged again. How can I support her now? And I still have my mother to care for. If only…" John ended. The look of desperation covered his face.

At his desk, John gathered his things to leave. Bryce became concerned for him. It was John who had taught Bryce the signs to look for when a person was at risk for suicide. Losing his nurse's license and his job, the pressure of caring for an ailing mother, and thinking that his girlfriend would not accept him caused John to act suspiciously.

Bryce said goodbye to John and then wasted no time calling Allison. Even though Bryce knew that John would want to personally tell her about his plight, Bryce wasn't sure what John might do. If anyone could lift John's spirits, it was Allison.

Mrs. Brown's death had an odd effect on Monique. The unfounded guilt she originally felt about her mother's death lingered. She tried desperately to force it aside by keeping herself busy. She did chore after chore. Some days she would set up the card tables and put out refreshments. This is what she used to do for her mother's card parties.

Brenda visited Monique daily. When she noticed this peculiar behavior, she phoned Bryce. "Monique has been acting a little bizarre," she reported.

"What exactly is she doing?" Bryce asked.

"I've noticed that for the past few days she's been obsessed with cleaning. And believe me, this house is not dirty. She's the only one living here. That's not all. Today she set up the card tables as if Aunt Martha was hosting one of her card parties."

"It sounds like some type of post-stress trauma or prolonged grief. She may need counseling to get through this. I wonder if the pastor from your aunt's church could come over to talk to her. And if that doesn't work, we'll look for professional help. Do you think you can call him?" Bryce asked.

"I'll do that now," Brenda said. She hung the phone up and went to look for a telephone book. Brenda found it on a shelf in the den. Next to it she discovered a pile of unopened bills and other mail. She then realized that Monique's problem was more serious than it seemed. She was unable to care for herself and manage the house. Monique was seventeen now, and everyone took it for granted that she would be able to live alone. However, the way she acted was clear evidence that she was not in control of herself yet.

Besides that, no one had given thought to how she would pay her household bills. She had no income source. Where would the money come from? Would she be able to keep the house? These questions bothered Brenda, and she knew that they needed to be addressed by the family.

Brenda sorted through the bills and letters. She noticed one from the Veteran Administration Benefits Division that stated: "**IMPORTANT: OPEN IMMEDIATELY.**" Brenda opened the letter. It said that the surviving members of the deceased person must call the VA as soon as possible. Brenda showed the letter to Monique. Monique read the letter and then stared at it as though looking at a blank piece of paper. Her face grew blench and she clamped her eyes shut. She asked Brenda if she could take care of it for her.

The VA representative told Brenda that Mrs. Brown's check, which was originally her husband's disability check, could continue for any surviving minor child under age eighteen. The person on the phone explained that when the minor child turned eighteen, he or she could continue to receive the benefits if enrolled full-time in school. But the check would not be made out to the survivor alone. An adult guardian would have to co-sign for the benefits.

Brenda tried her best to explain this to Monique. Monique's face remained unexpressive, and Brenda was not sure that she understood. She called Bryce for advice. He suggested having a meeting with the aunts to discuss the matter. It was too important to proceed without planning and input from them.

Later that day all the family members that were concerned about Monique gathered at her house. Bryce was there, too.

"How do we know that Franklin can handle this money business?" Mabel asked right away.

"How do we know if Franklin wants to be responsible for this? I mean, we just assumed that an adult guardian meant Franklin," Jessie Mae added.

"He's gonna have to do it. He's the adult of the two," Brenda said.

"Wait a minute, wait a minute. I'm not sure if Franklin is allowed to be Monique's guardian," Bryce interjected.

"And why not? He's her brother," Jessie Mae asserted.

"Yeah! What do you mean, Bryce?" Mabel asked curiously.

Bryce looked to Brenda as though he was saying "help me." Brenda raised one eyebrow and threw her hands up in the air. "I'm with them," she said. "What do you mean? Franklin is her adult brother."

"Don't forget that Franklin is diagnosed with a mental illness, and he is in a rehabilitation center for treatment for drug abuse," Bryce explained. "Maybe you should call back, explain the situation, and ask if he's still qualified to be Monique's guardian. I think you should do this before you ask him. Franklin doesn't take disappointments well."

"That's a good plan, Bryce. I see why Brenda invited you," Mabel commented.

"Okay, Brenda. You heard the man. You call. We're gonna go in the kitchen and see what's left to eat around here," Jessie Mae said.

They all had forgotten that Franklin might be on his way to prison for the slaying of Ray-Man. This, too, may disqualify him for the benefits.

Brenda called the VA representative, and he informed her about what Bryce had suspected. Franklin's illness made him unqualified to be Monique's guardian. This left the family with a problem. Who would be Monique's guardian?

"This is no problem," Mabel announced. "We'll just ask Monique who she would like to be her guardian."

Monique had become ill and was upstairs lying down. She complained of feeling light-headed. She was nauseated, and her energy had begun to fade.

Brenda helped her downstairs. Her face was still pale, and she said that she felt a sudden stab of anxiety in her belly. Everyone there seemed more interested in who she would choose as a guardian.

"Well, first on my list is Brenda," Monique started. "Brenda is my favorite cousin, and she understands me. Second on my list is Allison. I hope you're not mad at me for not choosing Aunt Mabel or Jessie Mae. I love you both but you are family and will always be around. Allison is a good friend."

"Praise the Lord! Don't worry about me being mad. It would have been too much for me anyway. If anything happened to you while I was your guardian, your mother would come out of her grave to get me," Mabel declared.

"Amen to that!" Jessie Mae agreed.

"Well, Brenda, what do you think? Are you willing to be Monique's guardian?" the aunts asked.

"According to the letter, we don't have any time to waste. So, I'll say yes."

It was good news for Monique. Her eyes sparkled, and her face brightened. She stood, skipped over to Brenda, and put her arms around her. She acted as though this was just what she wanted to happen. She was probably feeling lost and alone after her mother's death and with Franklin far away.

"I think it would be better if I gave up my little apartment and moved in here. It'll be difficult trying to manage two places," Brenda stated.

"Besides, Monique shouldn't continue to stay here alone with that stalker out there," Mabel reminded.

"Stalker!" everyone else said almost simultaneously.

The stalker had not been a threat to Monique through all that had gone on. It had been months since she reported seeing him. However, the thought of Brenda living with her was very comforting to Monique. She now felt safe.

"It's funny," she said. "Since Mama died, I haven't been able to write any poems. Tonight I feel like I can start to write again."

CHAPTER 19

The end of summer was near, and the New England scenery was changing. The beautiful red, yellow, and orange colors of the fall foliage season would be witnessed by thousands of tourists. They flocked here from the inner cities. The ride north on Route 272 was crowded with visitors jocking for the right viewing spot.

However, Bryce paid little attention to the colors and the tourists. His long face reflected a downcast mood. Bryce was not experiencing seasonal affective disorder. That had haunted him for years, but lately it was just a thing of the past. Bryce's present unsettled mood was because he was thinking about Franklin's trial. Franklin's day in court was rapidly approaching.

Bryce had met regularly with Franklin's public defender, Attorney Peter Silverman. They had been trying to work out a plan for Franklin's defense. Franklin was asserting his innocence despite the heavy evidence against him. The people who might have testified to his good behavior up to the point of the stabbing were the very ones that found him standing over the body with the bloody knife in his hand. These weren't ordinary eyewitnesses. They were trained professionals. The police and the drug enforcement agency members were there. Bryce and John were also trained to assess the scene surrounding their clients. Even if they just reported what they had seen, it would be damaging to Franklin.

At the pre-trial hearing, Franklin sat at the table with his attorney. Franklin had a casual expression on his face. From the row of seats behind them, Bryce watched Franklin's mouth tighten into a stubborn line when Attorney Silverman suggested that he plead temporary insanity. The attorney felt that Franklin's chances of a lesser sentence was better by going this route, especially since Franklin had a mental disorder diagnosis. Besides, everyone knew the circumstances that led up to the stabbing. Franklin was not the bad guy in this case. The bad guy was dead, and even the police and the DEA could attest to that.

Attorney Silverman wanted Franklin to have a competency hearing. Franklin flat out refused. He became outraged. He turned his head and gave Bryce a scorching look. His face was hot and singed with anger. He stood up and started to spew out words with bitter resentment. He only calmed down after he was ordered by the judge to do so.

When Attorney Silverman was asked to approach the bench, the judge asked what had made Franklin so upset. The attorney told him how Franklin had refused to let him request a competency hearing. The judge said that he would look into that matter and get back to him. Franklin was still breathing fire when the judge ended the session.

Later that week, the judge phoned Attorney Silverman. He told him that according to the law, Franklin would have to go for a competency hearing before they could go forward with the trial. Attorney Silverman thought it would be best to let Bryce break the news to Franklin.

Bryce found Franklin sitting in the circular lounge of his cottage. He was reading the manuscript to Korianne. It was difficult for Bryce to tell if her interest was in the manuscript or Franklin. Her eyes were dark and smoldering, and she stared at him intently. The two of them were startled by Bryce's unannounced arrival. Like the proverbial cat that ate the canary, Franklin stammered, "Bryce, I don't remember if I've ever introduced you to Korianne. She's my roomy. I mean we share the same cottage."

Franklin's sudden nervousness was due to a policy at the retreat that absolutely forbidded the sharing of rooms between male and female residents. They could only share the lounge area. The fastest way to get kicked out of the program was to be caught in the room of a person of the opposite sex. Ms. Langdon put great emphasis on the irrefutable policy of no physical intimacy between residents. It was her feeling that such relationships would hinder the progress of the resident's recovery. Bryce was glad to see that Franklin and Korianne were following the rules.

There was a deep look of concern on Bryce's face. Korianne recognized it and figured that Bryce had some disturbing news for Franklin. She excused herself and returned to her room.

"Why are you so grim-looking today?" Franklin asked.

"It's about that competency hearing the attorney wanted you to take," Bryce replied.

"Well, what about it?"

"The judge has ordered you to take it. The trial can't proceed until it's done."

"Why does everyone keep trying to make me out to be crazy? I don't mind taking the test. I just don't want to be declared incompetent. That would mean that I might have done the stabbing, and I swear I didn't do it. Besides, going away to one of those crazy houses will make you crazy even if you're not," Franklin said in a huff.

"Listen, Franklin, there is a time to fight, and there is a time to use your head. I want to believe that you are innocent, but when they call me to the stand, I'll have to tell them what I saw. That alone will be detrimental to your defense. Everyone that was there will have to tell what they saw. When we all got there, you were standing over Ray-Man with the knife in your hand. We didn't see anyone else. Do you want to spend the rest of your years locked away in some prison?" Bryce appealed.

"Okay, okay. Let's do the dumb test," Franklin said, giving in to the reality of the matter.

Bryce and Attorney Silverman thought that Franklin's chances of being found incompetent were good. Their contentions were based on Franklin's long history of depression and mood swings. He also had just cause to be angry, which set off the rage. Attorney Silverman's plan was to argue that it was the duty of the state to commit Franklin to an intensive state-run psychiatric treatment program.

They were surprised when after only two days of testimony, a panel of three psychiatrists found Franklin competent to stand trial. It was a devastating blow to their defense. The panel agreed that Franklin was in clear control of his senses when he went after Ray-Man that night. They stated that Franklin had plenty of time to cool off during his drive from the Eagles' Nest.

In just another two days, Franklin would go on trial for manslaughter in the first degree. Attorney Silverman and Bryce scrambled about trying to come up with another angle on which to build Franklin's defense.

The bad news about Franklin's competency hearing traveled like an out-of-control brush fire, and it was equally disturbing to his family and friends. Still, there was a large gathering at the courthouse the morning of the trial. Allison and Brenda were seated at Monique's side. They took turns comforting her. Dark shadows surrounded Monique's eyes. She had been crying since hearing the news about the competency hearing. She now sat with her head hung down, and her face was scarlet and swollen.

Attorney Silverman and Bryce were at the defense table with Franklin. Franklin kept turning around trying to get Monique's attention. He was gesturing to her that everything would be alright, but his own face was growing drawn and pinched. He was sitting straight up as if his body was stiffening in apprehension.

The trial began, and the prosecutor wasted no time calling all the witnesses that were at the scene to the stand. One after the other they took their turn explaining what they had seen. Then the prosecutor called Bryce to the stand. Bryce sat in the chair facing the crowd. He put his left hand on the Bible and raised his right one. He had dreaded the day when he would be called to tell what he saw. Bryce's face was lit up with bitter anguish. When he spoke he grinded out his words between clenched teeth. His quavering voice was edged with tension. Several times he was asked to speak up. Bryce's testimony, the other eyewitnesses, and the physical evidence all seemed overwhelming. The prosecutor finished his presentation, and now it was the defense turn.

Franklin's attorney tried to build his defense by calling on those who could testify that Franklin had begun to change his lifestyle for the better before the crime occurred. Among those who took the stand for Franklin was Bryce, Allison, and Ms. Langdon. The judge, out of respect for her, let Ms. Langdon give a lengthy summation on overcoming substance abuse. But her testimony was not that effective. She seemingly lost her thought too often, and her speech was interrupted by periods of long pauses. It was obvious that her recent illness had affected her mental sharpness.

After three days of testimony in Franklin's behalf, Attorney Silverman presented to the jury the circumstances that led to the stabbing. Monique was called to the stand at this time. With Brenda and Allison on opposite sides, she was escorted to the witness stand. Her face was ashen, and her eyes were bloodshot from crying. In a voice that was wooden and distant, she was only able to tell what she remembered before and after the crime. After her testimony, the attorney rested the defense 's case.

The jury was dismissed to deliberate the case. The judge recessed the court pending the return of the jury with a verdict.

Only two hours had passed when everyone was notified to returned to court. It didn't take the jury long to decide. It was a clear-cut case. All of the evidence pointed toward Franklin. The most the defense could hope for was a reduced sentence. The courtroom was tensed. Monique could be heard crying. She was delirious with grief.

The judge asked Franklin to stand. Franklin had a remote, pinched facial expression. He turned to look for Monique. He winked and flashed a confident smile. The judge then asked the jury foreman to read the verdict. Franklin's knees buckled when the word "guilty" was pronounced.

The courtroom quickly became chaotic. Some cried aloud. Others made harsh and angry remarks regarding the verdict. Even the DEA agents and some policemen were outspokenly upset. They all felt that they probably would have done the same thing as Franklin under the same circumstances.

Only Franklin remained calm after the reading of the verdict. Bryce and Attorney Silverman felt they had let Franklin down. The judge ordered the courtroom to be silent. He set the sentencing for the next day. He then invalidated Franklin's bond and ordered him held in custody due to his past history of suicide threats.

Chapter 20

The evening after the trial, friends and family gathered at Monique's to offer comfort and support. Bryce visited briefly, but then went to the lock up to be with Franklin. Franklin had asked him to bring the shoe box. Bryce cleared the box with the police, and they let him bring it in to Franklin. Ray-Man and his gang had caused a lot of problems for the community. Almost everyone was glad that he was out of the picture. Franklin was shown some favoritism for what he had done.

"Everyone is so upset with the outcome of your trial," Bryce said in his meeting with Franklin. "How come you don't seem to be disturbed by what's going to happen to you? I would think that you would be scared to death."

"I have my reasons not to be afraid," Franklin said. His voice was low and solemn, and there was an inappropriate serenity about his manner. He was too calm, too confident. "It's all here in the shoe box. It has come through for me in the past, and it will come through for me again."

Bryce was worried about Franklin's comment about the shoe box and about his behavior. Bryce wondered if Franklin was becoming psychotic or was using the shoe box to escape reality. At the same time, he had a certain amount of admiration for him. Franklin was acting with courage in a very difficult situation. His father also had possessed this quality. "Remember when I told you that there was a time to fight and a time to use your head?" Bryce asked him.

"Yes," Franklin replied.

"Well, this was what I was referring to. Your father was a hero. Yet he knew when to fight and when not to. He told me this story and made me promise not to tell anyone else. And I haven't until now. I think you need to hear this," Bryce started.

"Okay, okay, tell me, tell me," Franklin anxiously begged. He sat up on the edge of the cot, and his legs pumped up and down like a piston.

"This happened while we were operating along the famous Ho Chi Ming Trail, down in the Ashau Valley. We had been following a smaller trail and had set up for the night. The smaller trail led down to a river and continued on the other side of the river. Your father went down alone to fill his canteens from the river. He was not supposed to go alone. He was supposed to have another person along so that while one filled the other watched. Anyway, your father was bending over getting water. The rifle he had borrowed from me was slung over his shoulder. He looked up and saw a Viet Cong coming down the banks on the opposite side of the river to get water. He, too, had his rifle slung over his shoulder. The two enemies gave each other the once-over, and your father took off. Your father said he briefly looked back and saw that the Viet Cong was also kicking up dust going back his way. Your father said that once he got inside our perimeter he was too embarrassed to tell anyone what had happened. So you see, your father wasn't a coward because of that incident. It just wasn't a good time to fight. He used his head, and because he did, he lived to fight another day."

"That's a strange story," Franklin said.

"Yeah, but did you get the point?"

"Yeah, yeah, I got the point."

Franklin's face brightened, and his eyes widened. Bryce knew that he wanted to hear more, whether there was a point to learn or not. It really didn't matter to Franklin at this time. Bryce had given him something to draw strength from.

"How do you feel about tomorrow?" Bryce asked.

"I'm ready for tomorrow. For some strange reason, I feel really good about myself. I didn't kill Ray-Man, and if I go all the way to my grave, I'll go knowing that I didn't do it."

The sky was heavily overcast the morning of the sentencing. The gray and gloomy clouds were reflected on the faces of those who cared about Franklin. They had all gathered back at the courthouse to offer their last bit of support. Franklin's fate now rested in the hands of the judge. The judge could still refer Franklin to a psychiatric hospital if he deemed it necessary or appropriate. So there was a little hope that everyone was clinging to.

Franklin took his position before the judge's bench. There was an eery hush over the crowd. The judge, speaking in a take-charge, officious manner, warned the court that he would not tolerate any disruptive outbreak like the one at the trial. He started to read the sentence when a man wearing a hood over his head stood and shouted, "Wait, Your Honor." He started to walk forward but stopped midway in the aisle. He continued, "Excuse me, Your Honor, but Franklin didn't commit this crime. I did. I was in the alley that night. I stabbed Ray-Man." He then removed his hood.

The courtroom became ghostly silent. Monique turned to look toward the voice, and she immediately recognized the face. "That's the stalker, that's the stalker," she said. Her voice rose to a high and hysterical pitch.

"I saw that man on the side of the road as we were leaving the burial site after the funeral. I'll never forget that face. It looked like he had come out of a grave," Allison recalled.

"Who is he?" Brenda asked. Everyone wanted to know.

"What's the meaning of this?" the judge asked. "Sheriff, remove that man from the courtroom."

"Your Honor," Attorney Silverman shouted above the noise of the crowd, "my client claims he's innocent, and this man says he did it. We need to hear him out."

"Okay. Sheriff, bring him up to the bench. What do you know about this case?" the judge asked, pointing to the man.

"I stabbed the man in the alley. I was waiting for the right time to catch him alone," he confessed.

"Who is he? Who is he?" Everyone wanted to know.

"Who are you?" the judge finally asked.

"My name is Ricky Brown. I'm Monique Brown's father."

Monique stood. She struggled to swallow the lump in her throat. She felt her knees buckle and she fainted, falling over into Allison's lap.

Ricky Brown continued to tell his story to the judge. Franklin's heart was leaping. He raised his fist high above his head and waved it around triumphantly. He caused the crowd in the courtroom to join him in a premature celebration. Franklin was unaware that Monique had passed out.

The judge was unable to regain control of the courtroom. He asked the sheriff to bring Ricky Brown and Franklin, with his defense team, into his chambers. The judge listened as Ricky told about how he had watched Ray-Man mistreat his daughter and how he had waited in the alley to stab him. Ricky Brown was willing to sign a confession for the crime.

The judge returned to the courtroom. No one had left. They were all eager to hear from the judge. The judge announced that Ricky Brown had signed a confession for the crime, and Franklin was now free to go his way.

This time the roar from the crowd was tumultuous.

Monique awoke from her faint and Brenda told her the good news. Monique looked dazed and confused, raising her eyebrows in a questioning slant. Her feelings were mixed. She was glad that Franklin would be set free but felt sad for the man who said he was her father. As much as she thought she hated her father, an intoxicating feeling of good spirit overcame her when this man came forward claiming to be him.

The hugging in the courtroom was contagious. It started with Franklin and his attorney, then his attorney and Bryce, and then spread throughout the room. The courtroom was energized with a surge of elation.

Monique requested time with the stalker who claimed to be her father. She was still confused. She wanted to thank him for coming forth for Franklin and to challenge him on claiming to be her father. The judge granted her time with him.

Monique entered the room but kept her distance. She gritted her teeth as her eyes raked the room. The stalker must have felt a wave of disapproval when her eyes reached him. The breath of her voice was hot, but her words were as frozen as ice. "Why are you saying that you are my father? You're not my father. I have pictures of my father, and they don't look nothing like you. My father has been dead for years. How dare you claim to be him. You're nothing but a stalker."

Ricky Brown attempted to move closer, and Monique widened her distance. She began to study him critically. Again, tears trickled down her face. "Why are you doing this to me?" she asked.

"But I am your father," Ricky insisted. "I knew it would be hard for you to accept me after all these years. That's why I just followed you. I wanted to see you but not frighten you."

Monique was resisting him, but deep inside she felt there was some kind of connection with this apparent stranger. She was confused and frustrated. Something inside her wanted her to feel glad that her father was alive. At the same time, something inside her was pushing her to be angry because he had abandoned her and her mother. Things were happening too quick and too sudden for Monique. Anger was the strongest feeling she felt and the easiest to release. "Why didn't you call me? You could have picked up a phone and called me. You're supposed to be dead. I accepted that, and that's the way I wanted to remember you," she cried."

"I always intended to call you. Then there was a long period where I simply couldn't call. I was in bad shape. Why don't you sit down and let me explain what happened to me," Ricky pleaded.

Monique softened her heart and took a seat to listen.

"When I first met your mother, she would rarely have a drink. She was depressed over how Tyrone had died. I had such a bad drinking problem that I influenced her to drink. This only caused us more problems. I became very abusive when I drank. I also had resentments against Franklin when I drank, because he wasn't mine. That's partly why I came forward to tell the truth. I felt that I owed him for what I had done to him. But mostly I stabbed Ray-Man for what he did to you," Ricky confessed.

Monique sprung to her feet. Spasms of irritation and confusion crossed her face. A hint of impatience crept into her voice. "Why am I listening to you? You sound like you may be telling the truth, but still you don't look anything like my father."

"I'll explain. Just let me continue," Ricky requested. "After I left you and your mother, I went off and got into some really bad trouble. I was sent to prison to serve fifteen years. In my first year in prison, I crossed some real bad guys. One night they jumped me and sliced up my face. They could have killed me, but they used me as an example for others to see. I was looking a lot worse than this. A doctor volunteered his time to perform plastic surgery on my face. At the time I didn't know that he wasn't licensed to do plastic surgery. Neither did the prison officials or so they say. Anyway, this is the result of his work. There was nothing I could do about my face, so later I worked hard to change my personality and bad habits. For the next few years I did good. I was even let out earlier than I was supposed to because of my good behavior. I wanted desperately to see you, but I knew you wouldn't recognize me. So I started to follow you to make sure you were alright. One night I even made your tire flat so that I could offer to fix it and be close to you. The night that Ray-Man abducted you I was in my one-room apartment nursing a bad tooth. Later I had trouble finding you."

Monique finally gave in to her feelings. Her heart had been aching from an inner sense of belonging. All along she felt that he had been telling her the truth. She had to make him say enough to prove it. Her face flushed as she reached out and grabbed hold of him.

Ricky Brown felt euphoric. He became dizzy with glee. He had waited a long time to hug his daughter. For the moment they hugged he felt no disfiguration of his face. His eyes became moist with joy. "Now I can go back to jail peacefully. I am satisfied with life. I have my daughter back, and that's all that matters," he said proudly.

The sudden changes in emotion took their toll on Monique. Again her knees buckled. She became weak and collapsed. This time her father caught her and eased her onto a bench. He summoned the guards, and they signaled for Brenda and Allison.

Brenda and Allison decided to bring Monique to the walk-in clinic on the way home. They were concerned about her fainting episodes.

Bryce and Franklin headed back north on Route 272. This time Franklin was a free person. It was a cheerful drive, just the opposite of the drive down when Franklin was facing almost certain prison time. Franklin's face was flushed with happiness.

"What a difference a day makes," Bryce commented.

"You're right about that," Franklin agreed. "Even though I knew I was innocent, I was beginning to get a little worried about the sentencing. But I knew my shoe box would come through for me."

That statement bothered Bryce. It caused him to have concerns for Franklin. He turned to Franklin with a long, searching look. Franklin sat with a sheepish grin on his face. He was rubbing the shoe box much like one would rub a genie's lamp. "Does Franklin really think it was the shoe box that saved him? And what was it that I saw that made me think that Franklin did the stabbing? Ricky Brown did confess, and his statement covered every aspect as to what may have happened. So why can't I simply let it go?" Bryce worried.

"I know you've put a lot of hope in that shoe box, Franklin," Bryce said, "but it wasn't the shoe box that saved you this time. It was the truth. The truth always has a way of coming to light. I think you should also thank God for your release."

"I suppose you're right. I know that the shoe box isn't entirely responsible for my freedom. I do get a lot of inspiration from it, though," Franklin revealed.

Franklin lowered his head and was quiet for a few minutes. Bryce took this to mean that Franklin was thanking God for coming to his aid. However, Franklin was feeling giddy with joy, and he couldn't be quiet for long. "What do you think about Ricky Brown?" he asked.

"I think he was brave for coming forth like that. He showed how much he loves his daughter. He could have revealed himself to her without turning himself in for the stabbing. No one would have known. They had you red-handed, as they say."

"You're right. I didn't think of it that way," Franklin said.

"What did you think of him?" Bryce asked.

"He's not the same man I remembered. Not because of his disfigured face, but because his manner is different. He seems gentle and humble. The Ricky Brown I remember was cocky and brutal. Over the years, I've had nightmares about how he used to beat me. Later I learned that he had a bad drinking problem. The more I think about it, alcoholism has caused a lot of grief in my life. My father and mother both died from it, and it looked like I was headed down that same road. There's one thing that I don't understand concerning my father, and the manuscript doesn't answer that question."

"What is that?" Bryce asked.

"If my father was a hero, why did he turn to the bottle and drink himself to death? My mother could never answer that question for me. I thought I would find something in the manuscript to explain. So far I haven't," Franklin mentioned.

"The manuscript only covers your father for a few chapters, but everything that is written, he also experienced. When your father first came to our unit, he was very naive. He had a shyness about him. I don't believe your father never drank alcoholic beverages before going into the Army. In Nam drinking was not a big issue. It was too hot for alcohol, and the beer that was sold back in camp was always warm. Your father, like me and many others, turned to marijuana."

"My father smoked marijuana? Man, how cool is that?" Franklin said with silliness.

"Don't get too excited," Bryce continued. "That was the start of our problems. Marijuana flowed freely in Nam. It was so plentiful that nobody bothered to smoke joints. Practically everyone carried a pipe. We smoked marijuana everyday. Out in the jungle, we weren't hassled much for smoking. The captain, platoon leaders, and platoon sergeants all smoked marijuana. They didn't smoke it openly, but they did smoke it. There were occasions when the commanding officer would send out to the perimeter to borrow some marijuana. Everyone borrowed freely from each other without worrying about paying back. So, you see, marijuana was the start of our addiction. By the time we left Nam, everyone was hooked on something. That includes your father, even though he was sent home on a medical discharge after getting wounded. One of the biggest blunders that our government made was to bring us home and then just release us back into society. We weren't ready for that. We needed rehabilitation. It was a difficult transition. Marijuana was harder to get here and could get you in trouble. The little we were able to buy didn't have the same potency. Most everyone that I came back with turned to something else. A lot of guys turned to heroin. I turned to alcohol because it was legal. It seems that your father did the same. Our addiction to other drugs turned into alcoholism."

"Why is it if you and my father both suffered the same things, that you are still alive and my father is dead?" Franklin asked bluntly.

"That's a tough question to answer," Bryce responded. "As you know, I wasn't with your father the last few years of his life. Your mother told me that he wasn't the same after getting wounded. I guess that was hard for him, being the big, strong man that he was. We all came home with some depression, but I believe his injuries caused him to be more depressed than normal."

"How did you overcome your depression?" Franklin asked.

"Well, I also was headed for the grave. My drinking had caused me to hit the bottom. I had blown everything. I had no job. I was separated from my family. I was practically homeless, and I realized that I didn't want to live like that anymore. In Nam, I had a religious experience, one that gave me confidence that there is a living God. So I turned to God for help, and I was directed to a treatment center. While there, I continued to pray to God for help, and He took away my craving for alcohol and drugs. When I stopped drinking, my depressive episodes went away. I don't think your father made the same decision that I did."

"Thanks, Bryce. That helps me to understand why he took up drinking. Your story also gives me more incentive to stay sober. I have to continue living for myself and my father. There's a reason why he left me that shoe box."

They arrived at the Eagles' Nest. Just as they turned onto the dirt roadway, a shadow covered the entire car. It startled Bryce. It seemed to him like a huge plane was directly overhead. It worried Bryce that there was no engine sound. "Is there an airport nearby?" he asked.

"No!" Franklin answered. "That's not a plane. It's an eagle."

"An eagle!" Bryce shouted. He stopped the car and got out to get a better look. "That is one big bird. How often do you see them around here?"

"All the time. Why do you think they named this place the Eagles' Nest?" Franklin replied.

"Oh," Bryce said, sounding a little dumbfounded. "Where is that one going?"

Bryce's voice was high pitched. He was excited over the sighting, and he acted like he wanted to follow the bird.

"There's a nest on the north side of the retreat. There's a spot there where you can view the whole nest," Franklin told him.

"Man! That gives me a great idea. You have to forgive me, Franklin. I get excited when I see wild life in its natural setting."

Bryce parked the car, and a couple of the residents came over to encourage Franklin to come to the dining hall. Franklin entered the hall and was greeted by a loud round of applause. A welcome-home party had been arranged for him. Franklin's eyes widened in surprise, and he became speechless. Franklin spotted Korianne in the middle of the group. She blinked at him owlishly, and then continued as the leader of the cheers.

Brenda and Allison arrived just in time to join in the celebration. Bryce discreetly pulled Brenda aside. "How's Monique doing?" he asked.

"Not good, she's pregnant. She's been pregnant for two months according to the doctor. She was either afraid to let anyone know, or she was in denial. Some young women think it might just go away."

"Will she be okay at home alone?"

"She isn't alone. One of Allison's co-workers, who specializes in teen pregnancy, is there talking with her. Monique had so many questions that Allison suggested that we call her. I really didn't know what to say to her. My best advice to her is to be strong and continue with her education. I added that maybe she should make this her last pregnancy for a while. I don't know why I said that. It was dumb. It's not like she went out and intentionally got pregnant. Allison and her friend arrived just at the right time, or I probably would have made a bigger fool of myself."

"Well you did make an attempt to advise her. That's better than what I would have done," Bryce said.

"No, you don't understand. It would have been better to say nothing than to say something stupid and inconsiderate." Brenda plaused. Her face looked troubled. "Monique is confused, angry, and afraid. She stated some real concerns. She's awfully worried about having contracted AIDS or some other disease. That Ray-Man had a lot of sex partners, and many of them were drug users. Then she's worried that the baby may be harmed by her neglect. She's worried about how to care for the baby. She has mixed feelings about whether she should keep the baby or put it up for adoption. So you see how stupid my advice was to be strong and, to continue her education. This pregnancy will be another stressful ordeal for my little cousin."

"I see what you mean. I wonder how Franklin knew?" Bryce mumbled.

"What's that?" Brenda quizzed.

"Oh, it's nothing. I was just thinking out loud," Bryce answered.

"Does this mean that you also talk in your sleep?"

They both laughed.

"What a bittersweet day this has been," Bryce stated.

"And it's not over yet. Allison has an important announcement to make at the close of the party," Brenda revealed.

Bryce took Brenda's hand, and they glazed affectionately at each other. They strolled back to the party area. "Today I saw the biggest bird I've ever seen in my entire life. It was huge. Right away I got this great idea that I'm going to share with Allison. I'll tell you all about it on our way home."

The party started to cool down. All of the residents had gathered. Allison thought this would be a good time to break the news before they started to wander off. "May I have your attention, please," she began. "I realize that this gathering is for a happy occasion. We're all glad to have Franklin back with us as a free person. However, I must take this time to inform you that we are not yet out of the hot water with our debts. I was informed a couple of days ago that our grant did not rest entirely on the outcome of Franklin's verdict. As a matter of fact, our grant already had been given to another facility, even before Franklin went to trial. So that leaves us in a bit of a pickle. We may have to close and file for Chapter Eleven bankruptcy. I don't know of any other way we can pay off our debts. I'm sorry I have to tell you such bad news at a time like this, but I have to be straight with all of you."

CHAPTER 21

Before the night ended, everyone came forth with ideas on how to possibly keep the Eagles' Nest open. Bryce's idea was the one that appealed to Allison. His plan was the only one that was basically logical and required the least financial support to start up. Bryce suggested that the Eagles' Nest open its grounds to bird-watchers. They could bring in some revenue by charging an hourly or day rate.

The group liked Bryce's idea. They began to discuss it for approval. Someone suggested asking the Audubon Society for a grant. "Aren't the eagles considered a protected species?" one person asked.

"This idea sounds good. I believe we could put this plan to work. Unfortunately, I don't think we could get a grant from the Audubon Society big enough to erase all of our debts," Allison said. "At the same time, I realize that we must do something. Besides, bird-watching would add a nice feature to our program."

News of the Eagles' Nest's financial problems hit Franklin very hard. Just as he was settling down and feeling like a part of something, he might face another loss. He and the others realized that they would be leaving when their term was up, but this was eight months away. They hadn't expect to be tossed out without completing the program. For some, this was going to be the very first thing that they saw through to the end. Franklin threw his hands up in the air in a disgusted rage and said, "This is the one place that makes me feel like a human being. Now I'm going to lose this, too."

The Eagles' Nest had become Franklin's home away from home. He was treated well there. The residents at the Eagles' Nest had become like one big family. They all had the deepest respect for Ms. Langdon and Allison. Franklin vowed to do something about the Eagles' Nest's monetary problem even though he had nothing to offer. He began to look to his shoe box for answers.

Bryce's telephone flashed with messages back at the office. The one that interested him the most was from his friend James White. He left Bryce a number and asked him to return the call. Bryce called immediately. He was pleased to hear his friend's voice, and they jawed about the good old days for a few minutes. Getting to the matter of his call, James explained, "This information I have for you sounds very interesting. It seems that there was a secret project going on just as you was coming home from Nam. The government conducted a series of studies on Agent Orange. At first it concluded that only the children of veterans born with spina bifida were the ones affected by Agent Orange. However, the study later showed that others became affected and showed a variety of symptoms. The most common of the symptoms were similar. They included high fevers, excessive drooling, dysphagia, stridor, and projectile vomiting. Some, but not all, had a distinctive harsh barking cough (like croup), and they were born jaundiced."

"That's partly what I read in my client's file," Bryce said, his voice becoming tight.

"Here's the kicker," James continued. "The study showed that the individuals that had these symptoms were also connected to Agent Orange. The government tried to keep this finding secret. They were afraid that too many soldiers would come forward with sick kids. They acknowledged the finding by limiting it to those soldiers who were already granted disability. There was also a small window of opportunity for them to get registered. Those who did were issued a VA file number."

"Wow!" Bryce exclaimed. "Franklin has one of those file numbers. I saw it in his chart. Franklin's father must have gotten wind of that project. Does this mean that Franklin will be entitled to disability benefits?"

"Well, yes and no. It doesn't mean that he will be granted disability like a wounded soldier, but there was a large settlement from a lawsuit. He could be eligible for a part of that money," James informed.

"Can Franklin still apply for it?"

"I'm not sure. The project closed out some years ago, but I know that there's still some money in it. The project was so secretive that not many came forward to make a claim. If Franklin can prove that he was registered before it closed, he may stand a chance of collecting on his claim," James replied.

"What should we do?"

"You should have Franklin bring his VA file number to the nearest VA office. That's what I suggest."

"Well, thanks a million. You've been a lot of help, and I appreciate you getting back to me on this matter," Bryce said.

"Oh, I heard you were writing a book about Vietnam. How's it going?" James inquired.

"So far I haven't found anyone to publish it. I've been letting my young client read it.

He finds it interesting and somewhat helpful in his recovery," Bryce concluded.

If Franklin was among those found to be affected by Agent Orange, not only would he be entitled to money from the settlement, but he would be misdiagnosed all these years. His illness would be due to a post-stress disorder inherited from his father.

Bryce wasted no time in contacting the nearest VA office. Franklin was given an appointment, and the officer told Bryce that Franklin would have to bring the letter confirming his file number.

Franklin's voice sounded cheerful over the phone when Bryce related all that his friend had told him. Franklin's breath quickened, and it became hard for Bryce to tell if Franklin was more excited over the possibility of being awarded the money or discovering the cause of his illness. At any rate, it was good news for a change, and both were anxious to see if Franklin did qualify.

Bryce decided to ask Brenda and Monique to accompany him on this trip. Bryce hadn't had the opportunity to speak with Monique since he discovered that she was pregnant. He was also looking for the opportunity to spend time with Brenda.

Bryce felt relaxed as he navigated through the winding curves going north on Route 272. He pointed out all the beautiful features that made this a scenic road while beaming fondly at Brenda. His acting as a tour guide amused Brenda. Monique remained reserved. From the moment he had picked her up, she made no eye contact with Bryce, and she seemed aloof. Bryce's attempt at humor only seemed to distance her. He remembered how Brenda had made the wrong choice of words in her attempt to reach her. So Bryce decided to try a different approach, a more serious one. "How did your visit with the doctor go?" he asked.

It was difficult for Monique to talk. Bryce could sense that it was embarrassment and not anger that kept her silent. After a moment, she swallowed dryly, and her voice started as a childish whimper that got stronger as she spoke. "At first I was afraid, but the doctor helped me to relax. He's very good at what he does. I had an idea about what would take place, because Allison's friend had given me a detailed description of what would be done. She, too, is very good with people. She answered a lot of questions that had bothered me. We didn't hit it off at first. She gave me a lot of statistics on teen pregnancy, which I thought were boring. I thought she was there to lecture. I listened to her because she is Allison's friend. Then I began to find out some interesting things. Did you know that four out of every ten American females becomes pregnant before the age of twenty? And that most of these pregnancies will be unintended? Did you know that almost one million teenagers become pregnant each year and that only about 485,000 of them actually give birth? I learned that teenagers too often have poor eating habits. They neglect to take a daily multivitamin. Some smoke and drink alcohol and take drugs that increase the risk of their babies being born with health problems. Three million teenagers are affected by sexually transmitted diseases annually and could be facing death from AIDS."

Monique paused momentarily. Her eyes took on a haunted look. The thought of the dreaded disease of AIDS evidently had crossed her mind. She cleared her throat and continued, "I asked Evelyn why was she telling me these things, and she said that I didn't have to be a statistic. She said that even though my pregnancy was unintentional, I could still take control of the situation and move ahead with my life. Her words and speech was very encouraging and she enforced them by accompanying me to the doctor. Because she spent time with me, I was able to express my feelings on abortion. I had been struggling with whether I should abort the baby or not. I had heard a lot of girls in school had done that. When I was being examined by the doctor during the ultrasound, he pointed to a mass that was pulsating. I asked what it was, and he said,"That's your baby's little heart." He went on to point out the little feet and arms, still being developed. That's when I decided that I would not be another statistic. I also decided that my family had suffered enough losses. I wasn't about to add to that," Monique said with conviction.

"I'm sure you've made the right decision. I'm glad for you and proud of you. I'm going to do everything in my power to help you," Bryce said.

"And you know I'll be here for you," her cousin Brenda added.

Bryce was constantly looking up toward the sky as he got closer to the Eagles' Nest. He wanted to spot an eagle in order to point it out to the women. The eagle was a magnificent sight, and it had made a big impression on Bryce. He was sure it would brighten Monique's spirit. "Of all the times I came here it never crossed my mind why they called this place the Eagles' Nest. It wasn't until I saw that humongous bird that I got the picture," Bryce said.

Franklin was pacing in front of the administration building. His eyes glinted with pleasure on seeing that Brenda and Monique had come along with Bryce. Monique's face flushed with happiness on seeing her brother, but she also started to cry.

Bryce and Brenda made small talk while Franklin spent the entire ride to the VA office consoling his sister.

Franklin met his first road block after presenting himself to the officer seated at the front desk. In a smug and insensitive manner, the officer told Franklin he had no knowledge or record of an appointment for him.

Franklin's face grew hot. He threw his hands up in the air in disgusted resignation. He then slapped the desk smartly. Bryce quickly moved in to calm him down. The ruckus caught the attention of the duty captain. Bryce explained why they were there and they were brought into a small room and asked to wait. From the room they could see the captain making a number of phone calls. Bryce turned to Franklin and said, "Listen, these are Army people you're dealing with. You can't be showing these fits of rage. It doesn't mean anything to them. They'll just make things go harder for you. Not only that, but the one at the front desk was a highly decorated combat soldier. He'll kick your butt and not think twice about it."

"Oh yeah, well I know how to defend myself, a little, I think," Franklin said defensively.

After a short time, the captain came into the room and said, "We can't handle this matter here. Franklin will have to fill out this form, and someone from the Pentagon will get back to him. We'll make sure that they also contact you, Mr. Wright." He then showed them the way out.

At the front desk, the soldier was standing with his back toward them. Franklin looked at Bryce. His eyes widened incredulously, and he whispered, "He didn't look that big sitting down."

Monique had enjoyed Franklin's consoling. She no longer had that pitiful look of appeal. Her face now radiated with good cheer. However, both women stated that even though the scenery was great, one ride up

Route 272 was all they could take in one day. Bryce dropped them off at home, and he and Franklin headed back to the retreat.

"You know, Bryce, this money I may be getting has something to do with Agent Orange, right?" Franklin asked.

"That's right," Bryce answered.

"What if they ask me questions about Agent Orange? I don't know anything about Agent Orange. What's up with that?" Franklin expressed his concerns.

"You don't have to worry. They don't expect you to know about it. You're just an example of what it can do to people. The manuscript talks about Agent Orange, but I presume you haven't got that far yet. Anyway, we didn't think much of Agent Orange when we were in Nam. As a matter of fact, I don't recall hearing the term until I was out of the Army."

"So you didn't see it happening over there?" Franklin asked.

"On the contrary. I saw Agent Orange being sprayed numerous times. I just didn't know what it was, and I didn't think it would have a bearing on my health at that time."

"But there's nothing wrong with you. And you said that your children were born okay," Franklin reminded.

"That's true. My children were all born without any physical defects. But, I believe that Agent Orange was the cause for my years of depression. I was also hyper-manic for a few years after my discharge. I couldn't stay in one place for a long period of time. I got bored easily. I couldn't figure out what was wrong with me, but I didn't seek medical help," Bryce explained.

"So why did they use Agent Orange?" Franklin asked a second time.

"Let me see if I can explain it without getting too technical," Bryce began. "Agent Orange was the code name for a herbicide developed for the military. Its primary use was in tropical climates, like in Nam. The purpose of the product was to deny the enemy cover and concealment in dense terrain by defoliating trees and shrubbery where the enemy could hide. Did you get that part?"

"Yeah. It was supposed to kill all the bushes and trees so you could find the enemy," Franklin guessed.

'That's close to being right. It worked on broad-leaf trees, such as the dense jungle-like terrain found in the Central Highlands, where we were operating."

"Wow, you really know all about that stuff, don't you?" Franklin mused.

"Actually, when I learned about Agent Orange, it gave me some relief. I then had an answer to why I was so depressed and confused after leaving Nam. For a while I thought I, too, had a mental illness. Even though I was there and saw the spray coming down on me, I won't be compensated for it. That Agent Orange mess had different affects on individuals. It could have been the reason your father drank so much. It was probably his way of dealing with the depression. He didn't realize that alcohol in itself is a depressant. The good news is that, hopefully, you'll be compensated for your years of suffering. That will make me happy, and your father was probably hoping this would happen. Remember, he was the one that got the ball rolling for you. He was the one that got you registered. He just didn't live to see this day, but hopefully I will for him," Bryce said. His voice was ringing with optimism.

Bryce had really given Franklin something to think about. He sat quietly meditating on the words. His eyes were mirthfully crescent, and there was a childlike smile on his face.

CHAPTER 22

It was six o'clock in the morning when Bryce's phone rang, waking him up. He brushed the sleep from his eyes and peeped at the clock. "I've got another half hour to sleep. Who in the world can this be?" The caller ID displayed the name "Allison Langdon."

"Hello," Bryce answered without any further hesitation.

"Hello, Bryce. It's Allison. I'm sorry to bother you so early in the morning, but I'm calling about John. I just got a call from him, and he sounds awfully disturbed. He mentioned something about getting a gun. I don't know what to do? Should I call the police?"

"Where was he calling from?"

"He said he was calling from a phone booth and that he was going to the mental health building to wait for the employees to arrive. I'm really worried. He sounds serious."

"Don't call the police yet. I'll go there and see if I can talk to him."

"But I can't stay here and just wait. I'll meet you there."

Bryce found John sitting in his car in the back of the parking lot of the mental health center. John's eyes were narrowed with suspicion. He flashed a malicious smile when he saw Bryce. He had a crazed look and spoke with grave deliberation. "They're responsible for this. I'm gonna get them all, including Nick." He lifted the handgun from the seat to show Bryce his intentions.

"Why are you doing this, John? You're gonna lose everything. What about your mother? Are you going to leave her alone? And what about your engagement to Allison?" Bryce was trying to reason with him.

"After what I did last night, Allison wouldn't want to marry me. And my poor mother, I can't even help her anymore," John said sourly. For awhile, John's eyes darted manically, and then he couldn't stop blinking. Bryce knew that John was on the verge of losing it. He was close to having a mental breakdown.

John heard the brakes of a car squeal as it turned sharply into the parking lot. He got out of his car just as Allison came speeding up. When John saw Allison, he softened his murderous stand. He lowered his chin to his chest and shook his head wildly. He began to cry out, "Why did I do it? What made me do it? Why can't I stop?"

"What did you do, John?" Allison asked as she walked closer. "What is it that's causing you to act this way?"

"Oh, Allison. Why am I blaming everyone but myself? I came here to shoot innocent people because of my problems. They're not the blame. I did it to myself. There's no one else to blame but myself."

"John, I thought we talked about this. You shouldn't let this job cause you to act this way. You can always get another job."

"It's not the job, Allison. It's the money. The money that I lost. I lost all the money that I was going to use to support my mother and myself with."

"What money, John?" Allison asked.

"The money that I got from my savings, my vacation and sick pay, my 401K, and my pension money. I lost it all last night. I bought $50,000 worth of lottery tickets, and I only have a few low winners to show for it."

"Oh no, John," Allison said, her face glazed with shock. "You promised me that you would seek help for that problem. You said that by the time we were ready to marry that that would not be a problem. And I just can't believe that you came here to hurt these people because of that." Allison's face turned red. Her mouth crimped in annoyance. She placed her hand over her mouth to bridle her next remark. John could feel a wave of disapproval come from Allison and, for the first time, she turned her back to him.

"John, you're not going to solve this problem by hurting more people. Your life is not over just because you lost the money. But you do need help. Remember, John, you worked for the Department of Mental Health and Addiction Services. You helped people with addiction problems. That included gambling addiction, too. We can help you here," Bryce reminded.

John's eyes almost bugled from their sockets. He slammed his fist against the roof of his car. "No way! And don't you dare tell anyone in this building about my personal business. I'll get my own help somehow," John said acidly.

Allison turned to face John. Her eyes were swollen from crying. "Well, what are you going to do John? You promised you'd get help before, and look what happened. You've got to let us help you," Allison said.

Allison's willingness to help John made him listen. He thought he had lost her for good when she turned her back.

"It's getting late. Let's get out of here before people start to come in," Bryce suggested.

The three of them stopped at the coffee house down the street. John finally agreed to accept the help Allison and Bryce offered. Bryce would make an appointment for John with the psychiatrist he worked for. For the time being, John had salvaged his relationship with Allison, but he felt that she would not tolerate his gambling for long. She had her own money problems with the Eagles' Nest. Allison and Bryce left. John bought a newspaper and was searching through it for a job.

The bird-watching station attracted many of the tourists that had come to that area during the fall foliage season. It did bring in some revenue, unfortunately, as Allison mentioned, it wasn't enough to forego the almost certain closing of the facility.

Meanwhile, Franklin and Bryce anxiously waited to hear from the Pentagon regarding Franklin's Agent Orange claim. It had only been a couple of days since talking to the VA representative, but it seemed like weeks to them.

Early Tuesday morning, Bryce was sitting at his desk when the phone rang. The officer introduced himself as Captain Athas. He told Bryce that he had been assigned to Franklin's case. He said that Franklin's file showed that he had been awarded money from the lawsuit, but neither Franklin nor Tyrone came forth to get the money. So it was placed in an account under Franklin's name. This was done to keep the government from reclaiming the money after the project closed.

The Captain went on to say that if Franklin wanted to claim his share of the money, he would have to go to the VA office in Washington, DC. He would have to bring two picture ID's, a copy of his father's DD214 (Army discharge paper), and the letter confirming his VA file number.

This was the news Franklin and Bryce had been waiting to hear. Bryce became ecstatic. He suddenly had the feeling of being airborne. For awhile, it felt like he had been awarded the money. He returned to reality when he remembered that Franklin was at the retreat, biting his nails down to nothing. Without hesitation Bryce called the Eagles' Nest, and he was reminded that this was Franklin's group therapy hour. He left word for Franklin to call as soon as he could.

Bryce could measure Franklin's excitement by the cheerfulness of his voice. His blissful state was verbalized by a series of questions: "How much money will I get? When will I get it? Where do I have to go to get it?"

Bryce explained to Franklin the instructions he had received from Captain Athas and right away Franklin's cheerfulness started to fade. His face twisted in anguish. "I don't have my father's discharge papers, and I haven't seen any letter from the Army either," he said, sounding disappointed.

"These are very important papers. Maybe your father gave them to your mother to put away for safe keeping," Bryce said. "After work, I'll stop by and ask Brenda and Monique to search through the papers your mother left behind. Don't worry, they must be in the house somewhere."

"I certainly hope so," Franklin moaned.

"Don't worry. We can get a copy of your father's DD214 from the town clerk." Bryce remembered how he had to register his discharge paper there when he came home. "So, what are you planning to do with your money?" he asked.

"That depends on how much I get. Then I'll have to see how much is left after I pay the state back for their assistance. They'll probably take it all. I've been in treatment with them for a long time," Franklin whined.

Bryce was at Monique's house by five o'clock. Brenda had not come home from work. Bryce told Monique all that was happening to Franklin. But he decided not to ask her to look for the papers until Brenda was there. Monique looked like she was ready to have the baby at any moment, even though she wasn't due for a while. This made Bryce nervous. So instead, he asked her about the baby's condition, her school, and her poetry.

"I got good news from the doctor today. I want you to tell Franklin that all of my blood tests have come back negative so far for any disease. The baby appears to be healthy. I'm very happy about that. So it's off to school next month for me and my baby. Speaking of school," Monique remembered, "I would like you to read this poem that I wrote. I'm planning to send it to my father. I value your opinion, since you also like to write."

"You know, Monique, the way you've taken a responsible role in caring for your unborn baby and the effort Franklin is making toward staying clean and sober have made me really proud to have come to know you two," Bryce said.

"Thank you," Monique replied. "That's the nicest thing I've heard in a long while. It has been extremely rough for me and Franklin." She passed the poems to Bryce, and he sat back, crossed his legs, and began to read:

MY DAD
by Monique Brown
I now see my dad in shabby clothes,
a disguised man with a disfigured nose.
With a wearisome look, an appeal not so neat,
the by-product of living off the street.
My memories of him have faded away;
these are some things my mother used to say.
Always laughing with a joke to tell,
but around his family, he was not so swell.
Often grouchy and too often asleep,
cause at five every morning, he was on his feet.
He drove a truck for many years
socializing til he had too many beers.
Women chased him and caught his eye,
surrounding him til marital problems would arise.
Then my dad, quite set in his course,
pushed my mom to separate. And then divorce.
Through all this, I never knew him well,
now he tells me he's been in jail.
For a long time I thought him dead;
my love for him was only in my head.
I know I now must forgive;
with the past gone, it is time to live.
Sometimes I sit and reminisce with a frown,
sometimes sad but now glad I'm a Brown.

"So, what do you think?" Monique asked.

"Your poems are very good. They are inspiring. All of them have personal meaning. You write from the heart. I'm sure your father will be pleased to know how you feel about him."

"Yeah. I've had mixed feelings about him for years. Sometimes I hated him. Then there were times when I felt sorry for him. There were brief periods in my life when I felt love for him and wanted him to come back. I was glad to learn from him what had happened. I will definitely raise my baby to know and respect him as a grandfather."

There was a noise at the front door. It was Brenda. She tried to open the door, but her hands were full with bags, and she dropped her key. Bryce rushed to assist her. "Here, let me help you," he offered.

"I can handle these, but there are a few more in the car, if you don't mind," Brenda said.

"So, is this a social visit?" Brenda asked, as they were putting the groceries away.

"Well, sort of," Bryce asserted. "I always look for an excuse to come here. This time I have good news."

"Okay, don't hold me in suspense. You know how anxious I get. What is it?" Brenda urged.

"Franklin will get the money that his father filed for with the VA. The money had been put away, waiting for Franklin to claim it. He has to bring some important papers down to Washington, DC."

"Do you know how much money he will get?" Monique curiously wanted to know.

"We're not sure. The money has been in an account in Franklin's name since the seventies," Bryce answered.

"Wow!" Monique said. Her eyes danced at the thought, and she became unsteady and had to sit down.

"First we have to find the papers that Franklin needs. That's why I came by. We were hoping that Tyrone gave them to Mrs. Brown for safe keeping. Do you know where she kept important papers?" Bryce asked.

"Yes. There's a small file cabinet upstairs, hidden away in Mama's closet. That's where Mama kept everything she thought was important: things like mortgage receipts, insurance policies, tax papers. You know, things like that. If it's here, it's in there."

"Bingo! That sounds like where it may be," Bryce said in an energized voice.

"It's not heavy. Maybe you and I can bring it down. I don't like staying in Mama's room too long," Monique suggested.

"Oh no, not you," Brenda interjected. "Bryce and I will bring it down. You just stay seated, young lady."

"Bryce, don't you think she's a little overprotective?" Monique whined.

"No. Not at all. I think she's absolutely right. You shouldn't be lifting too much stuff. I hope you're not still running around this house doing chore after chore," he responded.

"Nah, I've slowed down some. I only do that when I'm upset or worried or nervous," Monique confessed.

The trio carefully searched through all of the papers that were in the cabinet. There was no letter from the VA or discharge papers. Bryce's face became twisted in a sorrowful expression. He felt like a trap door in the floor had opened, and he had fallen through. He had been certain that the papers were there.

They started to look at old pictures Mrs. Brown had stowed away to compensate for their disappointment. Monique's bottom lip began to curl, and her heart ached with nostalgia as she stared at her mother's picture. She missed her mother. Her eyes looked haunted with inner pain. She wiped the tears from her eyes and picked up a picture of her father. He was quite a handsome man before his disfigurement. "This one I'm going to have enlarged and place it on my night stand along with the one of Mama. And I think I will send him one along with the poem." Monique's eyes misted over again.

"Maybe we should stop if this is too much for you," Bryce suggested.

"No. It's okay. I have to face up to my mother's loss. I have to be able to look at these pictures just like I'm gonna have to be able to go in her room. That is something I have been afraid to do."

"What is going to happen now with Franklin's claim?" Brenda asked.

"Well, it's not hopeless yet. I believe that I can get a copy of the DD214 from City Hall. The confirmation letter is more of a problem. I'll have to call and inquire about that. I don't understand why they need the letter. Franklin has the file number. I have it in his charts," Bryce said. His voice was edged with bitterness.

Bryce went to the Torrington City Hall the next day. He asked the town clerk for a copy of Tyrone Cooper's DD214. After a long search, the clerk came back with nothing. Tyrone had not filed his discharge papers there. The clerk suggested that maybe he had filed them with the town from which he had originally gone into the Army. This was probable because Tyrone was not a native of this Torrington. Bryce remembered back when Tyrone used to tell stories about growing up on a farm in North Carolina. Goldsboro was the name of the town Bryce recalled. Bryce raced back to his office with that thought in mind. He got directory assistance and was connected to the town clerk's office in Goldsboro. But to his dismay, he struck out again. The clerk remembered Tyrone because a remnant of his family still lived there. However, he told Bryce that Tyrone had only visited there after leaving the Army. He did not make Goldsboro his home of record.

Bryce was feeling hopeless after running into so many dead ends. He reclined in his chair to think of how to get the papers. His face became blank as he stared up at the ceiling.

Nick noticed the puzzled look on Bryce's face and came over. "What's bothering you, Bryce? Franklin's not on a rampage again, is he?"

"No. Franklin is doing quite well in his recovery. He's come into some money, but we can't find the proper papers he needs to collect it." Bryce told.

"Why don't you come into my office and tell me the whole story. I haven't been updated about Franklin for a month now," Nick said.

Bryce told Nick all that was going on with Franklin. Toward the end of that report, Bryce decided to take the opportunity to clear the nagging thought that he had gotten from John. "You know, John was very upset that you didn't stand up for him at the licensing hearing."

"All of the problems that John has were caused by his gambling. Did he tell you that I've been after him for years to get help. He refused any help that was offered. We all know of his problem with those tickets. When I first came here, I thought it was strange that he would ask to borrow money from me. But then I found out that he had borrowed, one time or another, from most everyone here. For his sake, we had to create a policy about not loaning money to co-workers. He still didn't get the picture. This stealing drugs is something I won't tolerate. Hopefully, now that you and Allison have talked him into coming to see the doctor, he'll be able to stop."

"How do you know that Allison and I talked to John about seeing the doctor? I told her that he would only come in if it was kept confidential. You know how sensitive John is." Bryce was surprised to hear that.

"This is a state office. Everyone knows what goes on around here."

"That's too bad. He may not come in now." Bryce got up to leave. He reached for the door, and Nick called. "You know, if Franklin's father was on medical disability, he must have had to produce a discharge paper to be eligible for that."

"Thanks, Nick. That's a great thought."

Bryce called the disability department of the VA and was told that no discharge paper was available there either. Tyrone had been awarded disability on his discharge from Nam. Therefore, he never needed to show or file his DD214 with them.

Bryce's face turned red and then purple. He threw up his hands in disgusted resignation. He had no other choice now but to call Franklin with the disappointing news. He thought about that for a moment, and then he decided he should go and tell him in person.

CHAPTER 23

Bryce's mood was somber as he drove up Route 272. His heart ached as he focused on Franklin's problem. Bryce by-passed the administration office and went directly to Franklin's cottage. He found six dejected-looking people sitting in the circular lounge. Whatever the problem was, it affected all of them. It seemed that they had gathered to console each other.

Franklin had dark shadows under his eyes: an obvious sign that he had not been sleeping well. He peered up at Bryce lifelessly, and said in a monotone voice, "Oh, it's you Bryce." He then rested his head in Korianne's lap. She appeared to be the least dejected of the group. In a cheerier tone she said, "Hello, Mr. Wright. As you can see, it is a very sad day for us. We've been informed that it is absolutely certain that the Eagles' Nest can no longer afford to operate. Our cottage will be the first to close."

"That's really bad news," Bryce remarked.

"It's not too bad for me, because my parents are well-off. They can find me another place to go for treatment if I feel I need more time. All of the others were looking forward to completing the remaining time in the program. Most of them have never finished anything in their lives. Completing this program is a big step forward for them. They are afraid they will have to return to the streets and to drugs. It's so sad, because they're all here because they want a better life," she related.

Franklin suddenly remembered why Bryce might have come to visit. He felt a surge of elation, like a sunny feeling coming over his soul. He jumped up. "Did you get the papers? Am I going to get the money? What happened? What happened?"

"Maybe we should step into your room for a little privacy," Bryce suggested.

"You can tell me here. These are my friends," Franklin sputtered.

"It's okay, Franklin. We'll be right out here." They seemed to answer at the same time.

Franklin offered Bryce a chair and sat on the edge of his bed. He picked up his shoe box and brought it to his chest. He was preparing himself in case Bryce had brought more bad news. "Okay, let me have it. What else could possibly go wrong today?"

"I'm having trouble getting the papers you need to collect your claim. They weren't at your mother's house. The town clerk doesn't have your father's discharge recorded. It is not filed in North Carolina either. I called the place where his disability benefits comes from, and they don't have a copy. We probably could get the discharge papers from St. Louis. That's where they keep all military records, but that'll take a long time. However, it is absolutely impossible to replace or get another confirmation letter. That was your guarantee that the money belonged to you. The Captain said there was no way of getting the money without the letter, because the project has closed."

"So what are you saying, Bryce? I don't get the money? I was sure you would find them with Mama's things. What I am going to do? This place is shutting down, and no other rehab around the state wants to take us in. They want people with big bucks these days. I suppose I could live with my sister, but I feel like the others. I wanted to complete this program. I don't want to return to those streets. I was hoping that with that money, I could pay to get into another facility. What am I going to do now?"

"Don't give up so easily. You can get the money. We will have to fight for it. You have to get used to disappointment. That's what life is all about, getting over disappointment. These are tests of your sobriety and a part of maturity. Didn't you know that while you were drinking and drugging it was stumping your emotional growth? Instead of dealing with problems, you turned to something to get high on. You can't let things like this drive you back to where you came from."

"But I don't understand why my father would go through all that trouble to get me registered and then not leave the papers to complete what he started. It's like some kind of sick joke. You see, he really didn't care about me," Franklin whined.

Bryce saw that Franklin was getting himself all worked up. His eyes were narrowed with disgust.

"All this hope was for nothing. I shouldn't have started to believe in him or this stupid shoe box. Here he has me looking like an idiot by carrying around a dumb shoe box that's older than I am." Franklin spoke with a growing frenzy. His breath became hot in his throat. Franklin sprung to his feet. He took the shoe box and flung it to the floor. The contents spilled all over the floor, and the box came to rest upside down at Bryce's feet.

Bryce shot straight up in his chair, and his jaw dropped. For a moment he and Franklin eyed each other with a speculative glance. Their eyes then zoomed in on something neither had noticed before. There was an envelope heavily taped to the bottom of the shoe box. "Are you thinking what I'm thinking?" Bryce asked.

Franklin nodded but hesitated to pick up the box. His face grew ashen. His eyes became like saucers, and his heart fluttered in his chest.

"Well?" Bryce interceded. "Go for it."

Franklin carefully picked up the shoe box as though he was handling a newborn baby. He meticulously removed the tape securing the envelope. The return address clearly read "Veterans Administration, Washington, DC."

"Careful," Bryce said, "it's been there for an awfully long time."

Painstakingly, Franklin got the envelope opened. Inside was his father's medical discharge papers and a letter confirming Franklin's registration for the Agent Orange claim.

Both Franklin's and Bryce's eyes danced with excitement. The two men hugged. Then Franklin let out a loud cheer. He was bursting with joy. The people who were out in the lounge came crashing into the room. Franklin was eager to share the news of his good fortune.

The word spread rapidly across the grounds of the Eagles' Nest. Eager to inform Allison, Franklin and Bryce walked to the administration office, but the news had beaten them there. "Congratulations, Franklin," Allison greeted. "I'm so happy for you. I'm sure you could use the money. It couldn't have come at a better time. I can't wait to tell Auntie Lou. She'll be just thrilled to hear this."

"Allison," Bryce interrupted, "Franklin and I will have to go down to Washington, DC, to collect the money. They asked Franklin to bring his bank book. They need to verify the bank's name and account number. Franklin says that the bank book from the account that Ms. Langdon started for him is kept here."

"Sure. We have that. I will get it for you. What are you going to do with your new fortune, Franklin?" Allison asked. She opened a small safe and reached in for the book.

"Well, first of all, I don't think it'll be enough to be called a fortune. I just hope it's enough to get me into another treatment facility," Franklin answered.

"That's very good thinking, Franklin. Looks like your short stay here has taught you to think of your sobriety first. That's very good Franklin," Allison praised.

"Oh, Allison, since we'll be getting a flight out early in the morning, would it be okay if Franklin spent the night with his sister? That way I won't have to drive all the way back here tomorrow for him," Bryce noted.

"That's an excellent idea. I don't see why not," she responded. "The way it looks now, there may not be a cottage here for him to return to anyway. The banks are ready to foreclose on us. It's too bad. In just three months there will be ninety new people coming and with their tuition, we'll be able to operate, but it's the unpaid loan that's forcing us to close. We can't borrow more money from anyone."

Bryce waited at the administration office while Franklin went back to his cottage to pack his clothes. Allison's comment about not having a place to come back to had a devastating effect on him. He called out the people in his cottage and one by one he hugged them. He then took Korianne into his room. They exchanged a long kiss, and Franklin gave her Monique's phone number just in case they became separated.

Bryce inquired about Ms. Langdon. Allison told him that she was doing well. Since she gave up the responsibility of caring for the Eagles' Nest, her health had improved.

"What about John? Have you heard from him lately?" Bryce asked.

"John is still quite bitter. He only saw the doctor once. He did, however, go to work for a security company. He's not happy doing that, but he does have an income. For the time being, our engagement is back on hold," Allison said.

"Oh, Allison. I'm so sorry."

"Don't be sorry. This was John's idea. I don't think he'll ever be ready to marry. I'm beginning to feel like it's me. He keeps making excuses. After each excuse I lose a little love for him."

Franklin burst into the administration office with his suitcase full of clothes. A moment ago, he was heartbroken to have to leave his friends. The thought of him receiving money had him feeling bubbly again. He impatiently influenced Bryce to cut short his conversation with Allison, and the two headed south on Route 272.

Monique's face flushed with happiness at the sight of Franklin. She was thrilled to learn that he was allowed to stay the night. It had been a long time since the two of them had spent an entire night together. She also volunteered to pay for Franklin's plane ticket.

Bryce returned to the office to speak with his supervisor. He had not yet gotten permission to travel out of state with Franklin. Bryce began to form stress lines over his brow as he raced toward the office. "What if I'm denied? I've gotten Franklin all pumped up for the trip. How can I not go? How could I almost forget something as crucial as this?"

Bryce explained the situation to Nick about Franklin needing to go to Washington, DC. Nick began to make several phone calls. There was a sudden stab of anxiety in Bryce's stomach, and he could feel a bead of sweat trickle down the side of his face. While still on the phone, Nick nodded the approval, and Bryce relaxed back into his seat.

There was no place to park at the Brown's residence when Bryce returned. Aunts Mabel and Jessie Mae were among the many relatives that had rushed over after learning that Franklin was in town. The news of his good fortune had also reached them. "Hey, Brenda, I see you're still holding onto your Mr. Right," one cousin said as Bryce entered and searched for a seat.

"We heard that Franklin has come into millions of dollars," Mabel remarked.

"Yeah, and I came over to see if you needed someone to be his guardian. I'm not going to pass this one up," Jessie Mae announced.

"Hallelujah! Praise the Lord!" Mabel resounded.

Brenda suggested that they order food, and this took the focus off of Bryce. Franklin came over and quietly gestured for Bryce to follow him to a more private area. He then whispered, "I remember when I wasn't welcome at any of their homes. Now they all want me to visit and do this and that with them. You should hear some of the plans they have made for me. This reminds me of a story that my mother told me about my father. She said that when he used to get paid around the first of the month-I mean when his disability check would come-there were dozens of people that waited out on our front porch. These were his so-called drinking buddies. They waited like vultures. They greeted the mail carrier. They followed my father when he went to cash his check. They did all this because they knew that he would buy liquor for all of them. When he drank, they drank. When he left home to go down the street, he had a small parade of people following him. Too bad he had to die because of drinking."

"That doesn't surprise me about your father. He always had a crowd of people following him. Except in Nam, it was for a different reason. I followed your father, and he's the reason I'm alive today," Bryce related. "By the way, we shouldn't stay up too late tonight. We have an early flight in the morning."

"Oh, yeah, about this flight thing. Why do we have to fly? Can't we just drive down or catch a bus or something?" Franklin asked.

"Flying is the fastest way. We'll be there in less than two hours. Aren't you anxious to find out how much money you'll be getting?"

"Well, yes, but not that anxious."

"What is it then? Are you afraid of flying?"

"I don't know," Franklin returned. "I've never been in a plane."

"Don't worry. It'll be fun," Bryce said.

"Oh yeah, that's right!" Franklin remembered. "You and my dad were paratroopers. You guys jumped out of planes. No wonder you're not afraid."

"Yes, we did, but that was a long time ago. I get a little nervous about flying these days. I don't believe in taking unnecessary chances. I found out in Nam how easy it is to be killed."

Early the next morning, the two men were driven to the airport by Brenda and Monique. "Franklin, if you get enough money, we could chauffeur you around like this all the time," Brenda commented.

"Yeah, and while she's driving, I could be reading you some of my poems," Monique added.

Franklin did not comment. After a minute or two, Bryce leaned over and whispered in Franklin's ear. "Smart move. Now you're learning that there's a time to speak and a time to say nothing at all."

Bryce relaxed back into his coach seat to enjoy the short trip as the plane sped toward lift-off. Franklin was seated by the window. His face was glued to the pane. He expressed that he felt butterflies in his stomach. He struggled to control the quavering of his voice as he sung a chorus of "Ooh's and ah's."

The previous night had taken its toll on Bryce. He now looked for an opportunity to take a quick nap. Franklin was fidgeting in his seat and kept disturbing Bryce. He acted as though the plane would crash if Bryce fell asleep. "Man, oh man!" he said. "You guys must have been awfully brave to jump from this high up. You know, Bryce, the more I learn about my father the more I want to be like him."

Bryce peeped through one eye at Franklin. He stretched his arms above his head and straightened up in his seat. In a voice that was tinged with sarcasm, he said, "Yeah, I know. You tell me that every opportunity you get."

Franklin was too excited to be insulted. "My father wasn't afraid of anything."

"That's not exactly true," Bryce corrected. "There were a few things that your father was afraid of. But that's okay because everyone has at least one phobia. Your father's was connected to one of the elements that we battled in Nam."

"Oh, yeah. Well, what was my father's phobia?"

"Your father was an ophidiophobian." Bryce answered that way knowing it would only confuse Franklin.

"He was a what? Come on, Bryce, you're only trying to make up something for him to have been afraid of." Franklin laughed.

"No, that's not true. Your father was extremely afraid of snakes."

"Snakes?" Even though Franklin was surprised by the answer, he was somewhat relieved. He, too, had a fear of snakes.

"Yes, snakes. That's what your father was afraid of, and so was I. Your father was a hell of a fighter, but he was terrified of snakes. However, they were all over in Nam. In the jungle it was impossible to avoid them. To make matters worse, we walked through the jungle in single file. Communication was by word of mouth, passed up and down the line. Often word would come down from the front warning us to watch out for a snake in the tree. Those of us who were afraid had to watch every tree and bush we passed. Then, every hour word would come back for us to take a ten minute break. That meant that we would have to sit right where we were, and sometimes that might be under the tree where that snake or sometimes snakes were hanging out."

"Man! That must have been scary. What kind of snakes did you see?" Franklin asked. His eyes became as big as golf balls, and he said that his skin felt like it was crawling.

"During my one year tour, I saw three huge pythons in the jungle. All three measured twenty feet or more. But it wasn't the large snakes that terrified us. Almost every little or medium-sized snake that we encountered had fangs. The deadliest of those was the Bamboo Viper. We called it "Mr. Two-Steps." It had a bad reputation. It was said that if you were bitten by this viper, two steps could be all you took before you keeled over. We didn't find that to be true. But it was extremely venomous. Fortunately for us, it wasn't an aggressive snake. It would not come over to you just to bite you. You would have to be handling it for it to bite, or you would have to roll over on it while you were sleeping. For the most part, it avoided us. Again, that wasn't the way of all the snakes in the jungle. I found out the hard way that there was an aggressive snake out there."

"How did that happen?" Franklin asked. He still sat with dropped jaws and saucer eyes.

"After setting up our perimeter late one evening, I needed to go outside to make a toilet. I notified both sides of my position that I was going out, but I made the same mistake as your father by not bringing someone along. Sometimes when we were out for a while and didn't make contact with the enemy, we got careless or complacent. At any rate, I grabbed my little spade and my rifle and went out. I was squatting when I heard the sound of leaves being disturbed behind me. At first I was not worried, and I didn't look back at the time. Soon I heard what sounded like heavy breathing. The breathing got closer than the sound of the leaves being moved. I decided that it was time to investigate, and I looked back over my shoulder. A large cobra was swaying back and forth. I presumed that it was trying to get into striking range. For a brief moment, my eyes became transfixed with horror. My knees began to tremble, and my heart fluttered in my chest. I took off running from a squatting position and tried to pull up my pants at the same time. I left my rifle and spade right there. I made so much noise yelling that everyone thought I was being abducted."

Franklin's face was grey. The blood had drained from it. He looked like he was about to faint. It was the same reaction Bryce had gotten from Franklin's father when he told him what he had encountered. "Are you okay?" he asked Franklin.

"Yeah, I'm okay. I can't imagine that happening to me. I probably would still be running until this day." They both laughed.

"What happened next?"

"The platoon leader later sent out a squad to retrieve my rifle. I was petrified after that experience. Your father became terrified just from hearing me explain what had happened. I was told later that cobras aren't usually aggressive unless it is a female protecting a litter or a male during mating season. I was unable to sleep at night for a long while knowing that something like that was out there. I had terrible nightmares about that incident up until a few years ago. In my nightmare, the snake grew bigger with each episode. "

"How could you all function with all those things around and out to get you?" Franklin asked.

"One thing we learned while in Nam was that a person could get used to anything in order to survive. Besides that, the sound of one round from an AK-47 or the sound of mortar fire coming at you would make you quickly forget about snakes."

The plane began its descent for landing and Franklin commented, "Boy, that was a short trip. We barely got going. I want to hear more. I forgot we were in the air."

"There weren't many things your father was afraid of. He did mention one more, and we all were afraid of that, too," Bryce hinted.

The plane skidded on the ground and Franklin's eyes widened. His attention again focused on the outside. "Whew! I'm glad we're back on solid ground," he admitted.

Franklin and Bryce were met at the Veterans Administration office by a man in a green Army uniform. He introduced himself as Captain Athas. He had a lot of decorations on his uniform. Bryce was pleased to see that the captain belonged to the same Army units that he and Tyrone had served with. He wore the patch of the 82nd Airborne Division(AA) on his left shoulder. On his right shoulder, he wore the patch of the 101st Airborne Division(the Screaming Eagles). The one on the right represented his combat unit. Bryce pointed these features out to Franklin. Bryce thought about asking him if he had served in Nam, but he realized that the captain was too young. Bryce assumed that he earned his combat patch in the Persian Gulf War.

Captain Athas led Franklin and Bryce to an office at the end of a long corridor with dozens of glass-front offices on both sides. Franklin presented the documents to the officer seated at the desk. She then asked him for his bank book also. They were offered a seat and asked to wait while the transaction was being processed. It had only been a half hour, but it seemed like an eternity to both of them. Franklin chewed on his lips, while Bryce was busy biting his nails.

Finally, the captain and four higher ranking officers came out to congratulate Franklin. "Well, where's the check?" Franklin blurted out.

Captain Athas handed Franklin his bank book and reached out to shake his hand.

"This is it?" Franklin spoke without opening the book. His lips curled up in disgust.

"Yes. We couldn't allow you to travel with that amount of money. The money should be available for your withdrawal by the time you get back. There's a receipt in your bank book for the deposited amount in the event there's a problem," the captain informed him.

Franklin's hands trembled as he opened to the receipt. He lifted his head, and with a slow appraising glance at the captain, he asked rather brazenly, "Is this it? You asked us to come down here for a measly $375."

"I think you need to look again," the captain countered.

Franklin looked again, and this time his eyes widened incredulously. He flashed a forced grin but said nothing. He then handed the bank book to Bryce. "Wow! $375,000! Is this all his?" Bryce asked.

"This is the amount the claim accumulated to. This is the amount that is being transferred to Franklin's account," they were told.

Bryce was puzzled to see that Franklin suddenly seemed to lose interest in the money. He had shown more animation about being on a plane than he was showing toward the money. Franklin's face took on a look of suspicious bewilderment.

Bryce, on the other hand, had a look of blissfulness. He was reeling in delight. "Franklin! Franklin! Do you understand what has just happened to you?" he asked feverishly.

"Sure I do," Franklin responded. He had a dubious expression on his face, and his eyes had a far-off look. "That's why I need to use the phone."

"Franklin, we have more good news for you," the captain interrupted. "Your father's discharge papers have confirmed what we needed to know. Now we can go forward as planned."

"What's this all about?" Bryce asked.

"We'll be inviting Franklin and his family and friends to a ceremony involving the Vietnam War Memorial Wall. Some new names will be added to the Wall at this ceremony. Because his injuries did occur in combat and were a major contributing role in his death, the name 'Tyrone Cooper' will be added to the Wall," the captain announced.

Again Franklin did not react. He was uncommonly reserved, and he still had a far-off look in his eyes. Bryce was concerned about Franklin's lack of enthusiasm for all this good news. Bryce's own excitement prompted him to speak in Franklin's behalf. "That's great news," he said. "Did you know that I served with Tyrone in Nam? I knew him well. As a matter of fact, Captain Athas, we were in the same divisions as you were. I think that's just great. Tyrone is being added to the Wall. That's a fine tribute to his name and family."

Franklin leaned toward Bryce. His eyes widened innocently, and in a serene voice he asked, "What's the Wall?"

His question surprised Bryce. Franklin had done a lot of reading about Vietnam, yet he didn't know about the Vietnam War Memorial Wall. Bryce now understood Franklin's lack of emotion when the captain made the announcement. "I'll explain what the Wall is about on the plane," Bryce told him.

Despite the good things that had just happened, Franklin's face still looked troubled. "I need to use the phone before we leave," he requested.

Captain Athas directed Franklin to a room where he could use the phone in private. Bryce waited by the door. Franklin's bizarre behavior was beginning to worry Bryce even more. "What's with this secret phone calling? Is he setting up a drug buy even before we get back? Is all this money good for Franklin's recovery? Will it send him back into the streets? He is acting strange. What is it that he is focusing on?" These questions were driving Bryce bananas.

"What was that all about?" Bryce bluntly asked as Franklin came out of the phone room.

"It's a secret," Franklin replied with a sheepish grin. "It's one of the first things I must take care of when we return. Don't worry so much, Bryce. Now you'll have to trust me a little."

"I want to trust you, but you've been acting strange ever since the captain placed the bank book into your hands. You almost act as if you don't appreciate what you just received," Bryce scolded.

"It's not that I'm unappreciative. Everything that I've come to appreciate has been taken away from me. So now I don't get excited when I first get something. I'm afraid it will be taken away. It'll take a while before I really believe that it's actually all mine," Franklin confessed.

Bryce tried to understand. "Well, just show a little appreciation to the captain. He did a lot to make this happen."

Franklin listened to Bryce. He tried to apologize to the captain for his unexpressive reaction. "There's no apology needed, Franklin," the captain said. "People act differently when they receive a large amount of money."

The captain gathered the needed information from Franklin for the Wall ceremony and assigned a driver to take the two men back to the airport.

CHAPTER 24

The realization of the money began to sink into Franklin's mind. Once the plane was airborne, he felt he had slid safely into home plate with the winning run. Franklin's thought was that now they could not take the money back. His emotions began to run unbridled. He let out a loud victory yell.

"Are you okay?" Bryce asked.

"Oh yeah!" Franklin replied. "You said I needed to show some appreciation."

"Yes, but I didn't mean for you to shake up the plane." They both laughed.

"I was surprised to learn that you haven't heard of the Wall," Bryce commented.

"Don't forget, before I met you, I spent a lot of time just getting high. Even the things I read, I couldn't recall half of them. So what's this Wall thing about?" Franklin asked.

"It's a marble wall that has the names of those killed in the Vietnam War engraved on it. It's a memorial to those guys. We weren't that far from it when we were at the VA office. There's also a smaller traveling version of the Wall that is being brought around the country for those who are unable to go to Washington, DC, to see the original one. That traveling version of the Wall was in our area not long ago."

"Have you ever seen the Wall?" Franklin asked.

"No, I haven't," Bryce responded.

"Not even when it was right here in our area?"

"I had planned to go, but then I realized that I still wasn't ready to see it. Maybe this article that I wrote will explain why I felt that way. I sent this article to the local newspaper, and they published it in the commentary section."

Bryce reached into his wallet and took out a news clipping. He unfolded it and handed it to Franklin. "Read this," he said.

Franklin began to read aloud, starting with the article's title: **"Traveling Wall, a painful reminder."** The text read:

"I'm a veteran of the Vietnam War. I served in combat as a medic with the 101st Airborne Division in 1968.

"I was planning to go to Washington, DC, one day to see the Wall—the Vietnam War Memorial Wall. After all these years, I thought I was ready to see it. However, as I was driving to Torrington, where I work as a nurse for the Department of Mental Health, I heard over the radio that a traveling version of the Wall would be in our area for a short while over the weekend. Well, I cried all the way to work, just remembering the guys I cared for before they died in my arms. I canceled all thoughts of visiting the Wall for that weekend.

"Friday of that same week, as I was entering Route 8 from Interstate 84 west, I saw a billboard that said, "The Vietnam War Memorial Wall—The Wall That Heals," and again I cried all the way to work.

"If the Wall is a healing site to some veterans or their families that is great, and it has served its purpose. But for me, the Wall is not a healing. It only rehashes old memories, memories that I have worked for years to get rid of.

"The Vietnam War was about more than one or two years in a jungle for me. It was about years of confusion, depression, near insanity, and substance abuse. From these things, this Wall did not heal me. Only after turning my life over to God was I able to begin healing.

"Some seem to think that if you see the Wall and cry out your emotions, you will heal. Maybe that works for some, and that is good. However, my feelings are deeper than that, and besides, I 've been crying for years.

"To me, the Wall is close to a lie. The guys I can't get out of my head were killed by our own artillery. Then there was a captain who was liked very much by all his troops because he showed he cared for them. He died when a helicopter's rotor blade decapitated him.

"A lot of things like this happened over in Vietnam. And the sad thing is that the American people will never hear all the truth.

"I've found that talking and writing about those experiences has been a source of healing. Recently, I completed a book entitled, *"Fighting the Elements: A True Vietnam Substance Abuse Recovery Story."* This work is being reviewed by some publishers. I completed a couple of children's stories also.

"I was doing fine with my recovery from Vietnam. The Wall was away down in Washington, DC, for those who were ready to go and see it. But now it has invaded my space. It has come into my backyard. My faith in God will sustain me through this, but I wonder how many others feel as I do—or am I alone in my feeling?

Bryce Wright

"Man! That was heavy," Franklin stated. His face was sparkling. "Why do you think they took so long to add my father's name to the Wall?"

"Like the article said, the American public will never hear all the hidden things about Vietnam. They probably tried to cover over the manner in which your father was wounded. The part of the article that said those guys were killed by our own artillery, well your father was in the group that survived."

"What happened, Bryce? No one has ever been able to tell me how he got wounded. Were you with him at the time?" Franklin wanted to know.

"Yes, I was with him. I was one of the medics that worked to keep him alive. I can tell you exactly how he got hit. By telling you how your father got wounded, you will also find out the second thing that he was afraid of. Remember I told you that he and all of us shared this same fear?" Bryce asked.

"Yes, I remember. Now tell me. What was it?"

"Dying," Bryce said.

"Dying?" Franklin repeated. He was puzzled by Bryce's answer.

"Yes, dying. But not just dying in itself. It was the fear of dying so far away from home: dying without saying goodbye to loved ones. It haunted everyone to think of dying in a foreign land."

"I understand," Franklin said. "Now tell me what happened."

"Have you ever seen the Vietnam War movie 'Hamburger Hill?'" Bryce asked.

"Yes, I've seen it several times," Franklin answered.

"Well that movie is the closest to show how the real Nam was. As a matter of fact, those soldiers were a part of the unit your father and I was in. Hamburger Hill happened three months after I left Nam. Your father was shipped out a month earlier than me. Well, to make a long story short, let me start from the beginning. We began to make a lot of contact in that area. Everyday we were either getting ambushed or having short firefights. Finally, an all-out fight began, and it took us nearly a week to drive the enemy from a huge bunker complex. Afterward, we set up our positions in the complex that we had captured. During the night, we heard a lot of commotion outside the perimeter. We figured that they were building up to try to recapture the bunker complex. Our commander sent word around to every position on the perimeter to prepare for a turkey shoot at first light of morning."

"Okay. Wait a minute. I was following along quite well until now. What's a turkey shoot?" Franklin interrupted.

"A turkey shoot is where everyone fires off three magazines or more of ammunition, throws out a bunch of hand grenades, and sets off some claymore mines. We all do this at the same time, and we do it to clear out anyone that may have surrounded us during the night. From the amount of noise we heard, we thought this had happened. In order for us to all start at the same time, we needed a signal. The commander had called a nearby firebase for artillery support. Our turkey shoot was to start after the third round from the artillery exploded outside of our perimeter. Are you still with me?" Bryce asked.

"I'm still with you," Franklin returned.

After so many years, Bryce still found it difficult to speak about this part. His voice began to quaver, and eyes misted over. He continued, "Well, I never heard the three rounds hit. I heard each one leave the firebase with a distant bang. I did hear a wisping sound pass through the trees and I thought it was strange for branches to fall from the tree for what I thought was for no apparent reason. Immediately after that, I heard a cry for a medic. It came from several places, and inside our perimeter the scene became chaotic. The three rounds landed right in the middle of our perimeter. There were five guys that were killed instantly. The first person I came to had the back of his head missing. Most of the damage happened to the men out on the perimeter, because when a shell explodes it goes up and then comes back down."

"Where was my father during all of this?" Franklin interrupted.

"Your father came from the far side of the perimeter to help us with the wounded. He didn't know that he was wounded until someone pointed out to him that he was bleeding. Your father was a strong man, because he was up, and walking around. When I saw his wounds, they looked bad. He had been hit in his right shoulder and below his right rib cage. I remember asking him if he recalled what happened, and he said, 'I heard nothing but I realized that I was flying through the air. When I got up I felt no pain. I felt wet but I thought it was beginning to rain.' We had difficulty getting the medi-vac in, because the enemy was definitely out there. They prevented the helicopters from coming in. It was then that I talked to your father about dying, because it was a real possibility at that time. We didn't know how long we could keep the wounded alive. Fortunately for us, there were a couple of other companies on the way to assist us. Finally the helicopters were able to come in. They still were not able to land, so everyone was hoisted up. Even then they were being shot at. It was a very scary time for all of us." Bryce stopped and wiped tears from his eyes.

Franklin's face was also dark with pain.. He had heard the whole story about how his father had gotten wounded. He neatly folded the news clipping and handed it back to Bryce.

"That's why up until now, I had no courage to see the Wall. It will remind me of the guys killed in that artillery mistake. I have all those names etched in my memory, because I had to make out the death tags for the body bags. However, I need to close out that chapter of my life. With your father's name being added, I'm going to muster up the courage to see it."

The flight attendant came down the aisle offering refreshments. When she caught sight of the two men with the downcast look, she said, "Listen fellows, this a plane, not a roller coaster. You guys have been up and down with your emotions ever since boarding. First we heard someone shout out with joy. Now you both are sitting here sobbing away."

"She's absolutely right," Bryce agreed. "You should be celebrating. Your whole life has changed. What are you planning to do with all that money?"

"I have a lot of plans. One of them is to give you some money, because without your help and your taking an interest in me, I might still be out on the streets," Franklin said.

"You can erase that plan. This is my job, and it's against the rules to accept money from clients. Besides, I'm doing this for my friend TC."

"Well the way I see things with this new Agent Orange diagnosis and the amount of money I have, I will no longer qualify for state services. Then you will be taken off as my caseworker, and I will be free to give you money," Franklin said.

"That is a thought," Bryce agreed. "But I don't want any money from you. I want you to stay drug and alcohol free. You have so much to offer to society."

Franklin and Bryce were greeted at the airport by Brenda and Monique. Franklin described how the transaction went and started to share his future plans with the two women.

"There's a lot of people at the house waiting for you," Monique said. "They claim to be cousins, but Brenda and I don't recognize most of them."

"It doesn't matter right now. I have something more important to do before I can go to the house. Drive me to the bank, Brenda, then I need to get back to the Eagles' Nest as soon as possible," Franklin said. He was starting to act suspiciously again.

At the bank, Franklin withdrew $20 and asked for a receipt to see his balance. He asked the clerk if there was a mistake with his balance. She told Franklin that they were aware of the transaction and the money was indeed in his account. Franklin rushed outside and showed the receipt to Monique. Monique's heart leaped and she felt a kick from the fetus when she looked into Franklin's bank book. Her face flushed with happiness for her brother.

Franklin urged Brenda to speedily bring them to Bryce's car, which was parked at the house. Franklin's relatives started to come out as they pulled into the driveway, but he and Bryce quickly got into Bryce's car and headed for the Eagles' Nest. Franklin was silent on the ride up Route 272. Bryce did not question his actions. He now had an idea of what was on Franklin's mind.

Allison had everyone at the Eagles' Nest gathered in the dining hall. She had one of the residents pick up Ms. Langdon, so that she would be present. Ms. Langdon now spent most of her time confined to a wheelchair, even though she could walk with a walker. Allison had summoned everyone to the meeting. No one was to be absent, as Franklin had requested by phone from Washington, DC. "May I have your attention, please," Allison announced as she saw Franklin and Bryce coming toward the hall. "Franklin has ask me to gather you all here. He would like to make an announcement and hopefully it will effect all of us."

Franklin stood in front of the gathered residents. He had a broad grin on his face. His eyes danced as he glanced around the room. He stopped searching when he found Ms. Langdon, and he started to speak. "I have come to appreciate all that the Eagles' Nest has done for me. Ms. Langdon trusted me even when I was afraid to trust myself. Allison has always shown a sisterly love for me and my family. Those two are very special people. There is a need for places like this one with people like them. I'm sure you all will agree with me. I have also come to love each one of you, because when I was down and acting like an idiot, you didn't give up on me. As you all know, I have come into a little money. I want to give back to the people that helped me. So I will pay off the Eagles' Nest's debt. Now we will all be able to graduate together as it was planned."

This was the secret Franklin had tried to keep from Bryce. The idea hit him the moment he got the bank book showing his new balance. This act had Franklin reeling with joy. He had never felt this high from drugs. He also felt like a hero. He imagined this was the feeling his father had experienced from helping the troops.

Everyone rushed to Franklin, and he was lifted into the air. Bryce rushed to the phone to tell Monique and Brenda of the generous deed Franklin had just done.

CHAPTER 25

Franklin's mental status was evaluated by a psychiatric team at the mental health center, because his father's military records showed that he was born with Agent Orange. Franklin's illness was now considered medical rather than mental illness. However, he would still have to stay away from drugs and alcohol to avoid symptoms such as psychosis and prolonged depression. His medication would remain the same.

Franklin then had to pay back the money the state had spent on his care over the past years. It wasn't as much as he had thought it would be. Franklin was still left with a substantial amount of money, more than enough to fulfill his promise to the Eagles' Nest and pay for private medical care. Franklin was discharged from the services of the mental health center. Bryce was no longer his case manager.

"Even though we hope that everyone serviced by us will recover from their illness and be discharged from our services, it's particularly difficult for me to see you leave," Bryce said as he and Franklin headed north on Route 272.

"Why is it that I'm not happy about this discharge. I thought I would be delighted to be free of the state," Franklin admitted. "But I'm not happy and, worst of all, I'm afraid. I've been in this system for so long that I'm not sure that I can survive on my own."

"You're not going to be alone. You have Monique and Brenda. And there's a new family that you've helped to keep together at the Eagles' Nest," Bryce reminded him.

"Why do I have to lose you? I feel safe with you looking over me. You've become like a father. Who will I turn to now if I get depressed? The shoe box can't continue to guide me, or can it? What else could possibly come from it?" Franklin whined.

"You're only discharged from our services. This doesn't have to be the end of our friendship. Actually, it's better this way. We don't have to worry about work rules and we'll be able to do more things together. Besides, I plan to continue dating your cousin Brenda. Now that she's Monique's guardian, I'll probably be in your company more than you like," Bryce admitted.

"Speaking of Monique and Brenda, that reminds me of the second part of my plan. I have to make sure that they are taken care of. I plan to pay off the mortgage on the house so that we will always have a place to call home. I'm also going to put money into their accounts. Then there's Mama," Franklin remembered.

Bryce was confused. What could Franklin do for his mother? She was dead. "What do you mean?"

"Oh, Monique and I had discussed doing something about her grave site. She doesn't have a headstone, and it may get difficult to find her later. I promised that I would buy a marble headstone for her if I ever got the money. That's all Monique asked from me. I offered to have her poetry published, but she sternly refused to have it done that way. She said that she wanted her poems accepted on their merits."

The Eagles' Nest was again operating as a drug and alcohol rehabilitation center because of Franklin's investment. The instructors had returned, and classes were being taught as scheduled. The culinary school still provided students to the dining hall. The residents that worked at various jobs continued and were offered some pay for their services. Franklin was given a partnership in the business. He was given authority over maintenance and security, while Allison continued to work as the administrator.

John's mother finally died from congestive heart failure due to complications of her diabetes and other health problems. Bryce, Allison, and Franklin attended the funeral. Even though John had expected that she wouldn't live for a long time, it was emotionally upsetting to him. John didn't have a lot of relatives, and his mother didn't have many friends in the area. He welcomed the support of Bryce, Allison, and Franklin. The trio stayed with John through the entire funeral session, and afterward they invited him to dinner.

It was during the dinner that John revealed how he had lost his position as a security guard. His mother's debilitating condition during her last days caused him to be home a lot from work.

Again Bryce was impressed with Franklin's change of character, when Franklin offered John a job as head of the three-man security team at the Eagles' Nest. John had expressed to Allison how he didn't want to work for her, but he viewed working for Franklin as not being the same. He accepted the job. He looked forward to the opportunity to be near Allison. During the dinner, John felt that Allison seemed a bit distant. She did not look up to him with the same reverence she had in the past. John's gambling problem was still haunting her, but she didn't feel that this was a time to question him about it.

Friday afternoon Bryce rushed to finish up his work. He hurried home, changed clothes, and headed up Route 272. It was a lousy evening for driving. The rainstorm was forecast to last through the weekend.

Bryce made his way through the bad weather to be at a special gathering at the Eagles' Nest in honor of Franklin. Everyone there waited anxiously for a special announcement that was to be made by Ms. Langdon.

Ms. Langdon struggled to get up from her wheelchair. Two male residents came to her aid and assisted her to the podium that was set up in the dining hall. Ms. Langdon appeared disgusted by her weakness, but she wasn't the kind to let anyone know if she was troubled. She stood there a little unsteady but she made warm eye contact with everyone. Then she made a brief announcement: "For the contributions Franklin has made to make the Eagles' Nest the respectable place it has always been, we are proud to announce that one of the cottages will be renamed "Franklin House."

A loud round of applause was given, and Ms. Langdon invited Franklin to speak.

"I'm not much of a speaker, but I'll try," Franklin began.

True, Franklin wasn't much of a speaker, but in the past he liked to ham things up. This time, though, Franklin was serious and business-like. He had a hard, pinched facial expression, and he seemed to be trying too hard to choose the right words. "I really do want to thank all of you for your support. My recovery has been mostly due to you all. To tell the truth, I invested in the Eagles' Nest because I am really afraid to leave this place. Now that I've gotten my own cottage, maybe I won't. Just kidding. Anyway, this next announcement I didn't just come up with while standing here. I had already talked about this with Allison before I was given a cottage in my name."

Franklin stopped to clear his throat. His hands were balled into fists. He licked dry his lips and continued: "When I first came here, I was desperate, lonely, and afraid. I was at the end of my rope. I saw no way out, and I was ready to end my miserable life. I know that there are many young people out there who are facing the same situation, probably as I'm standing here rambling on. I want them to know that there is a place where they can come for help. Many of these young people are on the streets, and homeless, with no means of getting help. Therefore, I am dedicating Franklin House to those individuals. The six room cottage will be only for people with chronic drug addiction who are threatening suicide and have no means to pay for help. Every time a room becomes empty, we will fill it, and their stay will be for as long as it takes them to recover. That's all I have to say. Thank you for listening."

Franklin was the hero of the day. And rightly so, because he had done a good thing, and it earned him the respect of everyone at the Eagles' Nest. Franklin's only regret was that Monique and Brenda were not there to hear his speech. The weather was too bad for Monique to chance coming, and she was in a late stage of pregnancy. Brenda had stayed with her. However, they did send word by Bryce to invite Allison and Ms. Langdon to their house on the coming Sunday for a baby shower for Monique.

The celebration inside quietly came to a finish while the storm outside grew more fierce. Bryce was offered a bed for the night in the newly named Franklin House. Franklin inaugurated his cottage by keeping Bryce up late into the night with his attempt at being a stand-up comic.

Things settled down around the Eagles' Nest for the next few days. Everyone was hard at work adjusting to their new roles. John was happy to be working near Allison. As head of security, he only worked the shift when she was there.

When Sunday came, Bryce shuddered at the thought of entering a house full of women. He remembered back when Mrs. Brown was entertaining and how embarrassed he felt on that occasion. But his team had pooled together for a gift, and he was designated to present it.

There was no place to park from the corner of the street to Monique's driveway, just as it had been during the card parties. But this wasn't enough to use as an excuse for not coming. Bryce braved his way to the door. He could hear loud chatter, mixed with a lot laughter and snickering. Bryce's stomach began to contract into a tight ball. He rang the doorbell once and was greeted by Brenda. For a brief moment, they stared at each other adoringly. Her face eased some of the anxiety that was now crushing his chest.

"Who is it Brenda?" Bryce recognized Mabel's voice even though it was coming from three rooms away.

"If it's some of your cousins, just take the gift and turn them away. Just tell them that there's no place to sit and that Franklin isn't here anyway," Jessie Mae added.

Bryce trailed Brenda closely. He tried not to step on anyone's toes. The scene was all too familiar. The people there were those who had come to Mrs. Brown's card party. They had the card tables out, and the women were playing the same game.

"It's just Brenda's Mr. Right," one cousin said as Bryce finally reached the kitchen.

Monique was sitting at the table, peeling a piece of fruit. She struggled to get to her feet.

"For heaven's sake. Stop waving that knife around, child," Mabel roared.

"Yeah, your mother had that same bad habit," Jessie Mae added.

Bryce's eyes widened in surprised alarm. He was transferred back in time. He stood speechless, staring at the knife in Monique's hand. Flashes of an awful memory kept popping into his head. It went on flashing in intervals until the picture was as clear as day. The blood drained from Bryce's face. He asked, "What happened to that old broken handled knife that your mother favored?"

"Good question," Monique replied. "I don't know where it went. I haven't seen it since Mama first went into the hospital."

Bryce was uncertain how he would react or express himself after the series of flashbacks. He hurriedly presented the gift and turned to leave. He squeezed through the party, excusing himself at every opportunity. This time Brenda shadowed him. Everyone thought his actions were strange, but they also thought he had become shy before the women.

Bryce gasped for air when he reached the porch. Brenda could see color return to his face. "What is it? Are you alright? You acted and looked like you saw a ghost in there."

"I can't explain it now. Something that I saw jarred my memory, and now I have to go to find out the truth. I'll call you later."

CHAPTER 26

Bryce headed down the highway for home. An hour passed, and he found himself parked in front of his apartment. The car's lights were on, but the radio was silent. The radio was always the first to be turned on after the ignition. Bryce imagined he had stopped at every red light and stop sign and had driven on the right side of the road. There were no flashing lights from any police cruiser, but he had absolutely no recollection of driving home. He was still troubled by what he had seen at Monique's. "How could Franklin lie to me and keep it going for so long? I knew I was right. How could I let them persuade me to believe differently? I know what I saw. If Franklin didn't stab Ray-Man, why was he holding the broken handled knife that belonged to his mother? How could he let an innocent man go to jail for a crime he committed? How could he give that speech like he was a hero, knowing that he had gotten away with murder? Franklin used me, just like he used everyone that he came into contact with. But he has not outsmarted me yet. I'm gonna get to the truth. But how? How can I find out the truth once and for all? Ah, ha Ricky Brown. Yes, Brown knows the truth. But he confessed. Why can't I just let this matter stand? Why can't I let it go?"

Bryce sat in his car and contemplated these things until it was late into the night. He finally decided to visit Ricky Brown and, if he still confessed to the crime, then he would let the matter rest. But he knew he would have to sever his relationship with Franklin. There was no more trusting him.

Bryce could hardly wait for his shift to end that Monday. He headed for the state prison as soon as it ended. He hoped he would be allowed to talk to Ricky Brown. Bryce didn't know the prison's regulations on visiting. He knew that he wasn't on Brown's visiting list.

At the prison, Bryce presented his state employee badge and asked to have a brief interview with the prisoner. He was told that all prisoners were entitled to professional visits. Bryce was led into a small gray room with a table and two chairs.

Brown was escorted in and seated across from Bryce, who was surprised that they were left alone. He was not handcuffed and didn't wear any restraints. "Why am I nervous about this?" Bryce questioned himself. "I only came to hear the truth."

Despite Brown's horribly disfigured face, he was aglow with good spirit. Bryce wondered how could he be in such a good mood while being imprisoned in such a depressing looking place. "What can I do for you?" Brown asked. His voice was indifferent, and it was hard for him to make eye contact. The long scar that ran from his forehead down to his throat made his speech slightly impaired.

"Mr. Brown, you may remember me from the trial," Bryce started. "I was with Franklin. I'm his case manager from the state."

"You can call me Rick. I remember you. What can I do for you?"

"I was over at a gathering they were having for Monique," Bryce began.

"How's Monique doing?" Rick interrupted.

"She's doing just great. But while I was there she started to wave around a knife while peeling fruit. Suddenly I remembered what I had seen at the crime scene that made me convinced that Franklin had done the stabbing. So I need to know if you were ever in Mrs. Brown's house since you left years ago?"

"No, I've never been back in that house. What's this all about? Weren't you at the trial when I confessed? I thought you came here with a message from my daughter. Look, Bryce, that's your name, right?"

"Yes, I'm Bryce. Something doesn't add up about the knife. Especially if you didn't take the knife from the house," Bryce said, as he eyed Brown suspiciously.

"Why are you digging into this? I confessed, and the case is closed. It was a knife that I always carried with me. What's the big deal?"

Bryce's questioning angered Rick. His pale-looking face now flushed with redness. The veins in his neck stood out in vivid ridges. His disfigured face became frightening. But Bryce was determined to get to the truth. He continued, "What's bothering me is that the knife that Franklin was found holding was a broken-handled knife that Mrs. Brown favored. If Franklin did the stabbing, why are you covering for him? I don't think he appreciates what you have done for him."

"Listen, mister, there are a lot of men in this prison that claim that they are innocent. And there are a lot of them that really are innocent. I confessed to the crime. I want to be here. Do you know how hard it was for me living out there? From alley to alley I lived. I was afraid to even approach my own daughter. In here I'm safe, and I'm known. I don't have to hide my face in here. My face is a protection in here. Please, just leave this case alone. All that justice ask for is a life for a life, and I've given them that."

"Okay, Rick. If that's the way you want it to be, then I'll let it go," Bryce said and offered his hand. "But I still think Franklin should have come here and personally thanked you. You have more than paid back for the way you treated him as a child."

"You just don't understand, do you? Why do you keep saying it was Franklin? Franklin doesn't owe me anything. I didn't confess to this crime to save Franklin. I'm doing this for my daughter. It was Monique who came out of the dark and stabbed that hoodlum."

"What?" Bryce said out loud. He almost got the attention of the guard. Bryce felt a rush of heat to his face. His face glazed with shock, and he could no longer remain seated.

"Sit back down, Bryce," Rick said. "It is for Monique that I'm taking this rap. I was there in the alley. I was waiting for an opportunity to snatch her away from that gang. I heard the siren and the commotion. I saw Ray-Man running my way. I watched Monique come out of the diner. She called out to Ray-Man, and I guessed that he stopped to wait for her. Franklin had turned the wrong way at first. I was stunned to see her with the knife in her hand. She stabbed him and kept stabbing him with an uncontrollable rage. She then simply fainted. Franklin quickly found his way and was coming. I picked Monique up and brought her back into the diner. I brought her into the bathroom and started to wash the blood from her face and hands. Two women came in looking for her. If they would have come further into the bathroom, they would have spotted me hiding behind the last stall. I don't believe Monique will ever recall what she did. She wasn't herself. She hadn't been herself the whole while she was held captive. So you see, Bryce, I didn't give my little girl much when she was growing up. I can do this for her now. Justice only asks a life for a life. Let this one be for me."

The two men stood and shook hands.

"Every morning when I wake up and every night before I go to sleep, I read a poem I got from Monique that I had framed and placed on the wall in my cell. The joy that comes over me when I read that poem insure me that I did the right thing," Rick said. A tear dropped from his eye as he looked Bryce straight in the face.

Bryce left without saying anything further. He was dumbfounded.

CHAPTER 27

It dawned on Bryce that he had completed the full circle of seasons as he took in sights and sounds driving north on Route 272. The scenic road had become so familiar to him that he could practically picture what was around each bend. His familiarity with the road allowed him the opportunity to reflect on the past year. It had been a turbulent time, filled with ups and downs. Grief still tugged at his heart when he thought about Mrs. Brown and her untimely death. Bryce truly believed that if he had become involved in her life earlier, he might have convinced her to give up the bottle. To see her sink into alcoholism had been painful to everyone who knew her.

Bryce felt a sense of accomplishment in his work with Franklin. He was delighted that he was able to continue his friendship with Franklin after learning the truth. Franklin was doing quite well in his recovery. He hadn't suffered any major depressive episodes since he quit using drugs and alcohol. It was becoming apparent that his psychosis was due to his substance abuse and that his manic-depression could be controlled by compliance with medication. More importantly, the money he had gotten hadn't caused him to crave drugs and alcohol. His role as a partner in the Eagles' Nest had gotten him to act as a responsible person. Franklin was maturing.

There was an increase of tourism to the bird-watching station. Magazine writers, reporters, and photographers were among those flocking to the Eagles' Nest. They were treated there to a view of a new set of baby eagles. However, the Eagles' Nest wasn't the only place with new arrivals. Monique gave birth to a beautiful baby girl. She was born on the birth date of her grandmother, Mrs. Brown, had a strong resemblance to her. She had a little round face with large raven eyes. She had a full head of hair at birth, and it was silky black like Monique's. Her smooth downy skin was aglow with a warm spirit. With help from the people who came to the baby shower, Monique decided to name her Selena Martha Brown. It was likely that little Selena would grow up to be a talented person, because Monique would sit for hours reading poetry to her little bundle of joy.

The sight of Brenda could still set Bryce's blood aflame, but their relationship had stalled somewhat like a plane in midair with engine trouble. After Brenda was given the cold shoulder by Bryce's daughter Tanya, Bryce hesitated to bring them together again. This caused tension between the two women. Bryce had been in Brenda's company on a regular basis, but most of his attention had been directed toward Franklin's and Monique's problems. With them headed in the right direction, Bryce was determined to rekindle his romance with Brenda.

Bryce was late in arriving at the Eagles' Nest. The bus that Franklin had chartered for the trip down to the Wall ceremony was almost full. Franklin was pacing around outside. Butterflies had begun to form in his stomach, and the palms of his hands were growing clammy. On seeing Bryce, he opened his mouth to talk but had to swallow the lump in his throat first. His voice strangled as he said, "You had me worried. You know I can't go anywhere without you."

"I didn't realize I was running late. Tomorrow is a very important day. I was creeping along, remembering all the things of the past year that helped us get to this day," Bryce said.

"Well stop dreaming and get on board. Brenda has a surprise for you," Franklin said, flashing a broad smile. With Bryce there, Franklin's tension faded and his mood became buoyant.

Bryce stepped onto the bus, and his heart filled with joy when he saw his daughter sitting with Brenda. His son was holding an empty seat for him behind them. Brenda realized that this was an important event for Bryce as well as for Franklin. She knew that Bryce would want to share it with his children. She also didn't want to come between Bryce and his daughter. She took the first step in easing the tension and invited them along. This act of concern caused Tanya to soften her hard stand. She and Brenda were so engrossed in conversation that Bryce could hardly get in a greeting.

With everyone onboard, the driver flipped through the heading until he came to the one saying "Washington, DC."

Franklin had a seat in the front of the bus beside Korianne. He waited until things calmed down and the bus was well on its way. Then he stood up to make an announcement. "I have some bad news and some good news to announce," he shouted.

"Give us the bad news first," everyone agreed.

"Well, our dear friend Korianne, who's been with us through our most turbulent times, will be leaving the program to go home to her parents when we return. She thinks she's ready to leave. She will be back for graduation though," Franklin stated.

Franklin waited until everyone expressed their regrets over her decision to suddenly leave.

"Now what's the good news?" someone asked.

"The good news is that she's going home to tell her parent about their new son-in-law. We're getting married," Franklin said with a lively and spirited grin. He took Korianne by the hand, and she stood to face the group. Her face was flushed with happiness, and she flashed an affectingly innocent smile.

It was good news, but not everyone was surprised.

Also, John and Allison were sitting together on the bus. Allison tried desperately to smile after hearing the announcement, but instead there was a pained look on her face. Allison always had trouble hiding her true feelings. She wanted very much to be making the same announcement for her and John, but she knew that John was still struggling with his gambling problem. On her visit to the small security station on the Eagles' Nest's grounds, she found it littered with lotto scratch-off tickets. These had never been found there before John came. To make matters worse, John denied that they were his. Allison had begun to lose her trust in him. She vowed not to continue their relationship until he addressed his gambling problem.

The bus arrived at the Wall, and the group was met by Captain Athas. He led them to seats that were reserved for them. It was a beautifully sunny day. The group took their seats among several hundred others that had been invited to the special ceremony.

Franklin began to squirm in his seat. Bryce noticed Franklin's face becoming tight and pinched. He started to clamp down on his teeth. "Relax, I'm just as nervous about this as you are. We'll get through this together," Bryce said.

After several speeches by military officers with so many decorations on that people were shielding their eyes, they were invited to view the Wall. Bryce took the lead, and they began to walk past the Wall in single file. Bryce stopped several times as he recognized the names of those that were in his unit. It was very hard for Bryce. He had a look of incurable sadness on his face. Each name he recognized brought on more sadness. He tried to hold back the tears but was finally overcome with grief. Bryce's body wracked with convulsions of grief. He had come to the end of the names and to those added. There was the name of Tyrone Cooper. Brenda and Tanya rushed to Bryce's side. They supported him on each side. There they waited for Franklin.

Franklin stood before his father's name. His eyes danced, and a spirit of intoxication came over him. It was not the sad occasion that

Franklin thought it would be. He was proud to see that his father was finally recognized for the service he had given to his country.

The others returned to their seats while Franklin and Bryce took another look at Tyrone's name on "The Wall -That Heals."

"For the first time since leaving Nam, I feel a sense of relief. Maybe this wall does cause a healing," Bryce said. "I feel I can put it all behind me now. I think I can end that chapter in my life and move on."

"I feel a sense of belonging and purpose," Franklin said. "I no longer feel abandoned by my father. I understand why he acted as he did. For me, the Wall is just a beginning. I have found a place where I can come to when I want to remember my father."

The two returned to their seats. The ceremony continued and Franklin, along with seven others whose relatives names were added to the Wall, were called forward. They were each given a plaque in honor of the deceased relative. On Franklin's plaque was a symbol of the Wall and the words"Tyrone Cooper-An American Hero"engraved on it.

The trip back to the Eagles' Nest was tranquil. Everyone seemed to be emotionally drained. Those that didn't fall asleep were heard whispering about the event.

Back at the Eagles' Nest, Franklin approached Bryce with urgency. "Tomorrow I need you to accompany me on one final thing I must get done," he requested.

"What is it?" Bryce asked.

"I need to get into town to a shoe store," Franklin said. Again his eyes narrowed with suspicion: the look he always got when he was up to something.

Early the next morning, Bryce was up and eager to get going. This was his weekend off, and plans had been made for him by Brenda and Tanya. The thought of the two women getting along brought him good cheer. But first he had to help Franklin with another mysterious deed.

Bryce was reeling with nostalgia as he blasted music from the dancing classics station on the radio. He turned into the Eagles' Nest and spotted Franklin waiting outside the security station.

The two men headed down Route 272. Bryce noticed that Franklin had brought along his shoe box. He also had that faraway dreamy look in his eyes, the look he got whenever he wanted to know something. "Okay, what's on your mind?" Bryce asked.

"Well, since you asked," Franklin said. "I reread the chapter of your book entitled "Back to the World," but I'm puzzled by it. Could you explain why you, my dad, and so many other veterans had so much trouble adjusting to state-side."

"For one thing, many of us were very young when we left for Nam. We couldn't wait to get home to talk about the things we had experienced. We were surprised by the reception we received on coming home. We all had a story to tell, but unfortunately no one wanted to listen. We needed to talk about our problems. The Vietnam War was a sort of hush-hush topic, and most of the movies that were made about it did not depict how it actually was over there. It was very frustrating. Many Vietnam veterans were labeled as crazy. So we used that excuse to drink and take drugs. After God helped me to recover from drugs and alcohol, I began to write about my experiences. That was a source of healing for me. However, there are many soldiers that weren't as fortunate as I was. Many of them have died, and many of them are still drinking and taking drugs. They're only adding to their depression and confusion. Today many of them are still fighting the war. These are the ones who can be found hanging out on the streets. They are the homeless and of the mentally ill population. People are just starting to show more interest in Vietnam veterans. I now believe that viewing the Wall helps healing, but having the American people know the truth about Nam will help many. I believe that every American that had a family member serve in Nam has a story to tell, whether it's related to being there or coming home after and trying to adjust."

"I believe you're right. Your story has definitely helped me, and that gives me a great idea. I want to invest in your book. How about letting me produce it. That way the whole world can learn about the real Nam and read about my heroic dad at the same time. Maybe then they will come to understand and respect the things you guys suffered," Franklin said.

"That sounds like a good plan," Bryce agreed.

Bryce parked in front of the shoe store, and the two men went inside. Franklin asked the salesperson for the largest pair of boots they sold. The clerk came back with boots size fifteen. "These are the largest size we have in stock. If you want bigger ones, we could order them for you," the clerk said.

"Oh no, these will do," Franklin said, as he reached into his pocket for the money.

"Franklin!" Bryce shouted. "Have you lost your mind? It's turning into summer, not winter. Besides, I'm sure your feet are not that big."

"It's not the boots that I want," Franklin admitted.

Bryce didn't understand. He just watched with a puzzled face.

Franklin took the boots out of the shoe box and placed them on the back seat of the car. He then transferred everything from the old shoe box to the new larger box. "I need room to allow the spirit of the shoe box to grow," he said.

"What else could you possibly want the shoe box to do for you?" Bryce asked.

"Oh, this new shoe box is not for me. It's for Franklin Jr." Franklin announced with a grin as broad as Main Street.

"Aaah, do you know something that we don't?" Bryce inquired.

"Maybe," Franklin smiled.

They headed out of town, and Franklin suddenly asked Bryce to pull over. Bryce watched as Franklin grabbed the boots from the back seat and ran over to a homeless man sitting on the sidewalk. Franklin gave the boots and the receipt to the man and pointed in the direction of the shoe store.

Back on Route 272 something caught Bryce's eye, and he pulled over. "As many times during the year that I've traveled this road, I never noticed that sign. Did you?" he asked Franklin.

"No. I don't recall seeing it either. It looks so out of place," Franklin said.

The two were talking about a completely white billboard with these words in large print square in the middle: **"Read Leviticus Chapter 24: verses 17-20."**

"I wonder what it means," Franklin expressed.

Bryce reached across Franklin and opened the glove compartment of the car. He took out a pocket-sized Bible and read the verses: *"And he that killeth any man shall surely be put to death. And if a man cause a blemish in his neighbor; as he has done, so shall it be done to him; breach for breach, eye for eye, tooth for tooth: life for life."*

He then gave it to Franklin to read.

"I still don't understand its meaning," Franklin confessed.

"I do. I think I can let matters stand now. You'll understand it some day," Bryce said. This time his face had an-"I know something that you don't," look on it.

Monday morning Bryce was sitting at his desk working on Franklin's discharge papers when Nick came over. He flipped a large folder on Bryce's desk. "Good morning, Bryce. I want you to meet Cliff. He lives out on the Connecticut-New York border in a log cabin. He's a white male and a Vietnam veteran. He's afraid to come out of his cabin, because he believes that the VA hospital has placed communication disks in his head. He gets transmissions through the telephone and electrical wires overhead. He's schizophrenic. He's your new case."

Bryce finished his work with Franklin's discharge. He read through the file on Cliff. He then gathered his things and headed for the door. Nick stopped Bryce in the hallway and said, "Remember, Bryce, he may accept you as his case manager, or he may not. Either way, there are plenty of others here just waiting for you."